Persephone in Bloom

An Olympus Inc. Romance

Kate Healey

Karen Healey

Content Description

This book is primarily a romantic comedy with a guaranteed happy ending, but it does have content that you should be aware of. *Persephone in Bloom* contains emotionally abusive parenting of an adult, mention of past abuse of a trans then-teenager, a workplace assault, and sexual harassment.

There are also two flatly unrealistic things that are there because I wanted them:

1. The heroine is fat and works at a magazine publishing company. She is aware of fatphobia and has encountered it before, but no one in the story targets her body.

2. A lot of people have the names and aspects of Ancient Greek gods and heroes, and nobody thinks that's weird.

For the librarians of Te Kura o Waimairi-iri/Burnside High School, heroes all.

Chapter One

P ersephone Erinyes, not for the first time in her life, regretted listening to her mother.

Demeter had caught her at the door, taken one look at her sleeveless linen shift dress—perfect for the unseasonably warm September—and pointed out that while Persephone's tattoos were very *nice*, darling, perhaps they shouldn't be on display on her first day.

And so Persephone had started her internship at Olympus Publishing in a long-sleeved, drapey peach confection that, it was becoming very apparent, wasn't made out of breathable fabric.

She should have dressed for a marathon. The head of Human Resources, Mr. Hermes, apparently not only took a very personal interest in the intern program, but seemed determined to drag their intake of twelve through every inch of their new workplace. From his place at the head of the pack, he occasionally called something over his shoulder. Mr. Hermes had introduced himself as "British via the West Indies", and his rich voice and plummy accent easily penetrated to the back of the crowd.

They'd scrambled from their first getting-to-know-you meeting in the HR department, near the top of the building, down through the hallowed offices of the editors and through the labyrinthine cubicles of the copy departments where those editors' peons scurried through the maze with intent expressions and giant travel coffee mugs

They were allowed a brief peek into the famed wardrobe, which took up most of a floor. Even Persephone, who'd been in her mid-teens before she realized not *everyone's* mother had a whole room for a shoe closet, was awed by the racks on racks on racks of gorgeous fabrics, stunning accessories, and superb designs, all meticulously organized so that someone could find the exact belt that had adorned the cover model of the July issue six years before.

Of course, few of these clothes would fit her, but she could definitely see herself in some of the accessories...

A jolt shot through the group as something happened in an aisle further away, the respectful hum shifting to a more intense pitch. Persephone craned, but couldn't see.

"What happened?" she whispered to the girl beside her. Thalia, she thought, from the quick introduction icebreaker games they'd played.

Probably-Thalia listened for a moment, and then whispered back, "Someone saw Aphrodite Urania!"

"Is she doing a shoot?"

"She must be. I didn't see anything on her socials, so it must be a big deal."

Indeed, Mr. Hermes, smile gleaming in his dark face, was herding them back together and reminding them all of the non-disclosure agreement they'd signed. "There's always a lot going on!" he said. "And you absolutely can't talk about it. Not to your best friend. Not even your mum!"

Persephone winced. Her own mother wasn't going to be happy about that.

They were off again, through the beauty department, where two of their group fell upon the product display with reverent shrieks, and the book design department, where Olympus Publishing created glossy art books, beautiful cookbooks, and hefty coffee table tomes - all, of course, promoted by and derived from Olympus magazines.

Persephone could feel sweat gathering between her breasts and dampening the band at the back of her bra. At least her silver low-heeled sandals weren't a problem, though Thalia was easily keeping up in her sky-high stilettos. Thalia was also wearing a sleeveless shift dress, with a delicate watercolor tattoo of a butterfly flashing on the underside of her dainty light brown wrist. Obviously, *her* mother hadn't caught her at the door that morning.

Persephone nodded at the tattoo while Mr. Hermes extolled the virtues of the advertising department. "That's pretty," she whispered. "Who designed it?"

Thalia beamed at her. "My sister."

"It's great work. I like the—"

"We're moving!" their relentless guide sang. "Keep up, keep up! Move it, people, interns coming through! To the art department!"

Persephone quickened her pace. For six months, the intern program rotated the chosen twelve through various departments, making sure they knew who was who and, probably more importantly, how they liked their coffee. It had been made very clear to all of the interns that their first six months were going to be gofer duties - pick up this, order that, clear away this mess, call this car.

But after that. If they made it. If they didn't burn out or screw up or run away screaming, they would get a six-month placement in a department of their choice, and the tempting possibility of doing some actual *work*.

And Persephone wanted to work in the famed Olympus Art and Design department. She was a decent sketch artist and a better painter, but what she really loved was design; selecting and editing elements, turning a miscellany of objects into a composition that intrigued and delighted the eye. If she could just *show* people what she could do...

The Art and Design space was enormous, and crammed with people. Persephone scanned the room, trying to pick up as much as she could, but it was hopeless; she saw layouts for skin creams and tennis rackets, food photography and travel shoots, all passing before her dazed eyes as they jogged through the floor. One man adjusting the shading on a swimsuit shot gave her a vague half-smile; a woman leaning over a lightbox glanced up in irritation as the pack went by. Everyone else ignored them. They were busy. They were focused. They were creating beauty with purpose and drive, and Persephone wanted to be one of them so badly she could barely breathe.

Persephone had expected people to be grouped according to the publication they nominally worked for, but instead the departments appeared to be organized by the kind of work people were doing, not by which magazine employed them.

"Cross-publication synergy!" Mr. Hermes declared, in response to a question. "It's what makes Olympus so flexible, and our work so fresh and vibrant." He checked his watch. "Righto, it's nearly noon. And you know what that means!"

What that meant, apparently, was a charge downstairs to the test kitchens and the cafeteria on the second floor.

4

Kitchens was a gleaming expanse of copper pans, white tables and well-scrubbed stoves, loud with friendly shouting over the clatter of cooking. Here, finally, Mr. Hermes slowed down - there were apparently rules about running in the kitchens, as a large Black woman in pristine chef whites reminded Mr. Hermes, the moment he crossed the threshold.

"Yes, absolutely!" he said, and made exaggeratedly slow walking motions. The woman rolled her eyes at him, and turned back to her stove.

Mr. Hermes winked at the interns, but Persephone noted that he didn't pick up the pace again.

One corner was set up for a photoshoot, and she instinctively drifted towards it. An impressive array of lighting modifiers and gels were trained on a stunning wedding cake. It was four tiers high, embellished with silver sugar roses and elaborate curlicues of pearls curving around the luscious white icing.

The illusion was only slightly tarnished by the food stylist who picked up a spray can, shook it with a calculated expression, and coated the entire thing with a clear substance that didn't smell at all edible.

"Acrylic spray," a tall intern with a sharp pixie cut said knowledgeably. "To keep it looking pretty for the shoot."

"I guess no one's taking a slice home for dessert," Persephone joked.

"Oh, do you eat carbs?" Thalia asked.

"Only on days ending with y," Persephone said gravely.

"I'm on keto."

"That's okay. I never offer to share my sandwiches," Persephone said, and was a little surprised when Thalia laughed. Well, just because somebody was beautiful and perky didn't mean they lacked a sense of humor.

"Speaking of sandwiches," Mr. Hermes said, and Persephone jumped. How was he everywhere at once? "It's definitely lunch time. Let me introduce you to my favorite place in the building: the staff cafeteria!"

And with a flourish he flung open the doors, a gesture only minorly impeded by the man on the other side jumping back with a curse. Mr. Hermes ignored him and gestured the interns inside. "Today, lunch is on HR," he told them. "Try the beef!"

***

Hades knew it was bad news from the moment his second-in-command came into his office.

"He said no," Odysseus said, with no preamble.

Hades scowled. "How does he expect us to manage the increased demand on the servers without additional IT support?"

"He approved a three percent salary raise."

"That won't give them more hours in the day. IT need at least three additional full-time staff, not a tiny raise for the staff we already have."

Odysseus spread his hands. "I made the argument."

And it would have been persuasive. That was why Hades had sent Odysseus to the meeting instead of going himself.

"You could take it to the next board meeting," Odysseus suggested.

"No point," Hades said. "The board does whatever he thinks is best. Next?"

"He's also not happy about the profit to expenditure ratio on the video suite, but accepted the timeline projections—I got the feeling that they'd better be accurate."

"They will be," Hades said, with absolute confidence, and was rewarded with a wink. Odysseus had overseen those projections.

"Yes to folding *Farm and Country* into *Life Outdoors*, with HR laying off twelve staffers."

Hades sighed. "Tell Daphne to coordinate the severance packages with HR."

"Yes to contracting Peter Atlas as a speaker for the January retreat."

"Good." He waited.

Odysseus looked at him expectantly.

Hades broke first. "And did you ask him about those personal expenses discrepancies?"

"Absolutely not," Odysseus said. "That's definitely your job."

Hades stared at him gloomily. "You're my direct report. When I tell you to do something, you're supposed to do it."

"Write me up," Odysseus said, with a complete lack of fear. "Or you could email him, if you're too scared to go upstairs."

"I'm not scared of Zeus," Hades protested.

"Just his office," Odysseus said. "Thirty stories up, glass walls..."

"I'm not scared of heights, either."

"You know, you can really feel it when you get off the elevator. The building sways just a bit - I mean, it has to, to counterbalance the wind. But you can't help wondering what would happen if it just kept swaying, maybe if it started to fall—"

"I'll send the fucking email," Hades said, a little sharper than he meant to be. "Get out of my office."

He turned to his computer, fighting to put the idea of falling masonry out of his head. His email was brusque, even for him—"See attached.

Can you explain?"—but Zeus didn't pay him for his people skills. When he looked up, Odysseus was looking at him in concern.

"I'm fine," Hades said.

"Have you left your office all week?"

"I do have a home of my own." He seemed to recall it being quite a nice one, when he was there long enough to appreciate it.

Odysseus snorted. "Seen it in daylight, recently?"

"Sunday morning," Hades said. "I read the papers."

"Uh-huh. I won't ask whether you went anywhere except work, because I know the answer. And while you're at work, have you been anywhere except the basement? The boardroom, the cafeteria, the gardens?"

"Certainly," Hades said. He couldn't remember where, exactly, but he must have been. The head of departments meeting? No, he'd sent Odysseus to that. Meeting his sister-in-law for a coffee in the executive dining room? That had been... shit, last month. He entered "Set up coffee with Hera" on his PA's to-do list.

Odysseus pointed at him. "You're turtling," he proclaimed.

"No, I'm not," Hades said automatically, then frowned. "Am I?"

"Yes. Yanking your head into your shell." Odysseus gestured at the office walls. "I'm taking you out to lunch."

"There's a lot to do," Hades said. "I can't leave for that long."

"Fine. The cafeteria, then."

"I suppose that won't hurt," Hades conceded, and then caught the smile Odysseus didn't hide quickly enough. "You cunning dog. What's happening in the cafeteria?"

"The September intern intake is here, and noon is their scheduled lunchtime," Odysseus said, and winked at him. "You never know, some of them might be cute."

Hades rolled his eyes. "One, you're the most faithfully married man I've ever met. And two, if you ever did go mad and cheat, your wife would murder you. And then I'd have to bury your body."

"Not for me," Odysseus said, mock-offended. "Interns for you."

"I am forty-two years old," Hades told him. "I will not be ogling any interns."

"All right, then we can place bets on who makes the distance," Odysseus said, moving towards the door. He was heading automatically for the stairs—working with him for nearly a decade meant that Hades didn't have to come up with excuses to avoid the elevator.

"That would be almost equally unethical."

"Mark Hermes runs the book every year, and he's head of HR."

"Don't tell me these things," Hades said. "I always feel obligated to do something about them."

"I was an intern," Odysseus told him. "Penny was an intern. Hestia was an intern. You, sure, you got in because your family owns the place—"

"Thanks."

"—but my point is, probably half the people working at Olympus were interns. Betting on interns is a time-honored tradition. Don't take that joy away from us."

Hades scowled, but he could feel himself giving in. "You could talk anyone into anything, couldn't you?"

"Yes, and you'd better thank your luck," Odysseus said cheerfully. "Or there'd be no one who could get you to leave your dungeon."

Hades was not supposed to know that his underlings called the finance department "the Underworld." Honestly, he hadn't meant to keep the department in the basement, but when he'd first stepped in as Chief

Financial Officer, building a stable team had been his first priority. A lot of the people working for his father's CFO had had to go, but Hades was proud that he'd had to fire very few people since then. Mark Hermes might be leading an illegal gambling ring, but he knew how to select good employees.

And just when Hades had gotten his team together, and was starting to think that sunlight and fresh air might be nice, Zeus had ordered a renovation program for most of the building. The basement layer was the only one he'd been able to guarantee wouldn't be touched for a couple of years. Maybe the flighty art department types could adjust to scrambling to a new location every six months, but Hades's people benefited from orderly recordkeeping and longevity.

So they'd stayed in the basement. And stayed. And stayed. For... could it be? Nearly fifteen years.

Distracted, Hades followed Odysseus into the cafeteria and looked up, just as a beam of sunlight struck through the high windows of the mezzanine and illuminated the most beautiful woman he had ever seen.

She was sitting in the middle of a group of chattering children, like a queen among her court. She was lush and round in profile, golden-skinned and pink-lipped, and her body was draped in curving folds of peach. Her honey-blonde hair was piled on top of her head. When she turned slightly to talk to a girl beside her, he saw bright red flower petals peeking over the back of her gown's neckline.

Poppies. There were poppies tattooed on the back of her neck.

"Holy shit," Odysseus said, from very far away.

Obviously, Hades needed to touch those poppies. He took a step forward, and a wiry hand clasped his wrist, squeezing lightly.

"Not that this isn't very, very funny," Odysseus said, so quietly it was almost under his breath. "But if you throw yourself at her feet in the middle of the cafeteria, people are going to talk, and that might be a problem on her first day."

Hades blinked twice, and felt heat rush to his cheeks as he met Odysseus's eyes. "What?" he said at random. "I was just. First day?" Shit, shit, shit. She was an intern. She was sitting with the other interns, and he was a dirty old man.

He could feel his eyes returning to her as if dragged, and forcibly stared at the dining stations instead. "Soup looks good."

"You hate cold soups. Last week you called gazpacho 'chilled demon vomit.'"

"I should give them another chance. I'm open-minded. I'm flexible."

"Since when?" Odysseus muttered, but he followed Hades to the soup station. There was a peal of laughter from the intern table. It wasn't... there was no *reason* for the laughter to be at his expense, but he felt the anxiety prickle at the back of his skull.

"Chilled cucumber puree with feta and cashew crumble," Odysseus read over his shoulder. "So... baby food?"

The station attendant grinned at him. "Don't let Hestia hear you say that," she advised. "Besides, how many babies eat feta?"

"Mine did," Odysseus said, "He ate everything, before he decided to eat nothing. Rubber bands. Coins. I miss those days." He handed Hades a tray. Hades watched as the attendant ladled pale green glop into a bowl, and sprinkled a generous handful of cheese and nuts on top. Hestia's determination to test new recipes on a wide audience was probably admirable but to his mind, cold liquids in a bowl should be

11

desserts. He couldn't stop his eyes from fooling his tastebuds into expecting something sweet.

"I wish Hestia would get over this cold soup streak," Odysseus muttered. "Hasn't anyone told her it's nearly fall?"

"Do you want the job?"

"No more than I want to ask your brother what those unexplained items are in his personal expenses account." Odysseus paused, then lowered his voice. "You don't think he's having another affair, do you?"

"No," Hades said. "He hasn't done that since they remarried, and Hera's prenuptial agreement is iron tight. If the marriage fails because of infidelity, she gets half of everything."

Odysseus's mouth was wry. "If I'd divorced someone for cheating, I wouldn't marry him again, even with a prenup like that."

"She loves him," Hades said. It was, unfortunately, the only reason that made sense. "Anyway, Zeus never paid for his affairs on the company dime. My chief concern is that someone on his staff is hoping that he doesn't check his expenses list before it gets sent to Accounts Payable."

"Well, he doesn't," Odysseus said. "Good thing he's got you."

Hades knew very well what Odysseus was doing; distracting him with banter, creating a small, private space for the two of them as they moved through the hall. The space was much more crowded than usual, and the intern table was attracting a lot of covert attention; people trying to gauge the odds before they placed their bets.

Unwillingly, inevitably, Hades looked at her again.

She wasn't *perfect*, he told himself. No one was perfect. And she wasn't, on closer inspection, the most beautiful woman he'd ever seen, either; he worked in an industry that frequently put the most impressive human specimens (suitably Photoshopped) on display. If he put her next to Aphrodite Urania, she might even look ordinary.

True, it was hard to pick out a particular feature that was less than gorgeous, but she had flaws. Her left sandal had a mark on it. Her mascara had smudged under her eyes. A tendril of her hair had escaped and was wandering deliciously down the back of her neck, bringing his eyes again to those blood-red poppies, starkly outlined in black against the golden dream of her skin...

The completely objective appraisal had lulled him into distraction, Hades realized. Odysseus's wandering route had brought them a lot closer to the intern table. Hades stopped in his tracks. The soup bowl wobbled perilously on his tray.

Odysseus turned to give him a look of innocent inquiry. Hades wasn't fooled for a second.

"No," he said, nearly under his breath, but with all the command he could bring to bear.

"Okay," Odysseus said. "You go find a table, and I'll join you in a second. I want a closer look at the prospects."

Half-relieved, half-disappointed, Hades scanned for a clear table. There weren't many; apparently everyone wanted to assess the new crop of interns. Maybe he could persuade Odysseus that the trip to the cafeteria had been enough social interaction for the day, and retire to his office to eat in peace.

The wistful contemplation of this peaceful vision was torn away by a booming, cheerful voice with a British accent.

"Well, well! Right over there is Hades Kronion, our CFO. Come and say hello, Hades!"

Hades forced a smile through gritted teeth, and turned to face Mark Hermes, who was wearing a lavender tie that glowed against his brown skin, because Hermes had style. Hades was devoid of style. This usually didn't bother him, but *she* was sitting directly opposite Hermes, so that he was perilously aware of a blur of peach fabric as she shifted to look at him.

Unfortunately, he couldn't turn away from the intern intake without a word. It would give them a terrible impression of an Olympus owner, and Hermes would make him pay for it, using all the resources of HR. There would be meetings. There would be workshops. There might be *roleplay*.

Hades took three steps towards the group, casting about for some polite nothing phrases of welcome, and felt the toe of his sensible leather shoe catch on some hidden flaw in the floor.

It happened in slow motion.

There was the jolt of the impact as it travelled up his leg, halting his progress. There was the instinctive stagger to keep his footing, followed by the sickening realization that while he and the tray had stopped moving, the bowl had not. There was the futile reach after he dropped the tray and grabbed at the bowl as it described a low arc, rotating vertically as it spun and dropped, face down, in her peach-covered lap.

Hades looked into the face of the most beautiful woman he'd ever seen, who was dripping green slime from throat to thigh, and yearned for the earth to swallow him whole.

***

Persephone took a bite of the best salmon salad she'd ever had, and focused on Mr. Hermes, who was emphasizing the necessary bonding between the interns.

"It's one of the things that will get you through the first six months," he said, and waggled his finger at them. "The program is tough, and we make no apologies for that. You have to be able to rise to a challenge to make it in this business. Make your fellow interns your family, and you'll have the support to meet those challenges. These are your siblings now!" He smiled in reminiscence. "Mine was the very first intake, and several of our fellowship even married each other."

"So, we should marry our siblings," Pixie Cut muttered under their breath. "Check."

Persephone choked on a leaf of baby spinach, and hastily turned it into a cough.

"Enjoy your lunch," Mr. Hermes concluded, and sat down to engage with an enormous sandwich.

Pixie Cut turned to Persephone. "I'm sorry, I didn't catch your name earlier. I'm Terry. Pronouns he/she/they."

"I forgot your name too," Persephone admitted. "I'm Persephone, she/her. What department are you looking at?"

"Photography. You?"

"Art and Design."

"Oh, me too!" Thalia exclaimed. "Where did you go to school?"

"Eleusis U," Persephone said. Thalia seemed determined to make friends, which Persephone felt cautiously optimistic about.

Thalia's eyes widened. "Me too! I knew I'd seen you somewhere before."

"We probably didn't overlap," Persephone said. She'd been hoping that this topic of conversation would wait a few days. "I graduated five years ago."

Thalia blinked at her. "But you look so young."

Persephone gazed at her fresh-faced, beaming companion, and felt about three hundred.

Thalia dropped her voice conspiratorially. "If you don't mind me asking, how old are you?"

"I'm 27," Persephone said.

"Oh, wow. That's, like, nearly 30!"

"I guess so," Persephone said.

"Experienced," Terry said, nodding. "Smart. I took a couple of years off after college myself and travelled through Europe."

Persephone ate another bite of salmon and watched Thalia and Terry start a conversation about their post-college backpacking adventures. The rest of the interns were talking about their colleges, their senior year spring breaks, the work they'd picked up over the summer vacation. Mr. Hermes was looking at her, a warm gaze that was nevertheless clearly assessing her current performance. And no wonder; he'd just *told* them to make friends, and she was sitting here in silence. The least she could do was make an effort.

"Has anyone watched anything good recently?" she asked, and Terry turned back to her.

"Last week I saw this amazing Spanish documentary about endangered snake preservation efforts," they said. "Did you know that—"

"Well, well!" Mr. Hermes cut in, easily slicing through the chatter. "Right over there is Hades Kronion, our CFO. Come and say hello, Hades!"

He was looking over Persephone's head. Persephone twisted in her chair, and saw a tall man in a dark suit, hunched over a tray. He turned back towards them, his lips drawn back in a tight smile, and she felt a thump in the pit of her stomach.

This Hades Kronion had a *great* face. Strong cheekbones arching over slightly hollowed cheeks on either side of an interestingly craggy nose. His skin was marble-pale, a stark contrast to the neatly kept black hair and beard, and there were faint blue shadows under his dark blue eyes. She could do something with charcoals, maybe, or even muted pastel crayons, to outline the bones and smudge the shadows, but she wasn't sure what she'd do to capture that wary air, like a cat that wasn't sure of its welcome.

He took a few steps towards the group, and then everything happened too fast for her to understand what was going on. One moment she was wondering how you asked the CFO at your new workplace if he'd like to sit for some quick sketches, and the next she was wet from collarbone to knees with something that smelled minty green and tangy.

There was a suppressed snicker from her left, as Thalia valiantly stifled a giggle behind her hands.

Hades was staring at her, his eyes wide and appalled.

"I'm so–" he said, and swallowed hard. "I'm so sorry, I lost my footing. Are you hurt?" His voice was deep and resonant, his tone grave. He could have been apologizing for some mortal offence.

Persephone plucked the bowl from her lap and deposited it neatly on the table. The bowl was empty; the entire serving had managed to disperse itself over her person. "No, I'm fine," she said. "Don't worry, it was an accident. But I'd better go get cleaned up." At least now she had a good excuse to dump the damn dress without her mother saying a word. Not even the most talented drycleaner was going to salvage this one.

"Washrooms are in the–" Mr. Hermes started, but a short, wiry, red-haired man with the sharpest eyes she'd ever seen suddenly appeared, and held his hand out to her.

"This way," he said, giving her a charming smile, and Persephone found herself being raised to her feet. "Introduce yourself," he muttered at Hades in an undertone, and Persephone was being whisked off to the kitchens while the hesitant, deep voice behind her began a stilted hello to the interns.

"I'm Odysseus," her rescuer said, and raised his voice a little. "I need some towels over here, please! Any allergies?"

"No," Persephone said.

"Good." He handed her a clean pile of kitchen cloths. "Wipe the worst of it off, then head up to Wardrobe. You remember where that is?"

"Seventh floor," Persephone said, and was rewarded with a smile. He scribbled something on a piece of paper, folded it in half, and put it on top of the towel pile.

"I need to rescue Hades from your cohort, but if you give someone in Wardrobe that note, they'll show you the secret showers and find you something to wear."

Persephone's brain had taken a moment to get up to speed, but it was whirring into action. "Will they have anything in my size?" she asked, striving to keep her voice even and non-judgmental.

Odysseus looked at her with approval. "An intelligent question. I'm almost sure they'll have something. At the very least, they can wash and dry your dress and you could wear it home. But it'd be a shame to miss out on the rest of your first day."

That, Persephone could agree with. She wiped off enough of the green sludge that she could get into the elevator without dripping, and developed a practiced rueful smile for everyone who saw her on her way there. She truly wasn't offended or upset, but even if she had been, no one had to tell her that whiny interns who baulked at the first mishap that came their way weren't going to be employment material.

She flagged down the first person she saw in the wardrobe floor, a woman who gave her dress a single, disgusted look, and the note a surprised one.

"Follow me," she said briskly. "Don't touch anything."

Persephone didn't need the warning. She'd spent enough time around her mother's closet to appreciate how many thousands of dollars of dainty clothes she could destroy with an ill-placed soup smear. She tucked the flowing gathers of her dress tight around her thighs, and walked after the woman, trying to keep her shoulders and hips pulled in. It wasn't easy—the aisles were narrow, and she was pretty wide—but she made it to a glass walled office where a dark-skinned woman in her late thirties was frowning at a rack of skirts.

Persephone's escort rapped on the door and walked in. "Penny, this is an intern," she announced. "Odysseus says help her out, and he'll owe you a favor."

"Oh, good," the woman said, turning to smile at Persephone. She had acne scars and lopsided features, and wasn't what most people would think of as pretty, but her crooked smile lit up her face. "He's down to owing me half a dozen favors, and I like to have a few in reserve. Stand up tall, hon, let me get a look at you. I'm Penny Laconia, Head of Wardrobe. What's your name?"

Persephone dropped her arms by her sides and straightened obediently. "Persephone."

"Right," Penny said, giving her one comprehensive glance. "Diana, show Persephone to the shower, and then pull... let's see. The navy Siriano metallic suit pants, the Trelise Cooper Curate thing in orange, and the Elie Saab I altered for Ashley. No, the Saab's too sparkly for work, make it the copper La Femme with the ruching. All right, go."

Twenty minutes later, Persephone was in the navy pants and a drapey orange camisole top. Penny had given her a new pair of shoes, which Persephone was almost sure she wouldn't fall out of. Diana had presented her with a paper bag that contained the peach dress, hastily rinsed and run through a spin cycle, so that it was merely stained and damp instead of marinaded and dripping.

"That orange looks wonderful with your tattoos," Penny said. "All those stark outlines and bright watercolor fill are great."

"Thank you," Persephone said, touching her bared arms. "I, uh, I designed them. In senior year. I did some design work for the tattooist and she cut me a deal."

"Did you?" Penny said. Some kind of consideration moved in her face. "Ah, well, I'd better get back to work, and you'd better catch up with the intake. Diana, where are the interns?"

"Zeus's office," Diana reported.

"Better scoot," Penny said. "You don't want to keep the boss waiting."

Persephone arrived on the top floor just as the last of her fellow interns was filing into the cavernous glassy space that was Zeus's office, and joined the end of the line. Mr. Hermes tipped her a wink and said, with barely a pause, "And finally, Persephone Erinyes, Art and Design candidate."

Zeus Kronion didn't look much like his brother, except perhaps for the height. Where Hades had hunched, he leaned back against his gleaming wooden desk, every inch of him radiating confidence and power. He wore his blondish hair swept back, and was clean shaven, exposing symmetrical features and piercing sky blue eyes. He was handsome, and that was all. Her fingers didn't itch for a pencil.

Of course, she'd seen him before, which was probably dimming any possible impact. She couldn't ever recall meeting Hades Kronion before, but Zeus and his wife were frequent attendees at her mother's more upscale events.

This was something she absolutely didn't plan on telling the other interns.

Zeus looked straight at her. "Persephone!' he said, flashing his teeth. "So great to have you with us. And how is your lovely mother?"

Persephone ignored the startled attention of her workmates, and plastered on the smile she used when she had to convince rowdier guests that they didn't need another glass of wine. "Fine, thank you, Mr. Kronion," she said, and hoped that he'd pick up on her cues. Formal greeting, casual acquaintances at most, please don't call any further attention to me...

Zeus laughed, a deep boom of genuine amusement, and made eye contact with Mr. Hermes to share the joke. Persephone noted that Mr. Hermes didn't smile back, and was grateful. He knew about her connections, of course, but he hadn't made an issue out of them.

"Mr. Kronion!" Zeus said. "As if she hasn't known me since she was this high." He waved a hand at thigh level.

Persephone was maybe ten or fifteen years younger than Zeus, not a whole generation behind him. She tried to think of a tactful way to remind him of this, when he spoke again:

21

"I'll be keeping an eye on *you*. You'll have to tell me how you like the program!"

None of the other interns physically moved, but Persephone could *feel* them leaning away from her. The mystery of her age was solved for them now--rich girl, well-connected, no doubt only got the sought-after slot because her mom made a call. Spoiled, untrustworthy, and probably reporting every move to the big boss.

Persephone swallowed. "Thank you," she said, wishing she could fade into the wall. "I'm so grateful for the opportunity."

Chapter Two

"So he called you out in front of all the others and made sure they all knew you were the favored candidate."

"He was just trying to be nice."

Hecate Jones shook her head and adjusted the cluster of clinking silver chains around her neck. "Persephone, I love you dearly, but you have *got* to stop thinking everyone has the best intentions at heart. That man is an apex predator in an industry that prizes killer instinct."

Persephone rolled her eyes. "Please, like law firms are any better."

Hecate pointed at her. "And that's how I know. He singled you out so the other interns will work harder. Properly motivated, they'll destroy themselves to prove they're better than you and take your place. Ah, here we go, thank you."

Persephone thought about it while the waitress delivered their coffees. It was depressingly believable. Hecate could make anything sound plausible, but her cynicism was hard-earned. She'd seen the worst of human nature, and she was so often right about people's darker motivations that Persephone had learned to take her advice.

Hecate was very small, very pale, and wore black. She'd worn black the whole time Persephone had known her, from their first day of college.

Somewhere, there might be photographs of a baby Hecate in a yellow hat or pale blue playsuit, but Persephone found it impossible to imagine.

In college, the black had been torn jeans, Converse and ripped T-shirts, with the occasional addition of a leather jacket (black), boots (black) and eyeliner (lots of it, and very black) when Hecate wanted to dress up or intimidate someone. Now the black came in the form of impeccable Tom Ford suits, and Armani dresses. At her law firm's formal dinner three months ago, Hecate had put on her single white silk shirt, climbed into her tuxedo, and walked out of the banquet with half a dozen phone numbers from the stunned dates of other people.

In college, Persephone had been the stable one, the girl who'd let Hecate cry on her shoulders after another call from home, the one who'd been able to cover meals and rent on the desperate weeks that Hecate had to fight to keep her head above water between work and study and scraping as much as she could from financial aid.

After college, Hecate had gone straight into law school with her head held high and a full scholarship. Persephone had travelled a lot, made a clumsy attempt to work as a freelance designer, and helped out with her mother's numerous fundraisers and charity balls.

Now Hecate was a couple of years from making partner, and Persephone was a first-time intern in her field who still lived with her mother. In her mother's guesthouse, of course, not actually *in* the house. It was a distinction that Persephone felt was important, but also hard to explain.

Hecate poured creamer into her coffee and stirred. "So, apart from that unfortunate encounter with Zeus Kronion, did you play nicely with the other children? Perhaps the situation is redeemable."

"They *are* children," Persephone said. "Most of them are 21 or 22."

"Most people wouldn't consider 27 ancient."

"That's, like, nearly thirty, as one of my new workmates informed me."

"That's your enemy. Take that one down"

"I don't think she meant to be rude," Persephone said, and then reconsidered. "Well, maybe."

Hecate raised her thin eyebrows. "It's a dog-eat-dog world, flower child. Kill or be killed."

"Any more cliches?"

"Sure. Be a shark or be chum. Take her down."

Persephone took a long sip of her mochaccino, and visualized the caffeine filtering into her veins. She was normally a four cup a day girl, but the work day hadn't afforded any coffee breaks. "Am I stupid to be doing this?" she asked.

"No," Hecate said. "You've got a degree, but no experience. If you want to learn how the work gets done, this is the way. I am not positive that publication design is your life's work, but this is how you find out."

"Mom wished me good luck this morning."

Hecate stirred her third packet of sugar into her coffee. "How kind," she said. Hecate had complicated feelings about Persephone's mother. Well, so did Persephone, but Demeter *was* her mother. And she'd never doubted Demeter's love; she only bridled about her expression of it.

"Then she reminded me that if I didn't get a job at the end of the internship, it didn't matter, because she'd always take care of me."

Hecate snorted.

"And *then*," Persephone went on, "she reminded me that the other interns likely wouldn't have my advantages, and would need post-internship jobs more than I did, and wasn't it nice that I didn't have to worry about that?"

Hecate laid her cup down with careful precision. "And there it is."

Persephone slumped. "It's true, though. I don't *need* it the same way they do."

"Here's another thing that's true," Hecate said sweetly. "Your mother would rather eat broken glass than let you be an independent adult, and she'll say anything—true or not—to make sure that doesn't happen."

"That's not fair."

"Isn't it? She's kept you on the leash of her money for your entire life."

"I'm not a dog," Persephone said sharply. "And she's not perfect, but she's still better than *your* mother."

Hecate's eyes narrowed to dark little slits, and Persephone held her breath.

Then Hecate picked up her coffee and took a measured sip. "All right. Although I'll remind you that's a very low bar to clear. Let's change the subject. Your boss made you a target and you met the other children, one of whom you must destroy. Anything else interesting happen?"

"The art department is incredible, and I can't wait to spend more time there. I met the fashion editor in charge of the wardrobe. And the company CFO dropped soup on me."

"Sue him," Hecate suggested. "I'll represent you."

Persephone laughed. "It was cold soup. Which is just as well, because I was absolutely drenched in it."

"Well, that explains the get-up," Hecate said, gesturing at Persephone's exposed arms. "It looks good, but not what I expected you to wear on your first day."

"It really wasn't a big deal, but he was so mortified he could barely speak. I was sitting there, dripping pureed cucumber everywhere, and

I felt sorry for *him*." She smiled, remembering, and then came back to herself to find Hecate grinning at her, cat-like.

"And he's cute," Hecate said.

"He's interesting," Persephone corrected. "Great bones. Strong brows. I bet I could do something good in charcoals, with that face." Her fingers twitched involuntarily.

Hecate's grin was getting wider and pointier.

"And," Persephone added, "he's definitely a lot older than me, and in a senior position at my new company, so forget about it."

Hecate gave that due consideration, then shook her head. "No," she said. "I don't think I'll forget about anyone who makes you want to draw. What's his name?"

"Hades," Persephone said, perhaps a little more warmly than was strictly appropriate. "But seriously, it's not a thing. I'm not the kind of girl who sleeps with the boss."

***

"Do you want another?" Odysseus asked.

"Yes. No, I'd better not." Hades eyed the empty wine glass. After what he had privately labelled the Souptastrophe, Odysseus had got him back to the office and head first into some nice, soothing, profit margin projections. When he'd surfaced, it was nearly seven pm, and Odysseus had insisted he come to the Happy Isles for a drink.

He'd had two, and drunk them fast. "Anyway, I'm your boss. I should be buying the drinks."

"I agree," Penny said, sliding into the booth beside her husband. She kissed him matter-of-factly, and opened the drinks menu. "Ah, they've got the new Ambrosia on tap. Thank you very much, Hades."

"You're welcome. I'll pay for it if you talk to the waitress."

"Bad social day?" Penny asked sympathetically, while Odysseus chortled.

"You could say that," Hades said, and tried to signal Odysseus with his eyebrows that he didn't want to discuss the cafeteria disaster.

"He fell in lust at first sight, and then poured soup all over her," Odysseus said. Hades kicked him under the table, hard enough to stop the cackling, but Penny was already looking at him, her brown eyes wide.

"Soup? Do you mean the new intern, Persephone?"

"Aha. We have a name," Odysseus said. "And what's she like?"

So Odysseus had sent her to wardrobe, where his brilliant wife could get a look at her. Persephone. A beautiful name. Old-fashioned, like his own, but with a musical air. Four lovely syllables that would drip from his mouth, like honey from the comb.

"Sweet, nervous, and a talented artist, if those tattoos are any indication," Penny said. She frowned at Hades. "A little bit young for you, don't you think?"

"I'm a little bit young for *you*," Odysseus said, leering.

Penny elbowed him. "You're only five years younger than me. And men die earlier, so it makes more sense for women to have younger partners."

"I'll have more stamina in my twilight years," Odysseus agreed.

Penny snorted. "Oh, please. You can barely keep up with me now."

"It doesn't matter how old she is," Hades said. "Obviously, I'm not going to... she's an employee."

"She's not *your* employee," Odysseus pointed out. "Finance doesn't take interns." He said this smugly, being the only intern Finance ever had taken – based on a recommendation from Penny.

"Well, at least you know she's old enough to drink," Penny said. She was looking over his shoulder.

With the return of the dread that had plagued him that afternoon, Hades turned, and saw Persephone walking into the bar.

She was wearing something else, naturally, since he'd ruined her dress with his clumsiness. Metallic blue pants hugged her strong thighs and wide hips. An orange top, barely a shirt at all, dipped perilously low at the front. Her round, smooth shoulders were almost completely bare, her arms...

Her arms were a flower garden. The tattoos spiraled up both arms from wrists to shoulders - bright red poppies, sunny orange marigolds, elegant purple irises. She was a woman in bloom, a beacon of color and life.

"You son of a bitch," he said, without looking away from her.

"I actually didn't arrange this," Odysseus said, sounding rueful. "It must be fate."

"She's seen you," Penny said, and tapped his shoulder. "You have to go and speak to her now, Hades."

He jerked, and made horrified eye contact with her. Her gaze was sympathetic, but firm. "It's good manners," she said. "Say hello, say you're sorry, offer to pay for the dress, and then you can leave. And Odie will be very nice to you tomorrow."

"Will I?" Odysseus asked, and then jumped, as some hidden wifely violence was enacted upon him. "Yes, I will. I'll be appropriately respectful for the workplace and not make any jokes."

29

Hades's heart was thumping against his ribs, and he took a couple of consciously deep breaths. He wasn't going to have a panic attack. This wasn't a room full of people staring at him, or a restaurant on top of a tower. It was an underground bar with a clientele much more interested in their own doings than his, and one nice young woman who'd already reacted calmly and politely to his incompetent fumbling.

And her companion, he realized, as he got closer to them. Persephone was with a small woman in sharp, business black who carried out a blatant head-to-toe appraisal of Hades, completed with pursed lips. Perhaps Persephone was on a date. Perhaps he was interrupting a long-term relationship with his inanity.

"Hello," he said. "I'm sorry again about today. Please allow me to cover the cost of replacing your dress. If you get a receipt to Accounts Payable they'll take care of it."

There, he'd got through the script. A few seconds more, and he could leave through the door so tantalizingly close behind her before his nerve gave out.

"Hello again," Persephone said. "I don't think you got my name before. Persephone."

"Oh. Yes. Nice to meet you. Properly."

"And this is my best friend, Hecate," Persephone said. "She works at Eule and Spindle. Hecate, this is Mr. Kronion."

"Hades, please."

"Good to meet you, Hades," Hecate said, and sounded as if she meant it.

"Don't worry about the dress," Persephone said, and smiled at him. "I kind of hated it anyway."

Quite without meaning to, Hades smiled back.

"She means, thank you very much, and she'll get you a receipt," Hecate told him.

Hades nodded. It was polite of Persephone to demur, but the interns barely made minimum wage. In fact, Zeus had fought against paying them even that, arguing that the prestige of interning at Olympus ought to be enough. It had taken both Hades and Hera to make it clear that if you didn't pay interns, you would get only interns who didn't need the pay—and those were often entitled trust fund kids with low work ethics and few useful skills. To develop talent into skill, you needed to be hungry for success—but you couldn't be literally starving.

Persephone was looking at her friend, a complicated expression on her face. Hecate gazed calmly back. Persephone's mouth went wry. "Then yes, thank you very much," she said, and offered her hand to shake on it.

Hades firmly held the shattered rags of his dignity together and touched her for the first time. Soft, warm flesh, with strength underneath. She didn't match her grip against his, but clasped and released. He caught a whisper of sweet jasmine and cool mint as she moved back.

"I guess I'll see you at work," Persephone said, and he gratefully seized at the opportunity to exit the conversation, nodding at Hecate on his way past. She had that assessing look on her face again.

Hades flagged down the host as he headed for the door.

"Mr. Kronion?"

"Those two women there?" he said, jerking his chin in the right direction. "Put their evening on my tab."

And, feeling that for once he'd made the right move, he escaped up the stairs, into a town car, and fell into the blissful, cool silence of his solitary bed.

If the brief thought that his bed could be even more blissful with the addition of some color and warmth flickered through his mind, he'd forgotten it by the morning.

***

Persephone didn't think she was imagining the slight pause in the conversation as she joined the rest of the interns for their second day. The voices rose again, and she slunk towards the back of the meeting room, where two giant urns of coffee and tea were waiting. Most of her colleagues were clutching paper cups and looking bleary.

Also, most of them were *here*. Persephone had congratulated herself on arriving fifteen minutes early, a sure sign that she was genuinely ready to work. But most of the intake had arrived even before that - from the paper debris in the wastebasket, some of them were already onto their second or third cup. Maybe Hecate was right. Maybe they'd all turned up so early because they were determined to prove themselves better than her.

"Any reason why you're gazing into the trash like a crystal ball?" Terry asked from beside her. Their voice was neutral, but at least they'd initiated conversation.

Or... *she'd* initiated conversation, Persephone thought, as she got a look at Terry's outfit and mentally adjusted the pronouns. Terry had gone very femme today, with a knee-length pleated skirt, fitted blazer and spike-heeled ankle boots.

"Just trying to see my future," she said.

"I thought you already had that sorted," Terry said, and sipped her tea.

"I-- Look. Yes, my mom is rich, and she's connected. But when I applied for the internship, I specifically asked her not to make a call."

It had been a tough conversation, even with Hecate coaching her through it beforehand. Demeter had kept looking at her, eyes filling with tears, asking why she wasn't allowed to *help* her daughter. For once, Persephone had stayed firm, and Demeter had agreed—with a tolerant sigh—not to get in touch with that lovely Hera or charming Zeus.

"And I applied for other programs, too, and was accepted for a couple of them. But I wanted to work here, because Olympus is the best. Isn't that why you applied?"

"Hm," Terry said. "And what if Zeus just happened to see your name on the applicant list?"

Despite herself, Persephone snorted. "Seriously? Do you think Zeus Kronion looks at intern applications? Yesterday was probably the last time he'll ever speak to us."

"Speak to *us*," Terry said, and made a circling gesture with her free hand that covered all the other interns—and decidedly not Persephone.

Persephone was very aware that the other interns' conversations had died away. Whatever she said next was going to be important.

"Oh, sure, we talk all the time. Before yesterday, the last conversation I had with Zeus was me saying 'Mr. Kronion, sorry to bother you, but did you leave your wallet behind?' and him saying, 'Ah, there it is. Thank you, Patty.' Real deep and meaningful."

"Well, clearly you're best friends," Terry said. She still looked a little wary, but the judgement had faded. "That's practically texting each other memes and gossiping about the other girls in the group chat."

33

Persephone laughed, and didn't even have to force it that much. Terry tipped her a barely perceptible wink, and wandered back to the long table. Persephone sat beside her, nursing her coffee. The only person still missing was Thalia, who scrambled in five minutes before start time, looking frantic. "The fucking *train*," she said, to no one in particular, and flinched when she realized the only free spot was beside Persephone.

To give her credit, Thalia recovered almost immediately, stashing her bag and coat under the free chair, grabbing a cup, and sinking into her seat just as Mr. Hermes stepped into the room.

Yesterday, the head of HR had taken them through the hectic day by himself. Today, he was flanked by near-identical, unfriendly looking women with long black hair drawn into the same tight ponytails. They were holding a pile of envelopes each.

"Ah, here we are!" Mr. Hermes said, eyes scanning the room. "All of us, I see, very good. This is Phoebe and Debbie, and they're here to give you your assignments and department info packs. After that, you're off to your first department. Anyway, I must dash, so I'll leave you in these capable hands, but don't hesitate to come to me with any concerns, or anything at all." He flashed bright teeth at them. From the silence the offer received, Persephone suspected she wasn't the only one who didn't trust it. "And I'll see you at the three-month mark, if not before."

The door had barely closed behind him before the interns were on their feet. Debbie scowled at them all impartially. "Surnames A-M with me, N-Z with Phoebe. Your departments are expecting you now."

So when would they read the info packs? Presumably while they walked–or ran. Persephone's heartbeat kicked up a notch. She was third in line in her group, and ripped her envelope open with the same lack of calm her predecessors had shown. She saw the word Copy at the top of the thick sheaf of paper, and heard Terry say, "I got Subscriptions?" in tones of horror, but then she was gone, racing for the elevator and trying to remember where the copy department was.

The elevator map told her that Copy was Floors 17-21. She scanned her info pack, trying to see if someone had bothered to include helpful information, like the exact floor she was supposed to be on or the name of someone to meet there. Before she could get there, another intern, Carlos, jumped in and hit the button for the second floor.

"Hey!" Persephone protested.

"I'm in Kitchens," he said, looking terrified. "I don't know how to cook. Do you think that'll be a problem?"

"Do you know how to wash dishes?"

"Yes? I mostly eat take out, so cups and glasses, knives and spoons... Oh, and cereal bowls!" Carlos seemed to realize this wasn't a long list, and sagged.

Demeter had a chef and a full-time housekeeper. Persephone hadn't really worked out dishwashing herself until college, when Hecate had taken her in hand. "I'm sure you'll be fine," she said, trying to sound as if she meant it. "The same skills apply."

Carlos looked somewhat reassured. When the doors pinged open, he raced out like a cat escaping a cage.

Persephone hit the button for Floor 17 before anyone else could get in. Her own confidence had been shaken by the fact that her info pack definitely didn't include any of the information she wanted. Most of it seemed to be a description of Olympus's mission statement and publications, taken directly from the website she'd already read. 17 was a guess, an instinct that interns deserved lower status, and therefore lower floors.

Floor 17 wasn't just busy. It was chaos. There were no glass-walled offices; just a hive of grey cubicle walls and a lot of people in them. So many people, all of them typing or shouting into phones or intently scanning printed copy, marking it up with quick, savage red pen.

There wasn't anyone waiting for her, and no sign saying "intern, this way".

Persephone stepped out of the elevator before her knees could fail. "Hello?" she squeaked.

No one so much as looked up.

Okay, then. She squared her shoulders, took a deep breath, and tried to project her voice above the tumult. "Hello!" she shouted. "Intern here, ready to work!"

This time, several people looked up. Two of them dashed towards her; a ruddy-faced White man with thinning blond hair, and a very tall Black woman with long, straightened hair floating behind her.

"Can you type?" the balding man demanded.

"Yes."

"How many words per minute?"

"I'm not sure. Medium speed, I guess?"

The man rolled his eyes.

"Can you *spell*?" the woman asked.

This was not the time to admit that your roommate had proofread all your college papers. "Mostly?" Persephone tried. "Doesn't the, like, spellchecker—"

The woman interrupted her with an audible, disgusted sigh. "Any information literacy?"

"Um, I'm not sure what that—"

"Can you research? Fact check?"

36

"I did some research papers in college."

"Is that the intern?" another woman with an impressive Afro called, heading towards them. "Can she do a coffee run?"

The man took an impersonal, but possessive grip of Persephone's wrist. Surprised, she let him. "In a *minute*," he snapped. "You, come this way." He shot a triumphant glance over his shoulder at the tall Black woman as he towed Persephone away. Fortunately, he let go of her wrist once he seemed satisfied that she'd follow.

"Oh, okay. Um, I'm Persephone, by the way."

This information was greeted with a complete lack of interest, much less a name in return. She was guided to a cubicle occupied by a young man with floppy blond hair, who was listening to something through headphones, and typing very, very fast. The balding man pointed to a chair in front of a beat-up monitor, leaned over her and typed in a password, and Persephone found herself blinking at an email in-box. The emails had headings like "URGENT: IRONTOSSER/URANIA BACK TOGETHER INTERVIEW" and "NEED BY NOON: GREEN PARTY TAX POLICY COMMENTS" and "VERY, VERY URGENT HAUNTED HOUSE INTERVIEW UPDATE IS ANYONE EVEN CHECKING THESE??"

"Transcribe these," the man said.

"Uh, okay, sure, how do I—"

He was already leaving. Persephone stared after him, and swiveled back to search the screen for clues. Clicking around, she discovered all the emails had audio files attached. Right. Interviews. Which apparently she had to turn into written text. How was she even supposed to *hear* them in this chaos?

"Hey," the young guy said. "Here." He was dangling a spare set of headphones over her shoulder—plain black plug-ins, not like his cushy noise-cancelling wireless ones, but Persephone recognized help when it was offered.

"Thanks," she said, grabbing them.

He smiled slightly, and pointed at the taskbar on the bottom of the screen. "Run each interview through that app. That'll turn them into text. Not a lot of punctuation, and the spelling is bad, especially for names and jargon, so you have to check and correct them. Also, not great for anyone with an accent outside of Standard American -- if someone has a really strong accent, it's easier just to type the whole thing up yourself."

Persephone nodded, trying to look efficient. Another email had arrived while he spoke.

"Then you reply to the original email and attach the transcript. Don't worry about crafting a polite response. They don't care. They just want the interview so they can grab the quotes they want."

"Put interviews through the app, check and correct, attach and send," Persephone repeated. "Right?"

"Right. Oh, and I'm Patrick."

Persephone beamed at him. "Thanks, Patrick. I'm Persephone."

"I know," Patrick said, and went back to his station. "I put a bet on you."

Persephone tried to frame a question about that, but he'd already put his headphones back on and was industriously typing. She opened the transcription software, and, after a brief struggle, worked out how to open one of the downloaded audio files. Words started to appear on the screen. It wasn't too bad—about as accurate as closed captions on a live speech, she thought—but it was still going to take a while to get through even this one interview. It was going to be a long day.

The woman with the Afro popped up beside her cubicle. "Oh, there you are," she said. "Now, about that coffee run..."

***

Hades finished going over his schedule for next week with his PA, took an absent-minded bite of the sandwich she'd brought him, and discovered that the tomato had soaked right through the bread.

"I'll get you another," his PA said, correctly interpreting his grimace.

"I probably need the walk," Hades said.

Cherry shook her head, mock solemn. Her red hair had been bundled into two massive buns on either side of her head, and they waggled with the motion. "Can't have another incident like the last one, boss. You'll bring the whole department into disrepute."

"Did Odysseus tell *everyone*?"

"I heard it from three people before I sat down this morning. Granted, one of them was Odysseus."

"I can't do much damage with a sandwich," Hades said tartly. "Cherry, can we treat future iterations of the story as a non-event, please? I don't want to cause any embarrassment for the young lady."

"I'll put the word out," she assured him. "Rolled eyes and 'that old news?' by the end of the day."

"Thank you." He walked with her out into the main office, and paused. "Cherry? What's that thing on your desk?"

It was a phenomenally ugly construction of pebbled glass and aluminum, angled so that the glass was facing side on to Cherry's desk chair.

"Oh, that's my sun lamp. Daphne told me about them after she had that bout of SAD last winter."

"SAD? The seasonal depression thing?"

"Yeah, you know, we're heading into fall now, and there's less sunlight around. It gets a bit grim in the middle of winter, when you leave for work in the dark, and go home in the dark, and spend all day underground." She glanced at his face, and added, "Not that this is a bad workspace! It's just a little…"

"Grim?"

"Well. Sometimes."

Hades surveyed the cubicles. His team were busy, and seemed happy enough–no raised voices or sounds of strain. But now that he was looking, there were a lot of those pebbled glass and aluminum things, tucked in beside monitors or waiting on overhead shelves. "Cherry, could you please ask Odysseus to come see me?"

Cherry reached for the phone on her desk, then paused. "What about your lunch?"

"I'll grab something later," Hades said, heading back to his office. There'd been some kind of memo a few months ago… "Odysseus, please. At his earliest convenience."

Odysseus showed up six minutes later, with spinach stuck in his teeth. "What's up? Cherry sounded worried. Have we tanked the company?"

Hades snorted. "Not unless you've pulled off some really spectacular embezzlement."

Odysseus dropped into the chair across from him. "Give me some credit. If I were embezzling, you'd never know it. Penny and I would be in the Bahamas with fruity umbrella cocktails weeks before anyone caught on."

"I think someone would notice if *Penny* wasn't around."

Odysseus clutched his chest. "Ouch. So, what's the deal?"

"I'm wondering if maybe we should look into moving the department to another floor. What do you—"

"Yes," Odysseus said instantly. "*Yes*, excellent, please get us out of this hole."

Hades sat back. "Won't it be disruptive?"

"Stable team, stable processes, not a problem." Odysseus jumped to his feet. "I've got a presentation on my laptop, let me grab it."

"You've got a— Odysseus, how much do people dislike working down here?"

"A lot," Odysseus said. He was already halfway to the door.

Hades rubbed his eyes. "Why didn't anyone *tell* me?"

There was a pause. He dropped his hands.

Odysseus had walked back to the desk. "I did tell you," he said, his voice level. "You weren't ready to hear it."

"That's absurd."

"It's really not," Odysseus told him. "You get very focused, and you're not great with change. You know that. Unless I stood here and shouted, 'Hades, everyone hates the basement,' you weren't going to hear me."

"They *hate* it?"

"Yes. But they like you. You're a good boss. If you want to hide in the lower depths, then fine, they'll hide with you. But if you're saying you're finally ready to talk to Zeus and get us a space with some daylight, then yes, one hundred percent, everyone here will be delighted."

Hades scratched his chin. "Well, I was thinking an exploratory committee might be a good first step. Did you want to head it?"

"Committees are where good ideas go to die, Hades. And I appreciate the vote of confidence, but he's not going to listen to me. *You* need to talk to Zeus."

"Which department would he move down here?"

Odysseus spread his hands. "Not your problem."

"Right," Hades said. "Okay. Then I guess you better show me this presentation. Can you send Cherry in on your way out?"

"My pleasure," Odysseus said. "And I really mean that." He left, and Hades heard Cherry's quickly cut off howl of glee. She came rushing in, eyes gleaming.

"Is it true? We're moving?"

"I'm making the case for it," Hades said, and gritted his teeth. "Can you see if my brother has a few minutes for a phone call this afternoon?"

While he waited, he clicked through Odysseus's presentation. It was characteristically thorough, listing improved efficiency projections, benefits to staff morale and thus less demand on wellbeing resources, and had a nicely worded statement about perceived seniority. He hadn't made any claims for any particular space to serve as Finance's new home, but there was a brief note on transport logistics which argued that any move above the tenth floor would necessarily slow operations.

Hades grimaced. The bastard really had thought of everything.

His phone beeped.

"Mr. Kronion?" Cherry's voice said, at her sweetest and most professional. "I have Mr. Kronion for you on line one."

"Hello, Zeus."

"Hey there, big bro!" Zeus was clearly in one of his expansive moods. That boded well, but Hades knew how quickly the weather could change. "What can I do for you?"

"I believe it's time to discuss a move for the Finances department," Hades said, and launched into his argument. Well, Odysseus's argument. Zeus asked an occasional quick, cogent question, but was otherwise silent. Hades could hear the tap of his pen against his desk.

"The south half of the twenty-eighth floor is entirely empty right now," Zeus said, once he'd finished. "Might be nice, to work more closely together."

Hades's stomach knotted. "We're a big department," he said, trying to keep his voice neutral. "Productivity wouldn't benefit as much if we were crammed into our final destination. And there's the transport logistics to be considered."

"Good point," Zeus said. There was a trace of amusement in his voice. Hades let it slide. "Well, okay. Eighth floor is currently Archives and IT, and Archives keeps not so subtly hinting they want more space. They can have the basement, IT can go to the 28th floor, which should suit their inflated sense of importance, and the eighth floor is all yours. Have you got a timetable?"

Hades exhaled, making sure that it wasn't audible. "I was thinking around the end of January, right after the retreat. It's a slow fiscal month, and the retreat already disrupts processes."

"Can't put a price on a little team-building," Zeus said cheerfully.

Hades kept his mouth shut. The annual company retreat was one of the first things Zeus had instituted when he'd taken over the company from their not-so-dearly departed father, and one of the first things Hades had argued with him about. He could and did put a price on

43

hiring out an entire ski resort for four days, and it was an astronomical one. Zeus argued that after the way their father had left things, the demoralized staff needed a pick-me-up. Hades argued that for the cost of the yearly event, they could have a full-time counselling staff and install an office gym with a personal trainer, which would surely be of more long-term benefit.

But it was a company tradition now, and an argument he'd lost a long time ago.

"January might be tough," Zeus said, after a second. "Yeah, that won't work. End of February?"

Hades didn't have to pretend to be horrified. "March is tax season. That's non-stop work till the end of April."

"Okay, then May." Zeus said. "First of May, start moving day." He chuckled. "That'll give Archives some time to untwist their underwear." He sounded pleased. Tyra of Archives must have pissed him off.

Not his problem, Hades reminded himself. "May 1st, eighth floor," he said, and made a note. "I'll get things moving down here. Thanks."

"No problem," Zeus assured him. "A small piece of magic for my financial wizard. Anything else, while you've got me on the line?"

"No, I-- Oh, yes, actually. Did you get a chance to look at those unaccounted-for expenses in your last reimbursement claim?"

Zeus laughed. "Kind of busy up here, bro."

"For tax purposes, we need to keep close records of—"

"I'll remind my people to keep their receipts," Zeus said indulgently. "Oh, Hera told me to tell you that she expects you for New Year's Eve. No last-minute emergencies this time, you hear?" His voice was jovial, but he meant it.

"Sure."

"And bring a date," Zeus added. "Right, bye."

"How am I–" Hades scowled at the dial tone, and hung up.

Odysseus was hovering on the other side of his door, not even pretending to work. Hades waved him in.

"We're moving from the first of May," Hades said. "Eighth floor."

Odysseus let out a cheer that turned heads in the main room, and dashed into the middle of the cubicles before Hades could stop him. By the time he caught up, Odysseus was already standing on someone's desk, his arms raised in victory. "Esteemed workmates!" he declaimed. "Friends and foes! Rejoice, for this is our last winter in the Underworld!" Odysseus had been a theater minor in college, and sometimes it showed.

"Get down!" Hades snapped, uncomfortably aware of the excited murmurs running through the department.

"Absolutely not," Odysseus said, and effortlessly evaded Hades's futile grab at his knees. "My children! On May Day we rise with the green things of spring, and take our place on the eighth floor! We shall have windows. We shall have sunlight. And who shall we thank for this?"

His employees were abandoning their desks as word spread, clustering around Odysseus. There was a palpable sense of excitement. Cherry shouldered through the crowd and hovered at Hades's shoulder.

Odysseus pointed directly at him. "Our protector! Our king! Friends, let us show our appreciation for Hades!"

It was ridiculous. His employees shouldn't be cheering him for a simple, sensible business decision he evidently should have made years ago. But they were, and clapping too. Cherry hugged him, and that apparently broke some kind of boundary, because then he was being clapped on the back and grabbed for fervent handshakes. Daphne had actual tears in her eyes.

"You're welcome," he said, more or less at random. "Glad to do it. Should have made the change earlier." He gave Odysseus a look of mute appeal, and the man jumped down from the desk to usher him back to the relative calm of his office.

Hades took a deep breath. "You should be getting the credit for this."

"I prefer to be the power behind the throne," Odysseus said easily, and then grabbed his shoulder with uncharacteristic sincerity. "Seriously. You did the part I couldn't. And eighth floor is okay?"

"Certainly," Hades said, and busied himself with lining up his desk accessories. When he looked up again, Odysseus was still beaming at him. "What?"

"See, change can be good," Odysseus said. "Maybe you should think about making a few more?"

"Maybe you should think about getting back to work," Hades said sourly. But even when Odysseus had left and redirected the enthusiasm of the team back to their tasks, he found it difficult to concentrate on work himself.

Changes, hm?

For some reason, he found himself thinking of flowers.

***

"We give them ten minutes to clear the elevators, and then we go," Patrick said softly.

Persephone rubbed her eyes. "What?"

Patrick, his fingers still busily tapping, nodded at the rest of the room, now occupied by little more than scattered cups. Only the balding man

46

and older woman remained, arguing with each other about word limits on some copy. "We don't leave until Augie and Ness leave. But we can go after them."

Persephone's eyes felt like someone had poured sand into them. Her head was pounding; she wasn't sure whether it was concentration or dehydration, since she hadn't thought to grab water on one of her five coffee runs. Patrick had a water bottle. She'd bring one tomorrow.

"I'm nowhere near done," she admitted. It was nearly nine pm. She'd been there for over twelve hours.

Patrick snorted, and swiveled his screen so she could see the queue. "We're never *done*. The work never stops. But we're human, and we have to. How are your hands?"

Persephone stretched her fingers and rotated her wrists. There was a tension in her palms that kept dragging her fingers into claws. "Sore."

"Try to avoid using them tonight," he advised. "No food prep, no phone scrolling."

"Believe me, the most I'm going to do tonight is order take out and collapse in front of the TV," Persephone said.

"That's the spirit."

"Fine!" Ness shouted. "530 words, and not a single word more, Augie, do you hear me?"

"The whole building heard you, Ness! Are you coming home or not?"

There was some performative stomping and throwing of things into satchels, and then the two of them left, still bickering.

"They live together?" Persephone asked.

Patrick grinned. "They're married. Four kids. Can you believe it?"

"No! They act like they want to murder each other."

"Ah, true love," Patrick said, and stood up, briskly transferring his belongings to his own bag. "Not really my style, but it seems to work for them." He checked his phone. "Come on, my boyfriend's picking me up in five."

Persephone stood, her back cracking as she moved out of her hunch. "Owww."

Patrick gave her a look that was friendly, but not at all sympathetic. "You'll get used to it," he said.

Persephone privately doubted this was possible, but he hadn't pointed her the wrong direction once today. She meekly followed him out of the building and retrieved her car from the parking building across the street. She'd worried about whether driving instead of taking public transport was another thing that made her too conspicuous, but right now it was a luxury she wasn't willing to give up. She drove home, stumbled into the living room, and sat down on the couch for just a second.

Her phone woke her up half an hour later.

"Hi, Mom," she said, making a face at the taste in her mouth. Water. Water was needed now.

"Hello, darling. I need to speak with you about something important. Can you come over to the house?"

"I'm in my PJs, Mom." This was a lie. Her shoes were still on—gross—and her bra was digging into her ribcage. She reached behind to release the catches, and sighed in relief.

"At ten o'clock?"

"It was a long day. What did you want to talk about?" She stumbled to the kitchen and poured a glass of water, sitting at the table to drink it while she pulled her bra out of her sleeve.

"Well, have you heard about this thing with your little friend, Hecate? The one who wears all black?"

"I know who Hecate is, Mom."

"She'd look so pretty in florals."

Persephone put the phone on speaker and opened her fridge. Hm. Unless she wanted a saggy stick of celery and some suspect yogurt, it was going to have to be pizza. "Did you call me to talk about Hecate's wardrobe choices?"

"Hm? No. She's suing my friend Pontus."

"What? Why?"

"Because of Ceto's dolphins," Demeter said. "Honestly, I don't see what the fuss is about. I've never liked dolphins much. They always look like they're laughing at you."

Persephone mentally reviewed the clues before she tried the next question. Pontus was Miles Pontus, the CEO of Pontus Fisheries, who'd lately been in the news for mistreating their fishing fleet crews and overfishing. Ceto was one of her mother's acquaintances and occasional rivals, an energetic older woman with a taste for environmental causes.

"Do you mean that Hecate is representing an organization Ceto's involved with?" she tried. "One that's laid suit against Pontus Fisheries?"

"That's what I've been saying, dear," Demeter said. "Anyway, can't you have a word with her? She's always looked up to you."

Persephone grabbed an old sketchbook and a pencil. Her hands twinged, and she remembered Patrick's warning, but doodling was the best way to get through one of these calls. "What do you want me to say, Mom?"

There was a pause. Demeter loved pauses. Sometimes, Persephone thought that she wielded silence like a weapon. Then she felt guilty and disloyal for thinking it. She doodled a dolphin in the corner of a blank page.

"Well, you could tell her that Pontus is a good friend of mine," Demeter said at last. "He's practically your uncle."

"Mm," Persephone said, and gave the dolphin one of Hecate's metallic statement necklaces. "I'm not sure I've seen him recently."

"He came to the Friends of the Botanical Gardens auction last year!" Demeter said. "Honestly, Persephone, you've got to remember these things."

"Yes, Mom."

"It's vital to know who's who, and who's present. Even at your little internship."

"Right." Persephone made the dolphin's smile wider, and added a hint of sharp teeth.

"And who's connected to whom," Demeter said. "As we're both connected to Pontus, and you're connected to Hecate. Her taking this case is pretty much a conflict of interest, if you think about it."

Persephone didn't have to imagine what Hecate would think about this argument. She drew the logo for Pontus Fisheries under the dolphin, so that it was leaping joyously above it, and drew threatening tsunami waves in the dolphin's wake.

"I'm sure that they've checked all that in the due diligence, Mom," she said.

"But her firm might not be aware just how very close we are to the Pontus family," Demeter pressed.

"Maybe not."

"So you'll talk to her?"

"Sure," Persephone said. "I'll talk to her on Saturday." It wasn't technically a lie; she and Hecate had planned brunch. If her mother thought the substance of the conversation was going to be less about work gossip and mimosas and more about perverting the course of justice, that was on her. "Mom, I'm starving. I have to go figure out dinner."

"All right, darling. I love you!"

"I love you, too." Persephone hung up and looked at the dolphin. "Okay," she told it. "We survived the first day. Tomorrow, we do it again."

Chapter Three

"You're due upstairs," Cherry said, poking her head through Hades's door.

Hades didn't look up from his screen. "One minute."

"You were due five minutes ago."

"I just need to finish this one thing..."

"Hera called," Cherry said.

Hades flinched. Then he grabbed his tablet, straightened his tie, and headed for the elevators. The meeting was on the top floor, but if he focused on the agenda, and not on how high and how fast he was being moved, he'd probably be able to avoid panic in the elevator.

Getting out of the elevator and to the meeting was a separate problem he wasn't ready to contemplate yet.

And it worked–at least until his elevator was interrupted halfway up, and the doors opened to reveal Persephone.

He'd seen her around Olympus a few times. Interns worked long hours and were sent to almost every department, so it would have been strange if he hadn't. But it had been two months since their second, less disastrous meeting in the Happy Isles, and he'd been half-hoping his first stunned impression had been some weird trick of the fates, not to be repeated.

He immediately knew this was a false hope. Persephone had dark marks under her eyes, her hair was falling out of its bun, and she had a small coffee stain on the front of her violet dress.

And she was undeniably beautiful.

"Oh, hi!" she said. She looked actually pleased to see him, which he found foolishly encouraging.

"Hello," he said, and tried to smile. His cheeks felt stiff and strange, but she smiled back and took a place beside him. He could smell her, warm jasmine and cool mint. Could he hold his breath without looking like an idiot?

"Been a while, hasn't it? Thank you again for replacing my dress. And for covering our drinks."

"Oh. Well. The least I could do." This was a conversation, wasn't it? And awkward as it was, far better than thinking about the swooping sensation of rising through the air in a little metal box. "How are you enjoying your time at Olympus?"

"It's great!" she said, so enthusiastically that it rang false.

He crooked an eyebrow at her.

She relaxed a little. "You're not going to tell on me?"

"Wouldn't dream of it."

"Well, I really do enjoy the opportunity. And I've been in four departments already–it's amazing how much is going on."

"But?"

"But I'm tired. And I still haven't got anywhere near Art and Design."

"Oh, that. Mark Hermes makes sure that interns go into the departments that suit them least to start. Art for people who have no sense of color or layout, Wardrobe for people who don't know anything about fashion..."

"Kitchens for people who can't cook?" Persephone asked. "Copy for people who can't spell?"

"Exactly," he said, and the elevator dinged to a stop.

He'd forgotten. He'd been so focused on the conversation that he'd paid no attention to the rising numbers. He hadn't braced himself for the moment where the doors opened, and the merciless open space of the front office was revealed. The view hit him like a brick between the eyes.

The elevator opened directly onto the reception area, and it was designed to stun visitors from the moment they saw it.

The outer walls were all triple-glazed glass from floor to ceiling, discreetly held in place with white plastered columns that—he'd checked—disguised steel beams. The floor was black and white marble, polished to such a high gleam that even the weak beams of the wintry sun bounced light around the lobby. The window-walls provided an unimpeded view of the city–smaller buildings nearby, the trees of Ida Park, down to the river sparkling in the distance, and beyond that, the snowy mountains.

The effect was that of standing on top of a cliff.

Hades froze in the back of the elevator.

Persephone stepped out, and took a couple of steps. Then she paused, and turned back to him.

"You go ahead," he said, through lips stiff with terror. "I, uh. I'll be a minute."

Her assessment was lightning quick. He saw her eyes dart to his hands, clenched around the tablet, his position, pressed against the back wall, and his face.

He had no idea what his expression was, but her pose shifted, the stiffness in her shoulders relaxing.

"Does distraction help?" she asked, as if it was a normal question. As if what was happening to him was normal. "Do you want me to keep talking?"

"Yes," he said. "Distraction is good." He took a deep breath and forced a few steps forward, looking only at her face. His footsteps echoed on marble, not the elevator steel.

"Okay. Well, why do the interns spend their first weeks in departments Mr. Hermes knows they won't be good at?"

"Because the departments know that, too," Hades said. "They're never glad to see the interns they get for the first month or so, and you get a real baptism of fire. Mark is testing whether you can stick it out and try your best when you're out of your comfort zone and things go wrong. Because in publishing, no matter how experienced and skilled you are, something is always going wrong."

Her mouth fell open. Her lips looked plush and soft. "Wow. That's smart."

It was a lot easier to ignore the view when he could look at her mouth instead. "You'll get to Art. And by then, you'll be toughened up, and ready to show everyone what you can do." He nodded at her arms, covered in a navy-blue cardigan. "We already know you can do well."

Persephone blinked at him. "How did you know I designed my tats?"

"Penny told me," Hades said. "She was impressed." They were through the reception area, and had made it to the outer office. Zeus's two senior assistants had their desks here, and off to the right was Zeus's own enormous office. The internal walls were oak, but the outer walls were the same glass monstrosities.

One of the senior assistants looked up from his screen. "Oh, you're here, Mr. Kronion," he said, somehow making the statement of fact a chiding reminder of his tardiness. "Everyone's in the green meeting room."

Oh, thank goodness. The back rooms of the top floor were decently enclosed. They went down the corridor behind the assistant desks and Hades felt his shoulders relax as soon as the void was shut out.

"Tell me more about interning," he said, not because he was freaking out, but because he wanted to hear her talk. That renegade strand of honey-blonde hair was falling down her neck.

"Well, I thought I was doing okay with transcription on my first day, but on my *second* day I got the whole lot back, with sarcastic comments about my spelling and grammar in the margins."

"Oh no."

"Oh yes. I mean, they had a point. After that I was off to Subscriptions, although I spent most of my time calling people who had cancelled subscriptions, and didn't appreciate the follow-up call to talk about why."

"Don't they fill out an automatic survey when they unsubscribe?"

"Yes, but Subscriptions likes to apply the *personal* touch, or at least it does when it has interns to torment. And then it was Kitchens, which didn't throw me anything impossible, though it was hell on my feet and nails." She flashed a hand at him, her fingers spread wide, and he had the absurd desire to clasp her hand and brush his lips against the back.

"And now you're in Events," he said.

"Yes. Which is at least familiar."

He wanted to ask her about that—about the weariness in her voice, about what she'd done to give her that experience—but they'd come to a

56

halt outside the meeting room. There were walls in there, proper walls you couldn't see through, and the window to the outside would be smaller. He could sit so that he couldn't see it.

Persephone opened the door and gestured him in. He mouthed *thank you* as he passed.

"You're eleven minutes late," Hera said, looking up from her tablet.

Hades rather liked his sister-in-law, in a way where she also scared the crap out of him, but her eyes were laser-beam focused on the intern in his wake, and he couldn't allow that.

"My fault," he said. "I asked Persephone to help me with something and we got delayed."

"Hm," Hera said, and transferred her focus to him. It was unnerving, to be so minutely examined, and have no idea what she was thinking behind the carefully perfect composition of her face. As always, she looked impeccable, her dark hair styled into a bouncy wave that just touched the collar of her crisp pleated shirt-dress.

Technically, Hera didn't work at Olympus Publishing. Technically, she didn't work anywhere. She had inherited wealth of her own, and then married——twice—one of the richest men in the city, and as far as Hades knew, she had never had an actual job. Technically, she was a decorative example of the idle rich.

Anyone who had seen Hera in action knew that *idle* was the last possible word to describe her, unless you decided to go for *nice*.

Persephone, wisely, took the opportunity to slide in beside Joy from Events, and flipped open her notebook, looking the very image of a biddable and eager-to-please employee.

"We're all here now, honey," Zeus said, from where he was sitting beside his wife, and she instantly softened and smiled at him. They made a stunning pair and Hades felt a tug in the heart regions. He didn't want Hera, and he definitely didn't want the wrangling and bitterness that had so marred the years of their first marriage -- but he wanted that sense of understanding and partnership that they had now.

"Right," Hera said, and tapped a laptop key. The screen behind her displayed the Minos Centre banquet hall floorplan. "As you all know, the theme for this year's holiday event is Mystery in the Night Garden."

Hera didn't usually bother telling people things they should already know, so Hades assumed this courtesy was for him, since he'd missed the last three meetings. Hera started planning the Olympus winter holiday party right after she'd wrapped the Midsummer celebration, and while she casually conscripted Events staff to carry out her mandate, the vision was always hers.

"Titan's theme is Hawai'ian Dream," she added, and flicked through to a detailed events plan headed by the logo of the rival publishing company. The plan was clearly marked CONFIDENTIAL at the head of every page–and it had just as clearly been photographed surreptitiously on someone's phone.

"Where did you get that?" Joy asked. The Head of Events was a tall, dark-haired woman with jittery energy. She made Hades uncomfortable, possibly because he associated her solely with occasions where he was forced to make small talk with strangers.

Hera looked smug, but didn't reply. "They're going for something too similar with these floral photobooths. This is ours." She pulled up a mock-up of a garden arch, twined with ivy and jasmine, against a dark blue background full of stars, with a glowing full moon rising from the floor. "And this is Titan's." A square frame, covered in hibiscus, and a backdrop featuring a glowing bonfire on a beach. "We need an alternative -- a better alternative. Ideas?"

"Giant flowers," Joy said. "Lose the arch, cluster them together."

Hera shook her head. "Titan did that three years ago."

Persephone half-raised her hand, then hesitated when Joy frowned at her.

"Go ahead," Hera said briskly.

"Maybe a less literal interpretation would work? People can do really impressive things with papercrafting."

"Crafts," Joy said, in the same way that someone else might say 'slime'.

Hera frowned. "I don't want kitsch."

"No, I meant elegant lines and silhouettes, like profile cut-outs." Persephone was sketching something quickly in her notebook. Hades craned, and made out black trees with stark bare branches, layered on top of each other. "You'd build this out, and there'd be space in here for posing. It would look like people were lost in the woods, and they'd be the only color in here–like they were the only living characters in a spooky pop-up book."

Hera was pulling up images on her laptop, and they flickered over the projection screen. Zeus rested his chin in his fingers, looking thoughtful.

"Mystery in the Night Garden," Hera said. "Some props here, I think, leaning into the spooky book aesthetic. Ah." She paused on a picture of black masks on sticks, suggesting an owl, a black cat, a wolf. "We'll want the lighting to help integrate people into the space. Sharp shadows, perhaps a chiaroscuro effect." She smiled thinly. "That'll stand out on the apps. Yes. We'll do this, Joy."

The Events head was staring at her like a stunned rabbit in headlights.

"Good idea, Persephone," Zeus added.

Joy's stare turned puzzled, clearly wondering how Zeus knew this lowly peon's name.

Hades was wondering that himself. A nasty suspicion rose from the back of his mind, but he stamped it down. Zeus had stopped cheating. He'd gone to therapy and done the work and wooed Hera back, and ever since the second wedding he'd kept his hands and his dick to himself. Or, more to the point, exclusively for Hera.

Besides, Hera was carrying on with the next point on the agenda, while Persephone, head down, scribbled notes as fast as she could. Hades sat up straighter and tried to concentrate. Guests always tried to make conversation with him, and it was a lot easier if he could talk about the party details.

The meeting finished exactly eleven minutes past the scheduled time. Hades suspected Hera was making a point.

"Oh, I'll need that," she said at the end, gesturing at Persephone's notebook.

Persephone blinked at her.

"No notes leave the room," Hera said. "We don't want Titan scooping us, do we? Hope you've got a good memory." She walked around the table and plucked the book from Persephone's hand. Persephone made a faint noise that might have been a protest, and Hades bridled.

"She might have other notes in there, Hera," he said.

"Ah?" Hera opened the book and flipped through it. She stopped on one page and raised an eyebrow.

Persephone flushed all the way up to her hairline.

"Hm," Hera said. She turned to the back, neatly tore out several pages of notes in Persephone's flowing hand, and returned the notebook.

"Thank you," Persephone said. She was still red. Hades found himself moving instinctively towards her, and was smoothly cut off by Hera's hand on his wrist.

"Walk me out?" she said. It sounded like a suggestion, but Hades knew an order when he heard one. "Goodbye, love. I've got drinks with the girls this evening, so I'll be home late."

"Looking forward to it," Zeus said, and gave his wife a wink that Hades felt was definitely inappropriate in the workplace.

Hera kept up a barrage of light, impersonal chatter as they made their way to the elevator, and Hades used it as a barrier against the thought of the sucking void outside. In the elevator, he placed his back against the wall and sighed.

"We'll hold the next meeting downstairs," Hera said. "I'm sorry. I forgot." Her gaze was direct.

"It's not a big deal," Hades said automatically. The lighted numbers were ticking down. The muscles between his shoulder blades released some of their tension. "Honestly, it's fine."

Hera ignored that. "Did you have a chance to check out that therapist I mentioned?"

"I haven't really had the time."

"Hm," Hera said, and mercifully left it there.

"Is, uh, is Persephone somebody?" Hades ventured. "Only you and Zeus seem to know her."

"She's somebody's daughter," Hera said. "Her mother is Demeter Erinyes, chair of the Erinyes Foundation."

"Oh," Hades said. "I'm not sure I—"

"The Erinyes Foundation, Hades. The gigantic charitable trust. Poverty initiatives, housing, scholarships... Surely you've donated?"

Hades had a vague memory of glossy green cards with a gold embossed logo in his office mail, inviting him to various luncheons and fashion walks and galas. "I think so," he said. "Why is she an *intern?*"

Hera shrugged. "Her mother made a call and Zeus got her into the program."

"No, I meant... she was really good in there, wasn't she?"

"She had a good idea," Hera conceded. "Aren't you going to give me the nepotism lecture? I thought you were hell-bent on keeping the intern program a meritocracy."

"Well, she seems competent enough," Hades said. It was a shame that Persephone had thought she needed to use her connections, though. Surely she was good enough to have earned a place on her own merits? Not to mention perceptive enough to see he was distressed, and kind enough to talk him through the incipient panic attack.

Hera shot him a thoughtful look. "You know, you'd have met her before if you bothered to go to any of those charity events instead of just donating."

He smiled fondly at her. "You're my social manager. I'll go to whatever events you say are compulsory."

"You'll regret that," Hera said, and patted his arm. "So. Persephone Erinyes. Rich, pretty, clearly got some brains, and you stood up for her being late. This is interesting. You like her?"

"Oh. Well. I don't really know her, but she seems–" Lush. Vivid. "--nice."

"She has drawings of you in her sketchbook," Hera said. She stepped gracefully out of the elevator and looked over her shoulder at him. "Good ones. Ask her out."

And before Hades could point out that Persephone was a lot younger than he was, or inquire about what kind of drawings, or make his brain produce anything more coherent than an "uhhhh," Hera was off, sashaying through the lobby in her five-inch stilettos, taking no notice of the awed crowds that parted before her.

***

"Is that what you're wearing, darling?"

"Yes, Mom." Persephone took a few steps, watching the hemline in the mirror. Most of her clothes had been moved to the guesthouse, but her special occasion gowns were still stored in her mother's dressing room. The gown was tighter than the last time she'd worn it, but she didn't have time to find something else, and it was plain black and floor length, which fitted the brief.

Demeter shook her head and ran her hands down her own dress. She was heading out to a different holiday party, and wearing a deep ruby gown herself, with rhinestone detailing at her throat and diaphanous sleeve cuffs. The gown skimmed over her round stomach and substantial hips, outlining her curves. "Black really isn't your color, you know. You're not going to stand out in that."

One of the things Persephone liked most about her mother was that she'd never seen Demeter succumb to body shame or diet talk. When Persephone's private school friends had started being put on diets and exercise programs when they hit puberty, Demeter had scoffed, and encouraged her daughter to eat and move exactly how she wanted to. Whatever Demeter's private feelings about her own body–and it must have been hard to avoid having any negative thoughts in the high society circles she moved in–Persephone's mother had always modeled body-positivity for her daughter. And she always dressed to stand out.

"I'm an intern, Mom. We're not supposed to be visible. We're supposed to help with whatever needs doing and otherwise blend into the crowd."

"Well, you don't need to blend in *this* much, surely. You'll practically fade into the wall." Demeter brightened. "Why don't you wear my sapphires?"

Persephone tried to imagine Joy's reaction to her showing up with half a million dollars of jewelry around her throat. She was already on thin ice there; the Events head had not appreciated being upstaged at the meeting, and had made Persephone's work life more than usually hellish. "The sapphires might be a bit much," she said.

"Oh, I know!" Demeter said, and disappeared into the jewelry cupboard. She reappeared with a long strand of pearls, gleaming warmly in her hand. "There. Pearls with black are so classy."

Persephone wavered. Clearly, she wasn't going to get out the door completely unadorned. And the pearls were—relatively—understated. "Thanks, Mom," she said, and wound them around her neck three times. "How do I look?"

"Are you sure you don't want John to do your hair and makeup? He's here for me anyway."

Persephone kissed her mother's cheek. "I'm sure."

"You just look so *tired*, darling. I'm worried that this internship is too much for you. You've always been so delicate."

"I'm fine, Mom. Just a bit under-slept."

"Well, Kelly can drop you off and come back for me."

"Hecate's giving me a ride." Shit, her tone had been just a shade too dismissive. She heard the quality of the silence change, and tensed.

"You've got it all figured out, don't you?" Demeter said, every word bitten off. "I'm only your loving mother, trying to help you in any way I can, but what do I know?"

"You are helping," Persephone said. "These pearls are amazing, Mom, really. They make the entire outfit."

"I see you working yourself to the bone on these menial tasks, and when I try to give you advice you just push me away." Demeter sat down heavily on one of the plush dressing chairs. "Persephone, what more must I do to show you how much I love you? I've given you everything. You know I have! But you don't appreciate it a bit. We barely see each other anymore."

Persephone's chest squeezed. Her mother looked so deflated, sitting there with tears coming to her eyes. And she had been turning down a lot of invitations to the big house lately—all the late nights and early mornings hadn't left much time for what Demeter called "chatting, just us girls."

"Mom, I'm really sorry," she said, feeling her own eyes prickle. "I know I've been busy but of course I still love you. I'll love you forever."

"More than anybody?" Demeter asked.

"More than anybody in the whole wide world," Persephone said, completing the familiar phrase. It was a line from a book Demeter had read her every night as a child. Persephone couldn't remember much from that time, but she'd been struggling with her father's death, and her mother, no matter how busy she'd been, had always made time to come home and tuck four-year-old Persephone in. Persephone could remember her mother's hand on her hair, and her soft voice saying, "Persephone, will you love me forever?"

"Oh," Demeter said, in a small voice, and began to weep. Persephone embraced her mother, and resigned herself to being late.

Twenty minutes later, she slid into Hecate's electric sports car and said, "Don't say it."

"I wasn't going to," Hecate said, slipping her phone back into her silver clutch. "You only had another three minutes before I came in there, though."

Persephone winced at the thought and strapped herself in. "Shit, Joy's going to kill me. Can we break some speed limits?"

"Absolutely not," Hecate said primly. "I am an officer of the court." She grinned, her teeth flashing sharp and white. "I do, however, know some short cuts."

Persephone held onto the handle above the door for dear life and reminded herself she'd asked for this, as Hecate whipped through side-streets, hurtled through yellow lights, and at one point went down a one-way alley so narrow that Persephone was sure the car was going to lose its side mirrors. But they slid to a halt at the service entrance of the Minos Centre, having shaved seven minutes off the travel time, and Persephone tumbled out only slightly terrified.

"I'll see you in there!" she yelped over her shoulder, hustling to the door. The stupid trumpet-shaped skirt scooped in at the knees, making long strides an impossibility. For a brief second, Persephone considered hoisting the damn thing to her hips and making a run for it, but then she was inside, her eyes adjusting to the dim light of the staging area.

Joy spotted her immediately. There was a gleam of something approaching triumph in her eyes as Persephone made her apologies.

"Not a good look," she said, and snapped her chin at a passing Thalia who was burdened with a heavy snack tray. "But since you've finally made it, you can help her re-plate the hors d'oeuvres."

"Yes, Joy," Persephone said meekly, and hurried over.

Thalia barely spared her a glance as she set the tray down on a large trestle table. "Get the black platters," she snarled. "Big cardboard box by the kitchen loading doors, and whatever you do, don't drop them."

Persephone did as she was told. The platters were some kind of black glass, with glimmering points of sparkle embedded in them, and so heavy she needed to get both arms under the box and lift with her knees. "What's wrong with the hors d'oeuvres?" she muttered.

"Nothing," Thalia said, just as quietly. Her fingers were moving swiftly over the tray, to a platter and back again, as she shifted the small snacks, bare-handed. This probably broke about eight different food handling safety regulations, but Persephone didn't think this was the time to point that out. Instead, she moved the finished platters away as soon as Thalia was done with them, laying out new ones for her. "But your bitch of a boss decided that the caterer's trays weren't on theme, and only these stupid black ones would do. And she claimed that she didn't trust the center catering staff to redo it. Where the hell were you?"

"Family emergency, sorry. You're really good at this."

"I've had practice catering. I worked through college," Thalia said. Her tone said, *unlike you.*

Persephone didn't say anything. After all, it was true. And Thalia's stance relaxed as she stood back from the empty tray. "Did you see how I did it?" she asked. "Can you do it the same? There are another five big trays in there."

"I've got it," Persephone said, much more confidently than she felt. She braved the barely controlled chaos that was the kitchen for long enough to wash her hands and ferry the trays out, then set to work. She was definitely slower than Thalia, and she didn't have the same graceful efficiency of movement, but to her artist's eye, the plates at least looked the same.

Thalia came back with napkins and a tray of edible flowers and gave Persephone's work an approving nod before she started garnishing. Persephone dared a smile. "Your dress looks great," she said. It did–a full-skirted 50s style dress, with a scoop neck that made the most of Thalia's elegant collarbones.

"Thanks. So does yours."

They worked in a nearly companionable silence, and Persephone was wondering if she could broach a friendly conversation, maybe ask if Thalia had any holiday plans, when Joy returned, her eyes glittering with barely repressed fury. A man in black jeans and a white apron was staring after her, his arms folded across his chest.

"The servers are claiming these platters are too heavy," she hissed. "The catering manager says he won't make them carry them!"

Persephone looked at the empty trays in horror. "Do we have to put everything back?" she asked.

Joy stared at her as if she'd grown another eight heads. "No! These plates are *perfect*. You'll have to do it."

Thalia made a choked-off noise.

"You and the other interns," Joy continued, her eyes darting around the room. "Where are they?"

"Most of them aren't here," Persephone said. Only she and Thalia were working that evening, as the Kitchens and Events interns, and they were supposed to be general gofers, not stand-in wait staff.

"Well, call them!" Joy snarled. She stabbed a finger at Thalia. "And you! You take a plate and get on the floor. People are *arriving*. I'm going to see if these idiots will at least carry *drinks*." She strode off towards the kitchen.

"Shit, shit, shit," Thalia muttered. She hefted the platter onto her forearm. "I am not wearing the right shoes for this."

Persephone glanced down at her own strappy sandals and constricting skirt. "We're screwed," she said, and fished her phone out of her purse. "I hope everyone's got something black."

***

"Looking sharp, bro!"

"Thank you," Hades said, and suffered one of Zeus's enthusiastic back-slapping embraces. It was the same tuxedo he wore to every black-tie event. Hera had picked it out for him nearly a decade ago, and he could feel her inspecting it critically as she kissed his cheek.

"Remind me to take you shopping soon," she murmured. "No date?"

"Not tonight."

"Get a drink," Zeus said generously, his eyes already going to the next people in the reception line. "Mingle. Meet people. Cera! You look stunning!"

Hades ventured further into the party, already wondering when he could gracefully leave. He'd have to stay for the speeches and speak to some of the bigger names in the room, but he could probably get out after three hours if the timing was right.

At least there was plenty to look at. Hera had turned out another stunning event, transforming the nice-but-bland conference room into a hall of shifting shadows and starlit mystery. The bar in the corner was swathed in night-blooming jasmine and fairy lights that twinkled like fireflies. The string quartet on their greenery-swathed dais were playing something eerie in a minor key. Hades spotted Persephone's photo-booths to the side, where some of the younger attendees had already gathered, gleefully posing with the masks and pretending to scare each other by popping out of the paper forest.

He couldn't see Persephone herself anywhere, and the second he stopped moving, he became a target. Most of the guests were innocuously discharging their social responsibilities: he could make a few comments admiring the decor, accept some mild flattery about Olympus's successful year, and perhaps engage in a brief discussion of traffic, weather, or real estate before making his excuses and being swept into another group.

Some of them were more obnoxious, like Miles Pontus of Pontus Fisheries, who wanted to complain—at length—about a lawsuit, and only shut up when he spotted Minerva Eule heading their way.

"Can't she give me one night off?" Miles demanded rhetorically, and headed for the bar. Since he'd already drunk two flutes of champagne from the passing trays during the fifteen minutes he'd been monologuing, Hades didn't really think Miles needed another drink. He stayed where he was; Minerva was a senior partner at one of the most successful law firms in the city, and she was occasionally disconcerting, but always interesting company.

"Do you like Pontus?" she asked now, in her strong German accent. "He is not good company, I think."

Hades hid his smile in a sip. "He had a lot to tell me about some lawsuit you're bringing on behalf of an environmental group?"

"Hm, yes. This is a project for my juniors. We must do some good works, you see." She grinned at him. "It is not often so much pleasure. Hecate! Come."

Hades followed her beckoning finger, and found himself blinking at the same small woman he'd last seen with Persephone in The Happy Isles three months ago.

"Hello," she said to him now, perfectly poised. "Thank you for settling our tab that time."

"You're welcome."

"Hah! You know each other? Hades, Hecate is leading this suit against Pontus. She is young and fierce."

"I don't doubt it."

"Ah! Finally, I see something to eat. I will see you both later." Minerva disappeared in pursuit of a plate that was being swarmed by guests.

"Have you noticed the food?" Hecate asked quietly. Apparently she wasn't much for small talk either.

Hades scanned the room. Now that she'd drawn his attention to it, the caterers weren't putting out much of a spread. There were a lot of drinks trays in evidence, but only a few people with food platters, and every time one of them appeared, the tiny snacks on their plates vanished with alacrity. A few guests had taken to loitering near the door and pouncing on the hor d'oeuvres as they came out.

Come to think of it, some of those black-clad food servers looked familiar. "Are those the interns?"

"Yes."

Hera wasn't going to be happy about this. She had a genuine appreciation for the skills and experience that made good servers, and correspondingly high standards for the staff that worked her events. A group of amateurs drafted from the intern intake were not going to meet those standards.

He made for the nearest one, a young woman in a fifties-style ball gown. Her smile was professional, and she handled the platter with grace, but he could see the strain in her shoulders as the last blini was taken and she turned to go back to the kitchen. "Excuse me," he said.

Her eyes widened. "Yes, Mr. Kronion?"

Hades took the plate from her hands. It was even heavier than it looked. "Can you please explain this situation?" he said quietly. He was trying to project assurance, but she still visibly hesitated before she told him about the clash between the external catering team and Events, and Joy's subsequent choice to draft the interns instead.

"Persephone called everyone in, but we're still waiting for a few to arrive," she concluded. "Um. I'd better get back."

Hecate had tagged along behind him, looking both amused and concerned. She'd stopped what looked to be right out of earshot, but Hades had the impression that she'd taken everything in. Minerva didn't hire fools. He stepped over to her.

"Would you excuse me?" he said. "It was nice to see you again, but I think I'd better speak to my sister-in-law."

She regarded him for a long moment. "Good luck," she said, and it sounded too weighted for the moment. Hades didn't have time to think about it. He started moving through the crowd, muttering apologies and promises to catch up later as he went. He caught sight of the dark braids of Hera's personal assistant as she sped towards the kitchens, and winced. Hera had noticed something was wrong, but she and Zeus were stuck, still greeting people, and she didn't have all the facts yet. He could at least speed up the process.

He came up behind them and tapped her on the shoulder. She turned back to regard him quizzically. "There's been a little issue," he began, and then there was a stir from the receiving line as the latest guest presented himself.

Hades caught sight of him over Hera's shoulder, and felt his jaw actually drop.

"Don?" Zeus said, sounding genuinely shocked.

Hades had a very good view of Hera's face. Her eyes went wide and vulnerable as she heard the name. For a moment, she looked much, much younger. Then her practiced hostess mask reassembled herself, and she was once again the perfect gracious lady as she turned back to the reception line.

"Don!" she said. "How wonderful! I'm so glad you could make it."

The middle Kronion brother was grinning at both of them as Zeus released him from a hearty hug, but his question was for Hera. "Are you surprised?"

"Of course!"

"Did you miss me?" he demanded.

"Of course," Hades said, and found that he meant it more than he'd thought.

Don was wearing his tuxedo with no bowtie and the first two buttons of his shirt undone. The tousled waves of his blond hair brushed his wide shoulders. He'd put on more muscle, too–not the sleek, gym-toned muscle Zeus kept up, but the muscle of a man who used his body every day. He swept Hades into a hug and squeezed.

Hades squeezed back. "Behave," he said quietly, and Don winked at him as he let go.

"I had no idea the invitation had even reached you," Hera was saying. "I thought you must be in some forsaken place without wi-fi."

"I was," Don said. "But I got back to the internet last week and thought, hey, been a while since I caught up with the fam. Zeus, you look great. Hades, are you working too hard?"

"No," Hades said, at the same time that Hera said, "Yes, he is."

"Are you home for the holidays?" Zeus asked, putting his arm around Hera. "You must stay with us. We've plenty of room, don't we, darling?"

Unless something had changed a great deal, putting Zeus and Don in close proximity for more than a couple of hours was a disastrous idea. "Stay with me," Hades said quickly. "I'm sure Hera has a lot to do already."

"Yeah, won't inflict that brother-in-law energy on you," Don said easily. "Thanks, Hades. Catch up with you later? Later!" He grinned at them all and took off.

"That guy," Zeus said, shaking his head with tolerant amusement.

"Don't you start," Hera said. There was more color in her face. "If I have to, I'll put both of you at the children's table for New Year. Hades, what's the issue you wanted to discuss?"

"Hm? Oh." Hades relayed the facts about the catering situation as he knew them. Hera's expression didn't change, but there was a dangerous gleam in her eye.

"Excuse me, love," she said, and pecked Zeus's check. "I'd better have a quick word with Joy."

"Give 'em hell, babe," Zeus said. "Hades, stick around."

Hades startled. "Oh, no, I just came over to—"

"Nope," Zeus said firmly. "Shake and smile, big bro. I promise, it won't hurt a bit."

This, obviously, was a lie. Hades felt his will to attend diminish with every handshake, every enthusiastic greeting and pointless compliment. He lost track of the numbers after a couple of dozen new guests, and let Zeus handle all the names.

The appearance of Odysseus and Penny was one highlight, partly because he was always glad to see them, but mostly because Penny was wearing one of her own spectacular creations. She'd gathered layers of frothy green tulle into a long skirt, and rescued the look from being too prom princess by adding a tight strapless bodice in bright copper bronze, embellished with tightly clustered embroidery in green metallic thread. The embellishments looped and curled, suggesting stems and leaves without being outright representational. Penny's brown skin gleamed, and she'd teased out her hair into a glorious cloud of curls. She accepted their praise with well-deserved smugness, and Odysseus was so obviously enamored with his beautiful wife that he didn't even manage a dig at Hades for being on the reception line.

The line had dwindled considerably before Hera reappeared, looking calm and collected.

"Thank you," she said, and patted his arm.

He nodded and backed away, abruptly unwilling to exchange words even with someone he liked. But behind his usual self-recrimination—how hard was it just to smile at people? Couldn't he even act friendly for twenty minutes?—he was proud. He'd noticed a social problem and taken steps to fix it, and if he hadn't enjoyed the reception line, he had at least survived it.

Maybe Odysseus was right. Change *could* be good.

He wasn't quite sure whether that prickle along his spine was fear or excitement. Maybe both? He'd take a few minutes to recharge. Then he'd find Persephone, and suggest that they take a photo together, to celebrate her great work on those photobooths.

And after that, who knew?

***

Persephone was really regretting her wardrobe choices. Balancing the heavy platters was difficult already, but teetering on four-inch heels in a constrictive skirt felt like a circus act.

"I'm dying," she muttered to Carlos as she passed him on her way back to the kitchens.

"I'm dead," he returned. He was wearing a black suit with a red silk shirt, the best version of black tie he'd been able to pull together on no notice. Joy had seen the shirt and lost her shit. Only the pressing need for more servers had kept her from tossing him out to buy, beg, borrow or steal a white one. Persephone eyed his sensible black business shoes with naked envy.

There was definitely a blister forming on her left instep where the strap was rubbing. She let the platter hang by her side, no longer caring if crumbs fell on the floor, and limped over to the trestle table in the staging area, where mounds of food were still waiting. The catering staff were sympathetic, and happy to do the plating, but their manager was adamant; they would carry drinks trays only until Joy relented on the platters.

Frankly, they had a point. After ten minutes, Persephone's wrists had been aching. After nearly an hour, they throbbed constantly with the strain. She set her jaw and picked up the next laden platter, wincing as pain stabbed up the balls of her feet.

Thalia was hustling towards her, her eyes wide. "Brace for impact," she hissed. "Mr. Kronion just asked why the interns were serving, and he does not look pleased about it."

"Zeus Kronion?" Persephone said.

"No, the moody finance one."

"He's not moody," Persephone said indignantly.

Thalia rolled her eyes. "Whatever, that guy—he stopped me and was like, can you explain this situation?" She paused. "Kind of sexy, actually. Commanding. Anyway, I think he's going to do something about it. Honestly, just in time. People are getting *so* drunk out there without any food to soak it up. I saw Aphrodite Urania do three vodka shots in a row, and I don't care how hard she parties, if she doesn't eat something soon she's gonna regret it."

"Excuse me," Persephone said, and hobbled to the entrance, her platter wobbling precariously. The crowd was definitely loosening up. Most people weren't even waiting for her to offer before they started scooping things off her tray. She craned, and saw Hecate by a photobooth, but couldn't make out Hades anywhere.

"Hello!" someone caroled behind her, and she turned, smiling automatically. She had to look up, which was unusual, but the woman behind her was not only very tall, she was wearing skyscraper heels. Her dress was a sequined swath of gold silk that barely covered her breasts and fell straight down to brush the floor. Her long, slim thighs were exposed through two daring slits. Her hair was a spectacular red-gold shade that Persephone knew for a fact owed nothing to dye—because eight weeks ago she'd transcribed an interview that delved into Aphrodite Urania's beauty routine in excruciating detail. Apparently, readers were desperate to know what cleanser the world's top supermodel used.

"Thank you *so much*," Aphrodite said, and scooped three strawberries off Persephone's tray. "I am starving to *death*."

Persephone wasn't usually attracted to women, but Aphrodite in person was literally stunning. "Um, you're welcome," she managed, after a moment, and tried not to stare.

Aphrodite stepped in a little closer, hovering over the tray. "How's your night going?" she asked, and popped a stuffed olive into her mouth. Her eyes were a little glazed, and Persephone thought Thalia was probably right about the woman's alcohol intake, but she was still coherent and steady on her feet.

"Pretty good, thanks. And you?"

"My boyfriend's being a jerk," Aphrodite said blithely. "But that's nothing new." She grabbed a mini-quiche. "Is there salmon in these?"

"Yes."

"Perfect." Aphrodite took another one, then a third for good luck.

At this point, Persephone should have made a polite excuse and moved on—staying put while one guest monopolized the tray was something her mother had fired servers for before. But Aphrodite was friendly, and clearly very hungry, and it wouldn't do to let the guests get wasted, either.

Besides, her feet were screaming at her in deep, hot pulses radiating up her strained calves. If Hades was going to do something about the server situation, she really hoped it would happen soon.

She spotted him at last, standing beside his brother at the entrance, and felt her stomach swoop in a way that had nothing to do with booze. Hades in business dress was neat and professional, but Hades in a tux was... more.

He wasn't wearing anything flashy. That wasn't his style. But the traditional fit of his classic tuxedo elongated the sleek lines of his body, emphasizing the narrow waist and the flare of his shoulders. She'd noticed that he tended to hunch, like someone who was used to bending over a computer, but now he was standing straight, and for the first time she realized he was actually an inch or so taller than Zeus. His beard was a tidy frame around what she already knew were surprisingly lush lips, and she could remember very clearly the intensity he could summon to those dark blue eyes.

Oh, hell. Hecate was right. She had a crush.

"... told him that Aspen was too far from my next shoot and he basically had a tantrum," Aphrodite was saying, as Persephone came back to herself. The other woman either hadn't noticed she wasn't paying attention, or she was used to people going into a trance around her. "Yeah, he's hot, isn't he? Kinda dirty daddy vibes."

"Who?"

"Zeus Kronion. Bad news, though. Don't go there."

"I wasn't looking at—what do you mean?"

Aphrodite took another swig from her glass. "He hit on me when I started modeling," she said. "I was seventeen, and flattered. Granted, I was pretty dumb, even for seventeen, but he made sleeping with a dude in his thirties feel exciting, not objectively kind of icky. When my dad found out, he nearly murdered Zeus, and I think his wife wanted to murder me." She took the last of the strawberries, and looked briefly philosophical. "That was the bit that sucked. You'd think another woman would get it, but she sent me these disgusting emails, calling me the grossest names."

"But you still modeled for Olympus publications," Persephone said, and then felt very stupid when Aphrodite raised a perfectly filled-in eyebrow.

"You don't get a lot of choices when you have to pay the bills," she said. "Of course, now I make sure they pay through the roof. But if you want my advice, don't go near Zeus. They say he's stopped being a dog, but I don't think that mutt's been muzzled."

"I wasn't planning on it," Persephone said, and Aphrodite rewarded her with a smile that was blindingly beautiful. Persephone was still a little dazed when Aphrodite's boyfriend turned up and the shouting started.

Persephone wasn't a big sports fan, and knew less about soccer than she knew about personal finance, but even she'd heard of the football player Ares Irontosser. It was impossible to avoid him—he'd transcended football to become a genuine superstar, making cameos in movies, bringing out his own fashion line, starting a food truck fleet, and becoming the spokesman for an increasingly luxe series of brands. He was brutally handsome and famously brutal on the field.

Right now, he was drunk and angry, spitting out condemnations while stabbing his finger at Aphrodite, Persephone, and the empty platter. Persephone couldn't really understand him through the thick accent, and when Aphrodite started yelling back at him, she didn't have a clue what the actual problem was.

But people were starting to stare and pull out cellphones and she was absolutely certain Hera's post-event publicity plans didn't include celebrity fight exposes.

"Excuse me," she said, and then, when they didn't pause, she moved between them, using her plate as a kind of visual battering ram. "Hi," she said, making eye contact with Aphrodite. "I can help you find some privacy for this discussion."

Aphrodite drew in a sharp breath, ready to retort. But the pause gave her a moment, and Persephone saw awareness of her surroundings flood back in. Aphrodite nodded reluctantly.

"Who the fuck are you?" Ares demanded behind her, and then two meaty hands closed around her biceps with a strength she couldn't match, and moved her roughly aside.

To give him what little credit she could, Persephone thought later that he probably didn't intend to fling her down. He'd just wanted to get her out of the way. But the sudden motion caught her off-balance, and as she staggered, she stepped too wide. The skirt cut her off at the knees, and she tumbled, flinging her hands out to break her fall. The plate cracked as it hit the floor, chiming discordantly, like an untuned bell.

In the hushed room, she could clearly hear the gasps.

The silence was broken by the world's most beautiful woman absolutely losing her shit. "That's it!" Aphrodite shrieked, stabbing a gold-enameled finger at her boyfriend. "That's it, I'm done, I am so fucking done! Forever, do you hear me? We are over, once and for all!" She bent over Persephone. "I am *so* sorry. Are you okay?"

"I'm fine," Persephone said.

"Hey!" Ares roared. "Hey, you don't dump me! I dump you!"

Aphrodite hesitated, clearly unwilling to leave Persephone on the floor, but her presence wasn't doing anything to calm the situation. She turned on her precipitous heel and stalked away, her magnificent hair sailing behind her like a banner as the phone camera flashes caught every moment.

Sitting on the floor, Persephone saw the brief flash of uncertainty move over Ares' face, and then the return of his arrogant mask. "You'll come back," he yelled after her. "On your fucking knees." And then he too was moving, in the other direction, brushing right past the security crew who were finally arriving.

Persephone took a deep breath. The adrenaline surge of the confrontation and fall was subsiding now that the antagonists were leaving, and she was aware for the first time that people were taking photos of her too. She dropped her head to let her tumbling hair conceal some of her face and gingerly tested her wrists. Sore, but not sprained, she thought. Her mother was going to be so upset.

"Are you hurt?" a crisp voice asked. Hera Kronion had arrived.

"Not really," Persephone said. The greatest agony was still her feet. Abruptly angry, she tore her heels off and stood up, declining Hera's proffered hand.

"Watch out for the broken glass," Hera said. It was a practical observation, but Persephone wasn't feeling very practical.

She could see Hecate across the room. Minerva was standing beside her, talking very fast, her hand resting on Hecate's wrist as Hecate stared daggers after Ares. In a moment, Hecate would remember that she should comfort her best friend before murdering her assailant, and then Persephone would have to deal with awkwardly expressed sympathy when all she wanted was a private place to lick her wounds and maybe cry.

She murmured an excuse to Hera and headed for the kitchens, intending to find some band-aids and demand a bathroom break, but Joy caught her before she was even fully into the space.

"You!" she said. "Did you whine to Hera, hm? You think you know so much!"

Persephone could see her fellow interns over Joy's shoulder, all looking various levels of relieved and disgruntled. Thalia was looking apprehensive, probably afraid that Persephone would give her away for talking to Hades. Food was sailing out of the kitchen, carried on proper catering trays by the catering company's servers.

Hades had rescued them after all. Persephone smiled.

Unfortunately, Joy misinterpreted this as a confession. "I will be speaking to Mr. Hermes," she said, her face contorted with rage. "I have never had such a sneaky, untrustworthy intern, and I will be making my views very clear in your performance report. Do you understand me?"

At this point, Persephone knew, she was probably supposed to grovel. Joy was never going to like or respect her, but some abject apologizing might limit the damage.

But she was done groveling tonight. If she was going to get kicked out of the program after she'd been manhandled at a party, then she didn't want to work at Olympus, no matter how cool the Arts department was. "I understand," she said quietly, and maintained steady eye contact until Joy sniffed and turned away.

Thalia stepped forward, but Persephone fended her off with a raised hand. From her mother's previous events at the center, she knew there was an inner courtyard with a garden that the staff sometimes used for smoke breaks. She was going to hide there until she felt better, and if she could make it home without public tears or shouting at anyone, she was going to count that as a win.

Chapter Four

H ades was nursing a whiskey and loitering in a corner near an exit. He was almost enjoying himself, since he was sharing the corner with a fellow loiterer, Hephaestus Smith, who could always be counted on to avoid small talk.

"I hate parties," Heph said abruptly, breaking their companionable silence.

Hades leaned down and clinked his glass against Heph's. "Why did you come?"

"My sisters said I need to network more if I want Vulcan Consulting to take off."

"Are we not paying you enough?" Hades asked. He signed off on Heph's IT consulting fees, which were reasonable, considering his speed and expertise, but were also not cheap.

Heph shifted his heavy shoulders irritably. "No, you pay me plenty. They want me to have more clients, that's all. At places where I didn't already do most of the engineering. Expand my customer base." He looked gloomy. "Probably hire employees."

"But you'll still work for us, right?" Hades said, mildly alarmed. Heph had joined Olympus as an 18-year-old MIT wunderkind, graduating from college at an age when most people were starting. He'd spent six years at the company before going into business for himself last year, and Hades wasn't sure that IT had ever stopped mourning his departure. They still kept an office for him on the eighth floor. They'd probably get a new one for him on the twenty-eighth floor, after the move.

"Yeah, sure," Heph said, moving his shoulders again and shifting his weight in his wheelchair. Around the office he mostly used forearm crutches to get around, but Hades had noticed he preferred the chair for this kind of event. "I'm fine. I've got Olympus, and a half-dozen smaller clients. But you haven't met my sisters." He shifted again. "This padding is shit. I told the guy, but he wouldn't listen."

Hades looked around. "Would a cushion help?" he asked doubtfully.

Heph wasn't listening. He was looking towards the far side of the room where, Hades realized, voices had been slowly gaining volume. A current ran through the crowd as the guests succumbed to the dramatic potential and refocused their attention.

Hades's instinct was to stand back and stay out of it, but he was technically one of the hosts at this thing. "Excuse me," he said, and started towards the focal point. The incident was over before he could get near enough to figure out what was happening, though the upset redhead storming past him in a flurry of camera phone flashes gave him a clue. "Ms. Urania?" he said, and followed her. "Ms. Urania, can I—"

Aphrodite whirled on one spindly heel with the consummate grace that had made her a catwalk superstar. "What?" she demanded.

Her tone was pure fury, but those were definitely tears in her eyes.

"I'm sorry," Hades said. "Can I help you—"

"No!" She twisted again and strode off towards the exit, head held high.

She walked straight into Heph and his chair.

The burly engineer caught her instinctively, his massive arms going around her as she stumbled and fell into his lap. Her hair fell around them, a glittering red-gold curtain that concealed both of their faces.

Then Aphrodite tore free and pushed herself back to her feet. "I'm sorry!" she said, on a note that was almost a wail, and fled out the door.

Heph stared after her, looking as shocked as Hades felt.

"You okay?" Hades asked.

"Yeah. What the hell was that?"

"Hera's got it," Don said, walking past Hades. He plucked Hades's whiskey out of his hand, sniffed it appreciatively, and took a sip. "There's nothing she can't fix."

"What happened?" Heph demanded. He wriggled his backside and winced.

"Irontosser was being a douchebag, as per usual."

"You once described his left foot as a blessing from a bountiful universe," Hades pointed out.

"His foot is a blessing. The guy wielding it is a first-class asshole."

"Co-signed," Heph said, on a groan. "I've got to go, Hades. This chair's fucking me up. Can you grab the door for me?" Aphrodite crashing into him probably hadn't helped, Hades thought, and held the door as Heph wheeled out.

"Friendly guy," Don said, his eyebrows raised.

"He's brilliant," Hades told him. "He doesn't need to be friendly. Is Irontosser out of the building?"

"Yeah, he took off. Fuck knows what Aphrodite sees in him."

Hades rubbed the bridge of his nose. "Please don't attempt to seduce Aphrodite Urania."

Don gave him a lazy smile. "Why not? You don't think I'm her type?"

"I have no idea what her type is," Hades said. "I'm thinking about you, and your types."

"Stop worrying about me," Don said. His voice was affectionate, but the narrow-eyed look he directed at Hades was a clear warning.

"Sorry," Hades told him. "Habit."

Don grinned and held up Hades's whiskey glass, now empty. "I'm going to get another one of these, and then I'm heading outside for a smoke. Want to join me?"

"Certainly," Hades said, and automatically fell behind him as Don cut a swathe through the crowd.

Frankly, it was impossible not to worry about Don. He'd not only actively spurned every opportunity to get involved in the family business, he'd dropped out of college. The choice had infuriated their father, who'd cut Don off from his trust fund. Don had responded by effectively disappearing. The only contact he'd made with anyone during those years, as far as Hades knew, was the occasional email to his worried older brother.

Hades had always responded, usually with a money transfer attached. Sometimes the money had been accepted; sometimes it hadn't. After a year, Hades started getting transfers back, along with brusque updates. Don was working in shipping. Not the interesting, safe logistics work Hades could have handled, but the mentally and physically demanding work of a deck hand.

When their father had died, and Zeus had taken over Olympus, Hades had, frankly, been surprised that Don wasn't cut out of the will. But he'd been given the same twenty percent share of Olympus that Zeus and Hades had, and access to his trust fund had been restored. Hades was one of the trust managers, and he'd tried not to spy, but he had seen that some of the money had gone to course fees at a maritime academy.

Don had turned up for Zeus and Hera's first wedding, with a deep tan, impressive muscles, and a brand-new qualification as a third officer. Zeus had patronizingly offered to get in touch with some of his contacts. Don had rudely refused.

But he'd been a bigger part of their lives, as his shipboard time allowed. He got along well with Hera, and Hades, though always somewhat nervous around Don, nevertheless enjoyed his company. It was just Zeus and Don who mixed like oil and water, and it never took long for one of them to throw a match. When Hera divorced Zeus, Don had sent Hades a one-word email that read: "Good."

When they'd remarried, Zeus had demanded he attend. Hades had been privately sure Don wouldn't come, and then deeply alarmed when he'd shown up at Hades's home the night before the wedding, so drunk that he could barely speak, an incoherent tangle of misery and rage.

Hera and Zeus had remarried the next morning. Don had not attended the ceremony. When Hades got back from the reception, he'd left Hades's guest room in spotless condition, and vanished as if he'd never been there.

Don's visits ever since had been sporadic and brief. But if he were truly staying for the holidays, and yayfor Hera's New Year party, it was a great sign. Maybe he was ready to become a bigger part of their lives again.

"This way," Don said, and walked past a deferential security guard into a narrow passage. Trust Don to find the back way in and out of most places. The corridor led to an empty staff break room, and then out an unmarked door to a small, paved patio in a courtyard garden. The paving edges were planted with hellebore, and a weeping hemlock tree dominated the far end of the space, viburnum bushes clustered before it. The greenery was nice, but a couple of empty beer cans, a few candy bar wrappers and a worn pair of silver sandals abandoned at the edge of the paving stones bore mute witness to how little interest the users had in cleaning up their break space.

The foliage rustled in the cold night breeze. Hades took a deep breath, and felt his awareness expand. It was amazing how even the biggest room could feel like a cage when it was full of people.

"Want one?" Don asked. He produced a cigar case from his breast pocket and waved it in Hades's direction.

"No, thanks," Hades said. "And I'll stand upwind, if you don't mind."

Don shrugged. "Upwind's there," he said, pointing.

"You'd know," Hades said, and walked around him as Don plucked a cigarillo from the case. "How have you been?"

"Oh, you know. Good. Fine."

"Are you still, um, taking a break from shipping?"

"There's a lot of world," Don said. "Can't see all of it from a ship. Or a basement."

"We're moving," Hades said. "To the eighth floor."

"Of the same building," Don said, his voice deceptively mild. He lit the cigarillo and inhaled.

"Hey," Hades said, trying to keep his voice light. "I don't judge your work choices."

"No, you don't," Don conceded. He took another drag. "Sorry," he added after a pause.

"But while we're on the subject," Hades said. "If you are sticking around for a while, is there anything at Olympus you'd like to get involved in?"

"Thought you hated nepotism."

"Not a big fan," Hades admitted.

"Well, you don't need to stifle your principles for me. Not going to happen."

Hades tucked his hands into his trouser pockets and rocked on his feet. The stars were very bright in the sky, and though snow hadn't yet fallen in the city, the night air was piercing cold. But this was the longest conversation he'd had with his brother in months. "I guess I thought that maybe, with enough time passing after Dad died..."

Don's eyes were shadowed. "It wasn't just Dad."

"I figured. After–" he stopped himself. He couldn't say "after the second wedding." He couldn't voice what he only suspected. If it wasn't true, Don would be insulted. And if it was true, he had to trust that Don was doing the best he could.

"I know that to you, it's everything," Don said. Hades could feel the effort he was putting into sounding neutral. "But to me, Olympus is poison."

"I know Dad was an asshole—"

"Not just Dad," Don repeated. "Look, Grandfather was an asshole who made money in an era where newspapers made money hand over fist. Our dad was an asshole who lost money in an era where everyone bought magazines at the grocery store. Now Zeus is... Zeus. Somehow making money in an era where everyone gets their news online and magazines are scrambling for advertising, subscriptions, and audiences. And what really chafes my balls is that he's taking all the credit for it."

"He saved Olympus," Hades said. "He saved the family fortune."

"Yeah? Ever noticed how that cuts you out of the story? You're the one making money. Seems to me like he couldn't have done it without

91

you." He paused for a moment, and when he next spoke his voice was controlled. "You or Hera."

Hades rubbed the sore spot between his eyebrows. "I can't–it was the least I could do."

"The least you could do is what *I* do," Don said, with a strong dose of irony. "*You* work your ass off. It's never bothered you that Zeus gets all the credit?"

"If you haven't noticed, I can't *talk* to people," Hades snapped. "All the board meetings, the meet-and-greets, the networking–I couldn't do any of it. *I* couldn't save Olympus, Don! Zeus was the youngest, barely out of college, and he stepped up and took over. Somehow, he made it work. He *should* get the credit for it. I certainly don't deserve any."

Don looked at him for a long moment, then huffed a sigh. "The worst part is that you believe that."

"Why are you concerned with who gets the credit? You've made it very clear you don't care about the company, despite owning twenty percent of it."

"I don't give a rat's ass about the company," Don said cheerfully. "I'm asking because I care about you."

Hades stared at him.

"Seriously," Don said. "Are you happy?"

"Am I *happy*?"

"Yeah. Simple question, simple answer."

"I don't... It's not something I think about that often."

"Think now," Don suggested. He stubbed out his cigarillo, and immediately lit another.

Hades's usual instinct would have been to point out that two in a row verged on chain-smoking, but he was still chewing over the question. *Was* he happy?

He was content, certainly. He had satisfying work and he did it well. He had employees that he liked and respected, and he thought they liked and respected him, although Odysseus would probably rather be eaten alive than admit it. The books were balanced, bar the occasional expenses error. The profit margins were healthy. Projections indicated that Olympus would be able to continue navigating the precarious balance between digital and print production and…

And all of it was about work, Hades realized, with a grim sense of inevitability. When he thought of happiness, he thought of his work. When he thought of *himself*, he thought of his work.

"I don't think so," he said slowly.

Don nodded, as if this was what he'd expected. "So. Now that you know, what are you going to do about it?"

Hades sighed. "I don't know, Don. I just found out. Come on, it's cold out here, and it's nearly time for Zeus's speech."

"Oh yay," Don said, but after a final, deep draw on his cigarillo, he stubbed it out. Then he scooped up both butts, looked around for an ashtray, and, not finding one, tossed them both at the far side of the garden.

"Don't—Why would you *do* that?" Hades demanded. He crossed the courtyard and plunged into the bushes.

"Oh hell," he heard his brother mutter behind him. "Hades!"

Shaking his head, Hades scoured the frozen ground, shoving creamy white viburnum blossoms out of the way. He found the first butt easily enough, but the second had skidded and bounced under the weeping hemlock.

The cigarillo butt was resting beside a bare white foot, blueish with cold, marred by smears of dirt and small red wounds.

The breeze shifted. He could smell jasmine and mint.

Hades looked up slowly, along the curve of a strong calf, to the shadow of matte black fabric rucked up to full thighs, over the perilous folds and dips of her body until he met, at last, the shocked eyes of Persephone Erinyes, crouching under the tree.

With one hand, she was clutching a small purse against her hip. The other hand was clamped tightly over her mouth.

Her dark blue eyes begged his silence.

"Don't clean up after me," Don said, crashing into the bushes behind him. "You go back to the party. I'll find them."

"No!" Hades said. "No, it's fine, I've found them." He grabbed the cigarillo butt–his fingers brushed bare, cold skin–and dashed out of the bushes, nearly bowling his brother over.

"They weren't going to start a fire in there," Don muttered, but when Hades held out the butts, he obediently took them.

"You go back in and find a trash can," Hades said, trying to sound authoritative. "I'm going to clean up a bit." He swiped his hands together in a washing motion for emphasis.

"Fine," Don said. "Wouldn't want to miss Zeus's love song to himself, would I?" He gave Hades a single, dubious glare, and then headed back inside, muttering to himself.

Hades waited a few seconds. "He's gone," he said quietly.

The bushes rustled, and Persephone emerged, walking gingerly and tugging her skirt back into place. Her eyes were huge, drinking up every bit of the available light as she stared at him. "I am so, so sorry," she said.

For the first time, Hades allowed himself to realize what she must have heard. Don, talking about Olympus. Don, talking about Zeus.

Himself, admitting he wasn't happy.

He had a moment of overwhelming relief that he hadn't broken his private vow and gotten even *more* personal with Don before the anger swept over him.

"Why were you hiding there?" he demanded.

"I wasn't hiding!" she said. "Well, I was, but I didn't mean to be. I came out here to--uh, for some privacy, after the incident, and I heard people coming, and I wasn't really fit for company." She grimaced, and for the first time he saw the reddened eyes and flushed nose.

She'd been crying. And her feet, why were her feet bare and blistered? The abandoned shoes in the courtyard abruptly made sense.

"What incident? Wait, no, sit here." There were a couple of ugly resin mold chairs on the edge of the patio space, probably so that the staff could sit here and bitch about their guests in the summer. He hustled Persephone over to one of them and sat in the other.

"Oh, you didn't see that, huh?" Persephone laughed. It was too shaky to be genuinely amused. "Aphrodite and Ares Irontosser had an argument, and I tried to calm them down. But he moved me aside and I fell."

Hades felt the words slide into his heart like sharpened icicles. "He moved you aside," he repeated.

Persephone blew out a breath. "Yeah. I don't think he meant to hurt me."

"But you are hurt," Hades said. There was a feeling that resembled a blizzard in his brain, and then he was kneeling in front of her, holding one of her abused feet in his hands while he inspected the damage. Persephone was looking at him quizzically.

Hades froze. "I beg your pardon," he said. Why did he always stop *thinking* around this woman? He just reacted, without planning or gauging risks and consequences.

"That's okay," she said. "Your hands are warm."

He immediately closed them carefully around her foot.

"Besides, I did most of the damage myself," she said ruefully. "It turns out that my shoes were unsuitable for my duties tonight."

Hades frowned. He was moving his fingers in small, gentle circles, avoiding the blisters, hoping to improve her circulation. "Oh yes, the serving. I believe Hera was going to do something about that."

"She did," Persephone assured him. "That one's warmed up." She was untucking her other foot, looking hopeful.

Hades released the foot he'd been working on, and closed his fingers around the other. The cold paving stones were biting through his trouser knees, but he'd suffer a lot more than that before he moved away. Touching her, while at first motivated by genuine concern, was developing into something else. In other circumstances, if she indicated she wanted him to, it would be so easy to slide his fingers higher, stroke along those shapely calves, and tease at the sensitive nerves behind her knees. The dress was tight enough that he'd have to ease it up at that point, or maybe she'd yank down the zipper and step out of it, sinking down into his willing arms...

"Thank you," Persephone said, and retrieved her foot. He didn't think he was imagining the faint regret in her sigh. "Ooh, thank you," she said again, flexing her toes. "Much better."

Hades stood up and gave her some space.

"We keep bumping into each other," Persephone said. Her expression was hard to read, in the shadows, but her eyes were fixed on his.

Hades meant to make some comment about them working in the same buildings, or the capricious whims of the fates, but what actually came out of his mouth was, "Hera says you sketched me."

"Oh hell, she told you," Persephone said, and covered her face with her hands. When she took them down, her blush was obvious, even in the dim light. "Yes. I'm sorry. I should have asked. But you're—" she gestured at him.

"I'm what?"

"Striking," Persephone said. "You make a great model. I mean, not that I've been following you around like a crazed stalker or anything, but our first meeting was memorable and I picked up my charcoals."

"Striking," Hades said.

Persephone smiled, her cheeks still flushed. "And kind."

Hades took a moment to assess the situation. They were sitting in near-zero temperatures in a badly landscaped patio on chairs that were probably leaving all sorts of unsightly stains on their evening wear. She'd been shoved around by a meat-brained sports star, and he'd been pushed to the limits of his social capacity, barely navigating a fraught conversation with his wayward brother.

It was not, he felt, the most romantic setting.

But when he considered the history of their interactions thus far, he couldn't really see them ever having a better chance.

"*Are you happy?*" Don had asked. And, "*What are you going to do about it?*"

"Persephone?"

"Mm?"

"Would you maybe want—" He bit off the end of the sentence, and stared at his hands. "I've got to be absolutely clear about this; you're under no obligation whatsoever. And no matter what you say it doesn't affect your work at this company or your chances of getting employed afterwards–I don't have anything to do with HR or the intern program and obviously you're not qualified to work in Finance anyway."

Persephone's eyes were widening. Hades took a step back, then another. "This is stupid," he said. "I'm stupid. Sorry to interrupt your evening."

"You're not stupid and you're not interrupting," Persephone said. "But you haven't asked me the question."

"I can't," he said. "It's an inappropriate question. I'm sorry that I brought it up."

Persephone got to her feet, wincing slightly, and he froze in place as she placed one hand on his arm. "Hades," she said softly, and he shivered, both at her touch and at the sound of his name on her lips. "Would you maybe like to have dinner with me sometime?"

"I—" he said, and stared at her. "Like a date?"

"Yes. Would you like to go on a date with me?"

"Yes," he said. "Yes. I would really like that. Yes."

***

There was a moment, standing barefoot on the courtyard paving stones, that Persephone thought Hades was going to kiss her.

Her hand tightened on his arm, her head tilting back. His joyful smile was transmuting into something more intense. She felt more than saw his gaze focus on her lips, his stance shifting as he prepared to take her in his arms.

And his phone rang.

The sound cracked the fragile beauty of the moment. She let go of him while he fumbled in his pocket.

"Just a moment," he promised. "I'll tell them to—" His face stiffened as he glanced at the name, and he twisted to look at the building. "Hello. Yes. Yes, I know. Right. I took a break for some fresh air. I heard about it. *Yes,* Zeus, I'll be there. I'm coming now." He hung up and gave Persephone an apologetic look. "I'm sorry. I have to get back in there."

"Absolutely," Persephone said stoutly. "I should get back too."

"Can I give you a ride home after--no, damn it, I offered Don my place to stay, he'll be expecting to come with me." He looked at the center, then back at her. "Um, I could..."

"Can I have your number?" Persephone asked.

"Right! Yes, of course, you'll need that. To arrange the, um."

"The date."

"The date. Yes." He shook his head, in disbelief, rather than denial, then smiled at her.

Persephone was pretty sure he didn't know how devastating his smile was. Her knees weakened a little, and she wanted to grab him by the hand and say, *hey, let's go, let's just run away. Your brothers will deal.*

But he'd never do that–he was too responsible, and so was she. She pulled out her own phone and entered his number in her contacts list–there were a lot of unread texts she'd better get to–and texted, "It's Persephone :)"

Hades's phone beeped, and he beamed at it. "So it is," he said, and that breathless tension stretched between them again.

His phone rang again.

Hades hit the decline call button, shoved the phone in his pocket, carefully took her face in his hands and kissed her.

It was a gentle exploration, slow and tender, and every nerve ending in Persephone's body crackled to life at once. She gasped and went up on her tiptoes, needing to be closer to him. Her hands went to his back, pulling him tighter in.

He pulled back, hovering a few inches from her face. His thumbs stroked down her cheekbones, leaving little trails of sparks. "I have to go," he said. "I don't want to."

"Then stay," Persephone said, and dragged him back down to her mouth. This kiss was less gentle, and she slid her hands up and under his tuxedo jacket. Her fingertips slid over silk, tracing the muscle and bone beneath as she slid her tongue into his mouth, and felt his fervent response.

The phone rang a third time, and they broke apart. Hades, she was pleased to see, looked distinctly rumpled. She was feeling pretty rumpled herself.

"Augh," Hades said, throwing his hands up in an expressive gesture. He turned, scowling, and stalked straight-legged into the center.

Persephone fell back into her chair, fingertips going to her lips. "Holy shit," she whispered, and did a triumphant little wiggle.

There really were a lot of unread messages on her phone. She clicked through, and discovered that she'd been added to an intern group chat, titled THRIVING SURVIVING AND NON-STOP BITCH-ING [flame emoji] [skull emoji].

Carlos: :persephone in the chat!:

Ida: :welcome persephoneeeeee!!:

Thalia: [teary emoji] [big heart emoji] :saving my ass: [butt emoji]

Terry: :wtf happened?:

Carlos: :JOY: [finger emoji]

Thalia: :JOY: [finger emoji]

Ida: :persephone, just so you know, we all hate Joy (not joy):

Terry: :bitch with us Persephone:

Sophie: :oh no do u hate us?? Are we too babby??:

Sophie: :she doesn't have to bitch terry! She might be too classy to bitch!!:

Terry: :classy bitches are the best bitches:

Persephone laughed. It stung just a bit that she hadn't been added to the group earlier, but it appeared her fellow interns had taken her refusal to give Thalia away as an act of solidarity. She scrolled up, and saw hundreds of messages–a lot of bitching, a lot of encouragement, and some in-jokes it was going to take a while to assimilate.

Persephone: :hi: [smiley emoji]

Carlos: :hiiiiii!!:

Sophie: :hiiiiii!!:

Persephone: :I am not too classy to bitch:

Terry: :knew it:

Persephone: :am I in deep shit? Do you need me inside?:

Ida: :No, we're all good! Hera gave us the rest of the night off.:

Persephone: [sweatdrop emoji] [relief emoiji]

Thalia: :she took Joy apart: [knife emoji] [explosion emoji]

Carlos: :Hera our QUEEN: [crown emoji]

Persephone remembered Aphrodite saying that Hera had sent her emails full of slurs, and frowned. It couldn't be very nice to find out that your husband was pursuing a beautiful younger woman, but surely you'd take that anger out on the husband, not the actual teenager he was--well, that he was sexually harassing.

Shit. Her boss—Hades's *brother*—was a borderline predator. Or, maybe, had been a predator.

Obviously, this was all years ago, and if Aphrodite was willing to tell her, an absolute stranger, it couldn't be an actual secret. But Persephone had never heard the story before, and Aphrodite had obviously never followed up in any formal way–and no wonder, with a powerful couple like that to contend with.

No, Aphrodite's warning had felt like one of those things that women told each other in those informal whisper circles, to keep each other safe. There were a few people at college who everyone had known not to be alone or drunk with, a few men in her mother's circle who Demeter had adroitly dropped from her social life as Persephone hit puberty.

So if it was one of those, a secret-not-secret story, then Hades might not know about it.

But if he did. If he had dismissed or ignored or condoned Zeus's actions, where did that leave her?

"Don't sabotage yourself already," she muttered, but the magic was gone. She was no longer shivering with delight, but with the cold. Her feet were starting to chill again.

"Hey," she texted Hecate. "Do you have an idea when you think you might want to leave?"

The response was immediate: "As soon as Zeus stops giving himself a public blow job. Where are you?"

"Employee break space?? See you soon."

"You okay?"

"Yes. Got news."

Hecate's car was waiting for her by the staff entrance fifteen minutes later.

"What news?" she asked, without preamble, then assessed Persephone's appearance. "That piece of shit."

"I asked Hades out," Persephone said demurely. "And he said yes."

Hecate paused before she shifted gear. "Finally."

"That's what I like about you most. You're so supportive."

"I am extremely supportive," Hecate said indignantly. "I'm supporting your quest to bang that man like a screen door in a hurricane. Also, do you want to lay charges?"

Persephone blinked. "Sorry?"

"Ares Irontosser," Hecate said. "The guy who laid hands on you in front of four hundred witnesses."

"Oh, I think that was mostly an accident."

Hecate abruptly pulled over and braked.

"What is it?" Persephone said, alarmed. "Are you okay?"

Hecate lifted her head from the steering wheel, where she was rhythmically banging it. "Persephone," she said, and her face was completely free of the usual veneer of sophisticated insouciance. She looked nakedly concerned. "I love you, and I try not to worry about you too much, because I think you get enough of that already, but I desperately wish you'd stop making excuses for people who do bad things to you."

Persephone took a deep breath, her eyes stinging unexpectedly. "I love you too," she said. "And yes, okay, I was shaken. It wasn't a good time. But it's over, and I really didn't get hurt, and I don't want any more fuss." She thought about the pictures that would be plastered all over a hungry internet by now and winced. "At least, more fuss than I can avoid."

"Better reason," Hecate said after a second, and started the engine. "Okay. Let's get you home."

"Yes, please," Persephone said, envisioning a long soak in her bath.

"And tell me more about Hades."

"He kissed me!" Persephone said, brightening.

"Was it good?"

Persephone grinned. "Oh, yeah."

"Okay, go back to the beginning. So you went outside?"

They settled into a comfortable play-by-play. Persephone excised all mention of Hades's conversation with his brother, and if Hecate noticed any gaps she didn't say anything, instead demanding more detail about the important bits. ("Was there any tongue? And what did the beard feel like?") The result was that Persephone had recaptured the glow and was feeling pretty pleased with herself when Hecate dropped her off at the guest house. She hummed as she opened the front door and dropped her battered purse on the entranceway table.

And then a wailing Demeter rushed from the living room, and Persephone's mood abruptly tanked.

"Mom?" she asked, her arms instinctively wrapping around her weeping mother. "What's wrong?"

"How can you say that?" Demeter demanded. She was still in her evening wear, but her mascara had bled black marks down her cheeks, and her dark red lipstick was smeared across her mouth. "I've been worrying myself sick! I came home at once!"

"Oh," Persephone said. "Did someone tell you about what happened tonight?"

"They showed me! Such horrible pictures. Misty Achlys couldn't wait to tell me all the details. And you didn't call me!"

"I'm sorry, Mom, I didn't think you'd hear about it so soon. I'm fine, honestly."

Demeter drew herself up. "I just can't believe you didn't care enough to let me know."

"Did you call me?" Persephone glanced at her phone. "I didn't get any messages."

"Well, excuse me, I wasn't aware that I had to book an appointment!"

Persephone sighed. "I'm sorry, Mom. I didn't want to ruin your night."

"My baby was hurt! Of course my night was ruined. But I wouldn't mind, if I just thought you cared for my feelings at all."

"I'm sorry," Persephone said again. Every muscle was demanding a hot shower and a horizontal surface. "Mom, I'm really tired, and I've got one more day of work before the weekend. Can we talk about this then?"

"You're going to work tomorrow?" Demeter shrieked. "It's dangerous! You need to quit!"

Persephone let a faint prickle of annoyance into her voice. "Of course I'm going to work tomorrow, Mom. It was a one-off incident, and the job wasn't to blame."

The atmosphere turned arctic.

"Of course," Demeter said, every word icy sharp. "I can see when my advice isn't wanted. Please forgive me for caring."

She swept from the room, and Persephone heard the house door slam.

Persephone took a deep breath. She knew what was supposed to happen next—she was meant to chase after Demeter and reassure her. If she begged forgiveness and soothed her mother's feelings, Demeter would back down on demanding she quit, and all would be well again.

Normally, she would have done it without questioning. Knowing that her mother was hurt tugged at her like a fishhook in her heart.

But tonight, she was too exhausted to extract the barbs.

Besides, she wanted to focus on the good parts of the evening; the colleagues that had finally welcomed her, the good work she'd done with those photobooths, the kissing.

Oh, yes.

Definitely the kissing.

***

"Damn," Don said. "This Persephone must be something. I haven't seen you this wound up since junior prom."

"Thanks," Hades said, reknotting his tie. "Just what I need before a first date; a reminder of making an idiot of myself over twenty years ago."

"Hey, that's what family's for," Don said generously. "What are you doing on this date?"

"Dinner, and that new play at the Amphitheater."

Don made an evaluating sound. "Classic. Classy." He was lounging on Hades's bed, idly flipping through one of Olympus's home and design titles. "Hey, do you ever read these things?"

"Don, Olympus puts out six weeklies, eighteen monthlies and nine quarterly publications. I couldn't possibly read them all. I sometimes look at *Digital Digest* and *Modern Money*."

"Well, you need to read this one." Don held up a copy of *iHearthit*. Hades glanced at the cover. A living room, painted pale pink, liberally bedecked with fairy lights and swathes of colored fabrics.

"I don't think I want a pink bedroom."

"Any color at all would be good." He turned the page. "And plants. You definitely need some indoor plants. Says here that they keep the soul of the home alive."

"I don't have time to look after plants." The underlayer of the tie was still hanging too low. Hades undid the knot and started over.

"Theresa could do it," Don said.

"Theresa has enough to deal with." Hades had given his housekeeper a bonus to make up for her having to handle a two-person household with no notice. She'd assured him that it wasn't a lot of extra trouble, but he still worried that he'd added to her workload.

"Theresa loves me," Don said. "I think she wants to adopt me."

This, unfortunately, was true. Hades would have been happy to eat the same three meals every day, but Don loved food and had devoured local cooking on six continents. Theresa had taken this as an immediate challenge to her underappreciated skills, and ate up Don's extravagant compliments with almost as much vigor as he ate her meals.

Now the top layer of his tie was too long. And why was he wearing a tie on a date with a vibrant younger woman anyway? Too formal, too serious, too much. He ripped it off and threw it towards the bed. Now he was wearing an unadorned, white button-up shirt, and charcoal trousers. Boring. Old.

Don caught it out of the air and looked thoughtful at the subtle silver pattern woven into the grey silk. "Wear the blue shirt," he advised.

"I don't have a blue shirt."

"Hera had it delivered yesterday. Back of your closet."

Hades investigated. Behind the layers of white and cream and light grey button-ups was a dark blue one, right on the border between navy and midnight.

He stripped off his shirt and threw on the new one. "How did Hera know I had a date?"

"And you could do with some art, too. Maybe a gallery wall."

"Have you been talking behind my back?" The blue did look good. He looked pale, but his eyes stood out.

"Hades, listen to me."

Hades glanced at him in the mirror. "I'm listening. You want me to redecorate my home."

"I want you to *live* in it," Don said. He tossed the magazine on Hades's dressing table and prowled restlessly around the room. "Look at this place. It's all black and white and grey."

"It's minimalist. It's clean."

"It's *cold*. And you're not cold."

"Thank you?" Hades said. The words were complimentary, but the tone was disgruntled. On the other hand, Don showing interest in Hades's decor was a good sign. Maybe if he were invested, he'd want to stick around. "Look, if you want to make a few changes, go ahead."

Don whirled. "Really?"

Hades was slightly alarmed by the eagerness in his face. "Well, check with me before you do anything too dramatic. And stick to the upstairs."

"Absolutely," Don said. He was heading for the bedroom door. "Shirt looks great. Enjoy your date."

"Don't knock down any walls!" Hades called after him. He tugged at his shirt cuffs. Maybe even a button-up was too much. But he didn't have much in the way of informal clothing, and surely dinner and a show required at least a semi-formal outfit

He picked up his phone and scrolled back through the text messages he and Persephone had exchanged over the last five days.

Odysseus had offered his services as a Cyrano, composing the perfect texts to win her heart. Hades wasn't positive he'd been joking, but he'd tossed Odysseus out of his office anyway. As a result, Persephone's texts were light and charming, and his were leaden, but sincere. She'd offered to drive, and had seemed impressed by his immediate agreement.

Why hadn't he thought to bring up clothing choices?

The doorbell rang.

Hades shoved his phone in his pocket, grabbed his suit jacket, and headed downstairs before Don could do something appalling, like answer the door.

The sight of her, in his doorway, rendered him momentarily speechless.

Persephone was wearing dark green, a velvet gown that clung from throat to hip and then flared into a full skirt. Over it she wore an open cropped blazer covered in enormous tropical blooms. "Hello," she said.

"Hi," he managed. Oh, no, he hadn't thought about this. They'd already kissed, so was he supposed to kiss her again now, or was a hug appropriate or--

Persephone wrapped her arms around him and he was suddenly holding a generous armful of woman. He felt the soft pressure of her lips against his cheekbone, right above the line of his beard.

"I like your shirt," she said, releasing him and smiling shyly.

"You smell nice," Hades replied. This was an understatement. Persephone smelled so good that it was making his head spin. Not the jasmine-and-mint, this time, but something complex and floral, with some warm spice undertones.

"Oh, thank you. Aphrodite gave me this perfume."

"Aphrodite Urania? I didn't know you were friends."

"We're not. Well, not really. She sent me a gift basket as an apology for me being caught up in her argument with her ex, and I called to thank her. We've talked a few times since." She twisted her bracelet around her wrist. "I like her, though. She says exactly what she's thinking. That's something I wish I could do."

What Hades was thinking right then was definitely not fit for polite conversation. He was excruciatingly aware that they were hovering in the doorway to his home, and upstairs was his bedroom and a wide, cold bed.

There was a grinding sound from within, and Hades flinched. Lest he forget, his brother was also inside, and from the sounds of it, already embarked on some furniture rearrangement.

"Let's go," he said hastily, and took her hand before he could think too hard about whether his palms were sweaty. Persephone fell easily into step beside him. For a moment, Hades allowed himself the hope that this would be easy.

***

Persephone had chosen the play, so Hades had picked the restaurant. She'd been braced for a minimalist experience where each dish was supposed to be an experience, and maybe you inhaled a cloud of dessert instead of eating it, but Hades had gone for the Augean, an upmarket steakhouse where, it was clear, the staff knew him well.

The hostess's widened eyes when she realized Hades was on a date also made it clear that she was an unusual addition, and they were escorted to a corner table with ceremony.

"Do you eat here a lot?" she asked.

"Probably once or twice a week," he admitted. "My housekeeper does four dinners weekly and for the rest I either grab takeout or come here. Sometimes with Penny and Odysseus, if they don't mind me being a third wheel."

Persephone grinned at him. "You like routine."

"I really do. It's been put to me recently that I should embrace change more often." He looked around doubtfully. "But I like it here."

"You shouldn't change the things you like," Persephone agreed, and cut into her filet. It had been expertly seared, and the bright citrus dressing on the accompanying salad made her sigh in satisfaction.

When she opened her eyes, Hades was looking at her mouth, his own lips parted.

Persephone inhaled sharply.

"How is everything?" their waiter asked.

Hades waved at his sirloin with his fork. "Perfect, Jackson, thank you."

"Beyond perfect. I'm in love with this dressing," Persephone told him. "Jackson, I want to run away with this dressing and engage in a reckless affair."

"We've all felt that way," Jackson said solemnly. "Even though we know we're just begging for a broken heart." He winked at her, and then expertly faded back into the background.

Hades was smiling at her. "You're so good at talking to people," he said, and she remembered, with a small twinge, that he'd said in the garden that he *couldn't*.

"Lots of practice," she said, and smiled back. "You're good at talking to me."

"A rare exception," Hades said dryly. "The consolation of drenching someone in soup is that there really isn't anywhere more awkward for subsequent conversation to go."

"At least it was cold soup," Persephone said. "If you'd been carrying tomato, I'm not sure I'd be here now."

"To be honest, I don't even like cold soups. But I'd just seen you for the first time. I was so stunned I picked the closest thing." He said it lightly enough, but he was toying with his fork, the lack of eye contact making it clear he meant it.

Persephone's skin prickled. He'd walked into a room full of stylish and accomplished people, seen her sitting in the middle of a group of young and beautiful interns, and he'd been stunned. By *her*.

"For someone who's not good at talking, you're doing a great job of seduction," she heard herself saying.

His eyes found hers, and held. Persephone felt as if they were suspended in mid-air, the earth dropping away beneath them.

"I'm very glad to hear it," he said softly.

Persephone wasn't inexperienced. She had had a fair number of college flings, the occasional one-night stand, and a couple of longer-lasting relationships. She had wondered if one of them might have been interested in permanency, but then Mike had dumped her and run with no notice and no explanation. It had stung, but after a month, she'd realized she didn't miss him.

But she had never felt like this before, so openly and unhesitatingly *chosen*.

And there was a gleam in Hades's eye that said he knew it. He cut a piece of sirloin and placed it in his mouth, each movement precise and delicate. She shivered when his lips closed, and knew he saw her reaction.

His hands were incredible. Broad palms, long fingers, a challenge and a joy to render accurately in a sketch. In the low light, she spotted a few dark hairs gleaming at his wrists, disappearing into the crisp shirt cuffs. There'd be hair on his chest when she bared it, crisp against his pale, pale skin. How would his hands feel, cradling her breasts?

"How's work?" Hades asked mildly.

Persephone blinked at him, pulled out of the sensual fantasy.

"Joy requested that I be moved from Events," she said, which was a mild way of putting it. Rumor had it Joy had marched into Mr. Hermes's office and demanded her immediate firing.

When he'd called her into his office, she'd already been mentally packing a box.

"I'm moving you back to Kitchens for the remainder of this section," Mr. Hermes had said.

"Oh," Persephone said.

Mr. Hermes twinkled at her over the top of his glasses. "Disappointed?"

"No! No, absolutely, I'm grateful for the opportunity." She hesitated in the doorway.

"Yes?"

"Mr. Hermes? Did I get a second chance because of my mother?"

Mr. Hermes tipped his head to the side and regarded her calmly. "No. You get a second chance because your other assessments are fine to very good. We're aware that there are occasionally... clashes beyond an intern's control. One bad report doesn't sink your ship."

"Oh. Thank you."

"Two is bad, though," he'd added, and for a moment, she'd seen the steel behind the avuncular facade. "Don't get two."

"The other interns added me to the group chat," she told Hades now. The desire had faded a little with the workplace reminder, but she still tingled all over. "It's nice, but I feel super old."

"If you don't mind me asking..." Hades began.

"I'm 27. 28 in February. And you're 42." She read the question in his eyes and grinned at him. "Unlike you, I don't feel bad about using work contacts to do my due diligence." Sophia was currently interning with HR, and happy to use her limited access to staff files.

"We should probably talk about that," Hades said. "I mean, if we—if this—" He shook his head. "I'm sorry, I'm very bad at this. I don't date often, and I'm never sure how these conversations should go. I am probably moving too fast. But I like you very much, and although I'm aware there are barriers to do with my age and your workplace situation, I'm interested in exploring a possible relationship."

Persephone had definitely heard smoother approaches. On the other hand, no one had looked at her with that steady blue gaze, or so baldly admitted their interest in that deep voice. Or said "I like you very much" with no hint of an expected reciprocation. Honest vulnerability was an aphrodisiac, who knew?

"I like you too," she said, and reached across the table. Hades caught her hands in his. She shivered at the gentle touch of his thumbs, tracing circles in her palms. "Yes. Let's try."

Hades beamed at her, and her breath caught in her throat. His usual expression was serious bordering on stern, giving an impression of strength and maturity, with that wary look in his eyes an interesting challenge. But his smile was wide and unpracticed, and the kind of goofy that tugged at her heart. This wasn't a man who smiled when he didn't mean it. And he was smiling at her.

"I researched Olympus Publishing's romance in the workplace policies," Hades said. That should not have been sexy, damn it. But he was so determined to do this right. "The only thing that's forbidden is relationships that provide a conflict of interest in the direct chain of command. That's not us; you're not my direct report and I'm not your boss. The policy recommends we set up an appointment with HR to discuss any risks or other possible conflicts of interest, and the sooner the better."

Persephone flinched at the idea of sitting down with Mr. Hermes for a deep and meaningful discussion.

Hades looked rueful. "I know. It's not very romantic."

"No," Persephone said. "But you're right, we should do it. Could you, um, could you make the appointment? I feel like Mr. Hermes has done me enough favors lately."

"I'll get in touch with him first thing tomorrow," Hades promised.

Persephone wondered if he could tell she had plans for him tonight. But there was the rest of dinner and a play to get through before she could broach the topic. She bent her attention to eating, and to conversation. She made him laugh twice with her stories of workplace mishaps, and he told her about the changes he wanted to make in Finances when they shifted to the eighth floor. When they strayed from work, she was worried for a moment that without this thing in common, they would run out of topics.

But by the time they finished dessert, they had covered TV and movies, books and hobbies. Hades had confessed an addiction to mobile phone Match-3 games, and she'd told him some of her more bizarre experiments in attempting to cook for herself.

Hades paid for the meal, slipping his credit card into the black leather folder Jackson discreetly offered. "I asked you out," she protested.

He waved it away. "I picked the restaurant. You choose next time, and you get to pay."

Next time. The phrase lingered a moment.

When the receipt came back for his signature, it was accompanied by a small bottle of citrus dressing, hand-labelled.

"With the compliments of the chef," Jackson told her, and actually bowed slightly as she thanked him.

"Looks like you've been approved," Hades murmured. He held her blazer for her to put on, and reached for her hand with no apparent shyness as they walked into the evening air.

Persephone interlinked her fingers with his. "Good," she replied. "Because I can see we'll be going there often."

Now, there was only the play. Afterwards, their time would be their own, and she knew exactly what she wanted to do with it.

***

"Would you like a drink?" Hades asked, as the house lights rose for intermission.

"Oh, several," Persephone said immediately, surprising him into laughter. "Hades, I am so sorry."

Thank goodness, it wasn't just him. "It's not your fault. The play was very highly reviewed."

Hades liked theater. He enjoyed serious dramas and light comedies in equal measure. He took Hera to the ballet twice a year, and was her eager date to any musical Zeus didn't want to attend, though he drew the line at opera–he just couldn't suspend his disbelief in the ludicrous plots, or the physical impossibility of people belting out arias as they died.

What they'd just watched didn't match up to any of his previous experiences. In retrospect, review phrases like "bold experiment," "unconventional," and "brilliant exploration of the form's possibilities" might have been warning signs.

"Do we think they bribed the reviewers?" Persephone wondered. "Or do we just have terrible taste?"

"I think this is theater for theater people," Hades said diplomatically. Around them, there was a muted buzz, as people gravely offered their opinions. Hades's opinion of watching a masked woman screaming at a sustained pitch for two minutes while three actors circled her chanting nursery rhymes was "No, thank you," and also "Why?"

Persephone leaned in. "Do you want to get out of here?" she asked, her voice low. Her full breast pressed against his arm, and it was with an effort of will he kept his eyes on her face.

"Yes," he said. Did she mean... Was she offering more than just an early exit?

If so, she was going to have to be the one who made the offer, he'd decided before their date. Persephone didn't seem concerned by the age difference, and truthfully, neither was he. His experience of romance was slight enough that he suspected that there wasn't an imbalance there either, but the potential power dynamic worried him a great deal. He didn't want anything that smacked of coercion.

Persephone could certainly take care of herself, and was entirely capable of turning down any advance she didn't appreciate, but he didn't want to put her in a position where she'd have to.

So, no matter how much he longed to touch her, or see the full extent of her glorious tattoos, no matter how much her scent made his brain turn in dizzy circles, the first move had to be hers.

They hustled out of the auditorium and into the lobby. There was a small crowd around the bar–apparently they weren't the only people who thought this experience might go better with a drink–and one of them caught Persephone's eye and gave her–and him–a quizzical look.

"Shit," she said under her breath, and then they were outside.

"Um, who—"

"Terry. Another intern. It doesn't matter, since we're going to talk to Mr. Hermes soon."

Hades could imagine how much faster gossip would move than bureaucracy. "I'm sorry."

"I should be apologizing to you," she said, and grinned at him. "For dragging you into the intern gossip circle. Honestly, being seen in public with me was a serious risk." They were heading towards the parking building.

"I'm taking a lot of risks lately," Hades said. "For me, anyway. This evening, I gave my brother permission to redecorate my second floor."

"Zeus?"

Hades laughed. "Perish the thought. No, my middle brother, Don."

Persephone stopped. "About that night, in the courtyard, when I overhead you two talking..."

"It was an accident."

"Well, I want you to know, I would never tell anyone anything that I learned in those circumstances."

He smiled at her. "You know, I didn't think for a moment that you would. Isn't that strange?"

"My best friend thinks I'm too inclined to think the best of people."

"If anything, I'm the opposite. But I genuinely didn't consider it. I haven't yet told Don you were there, though I suppose I should. To be honest, though, I don't have the faintest idea of how he'd react."

"What's it like, having siblings?"

Hades automatically held the parking building door open for her. "Interesting. Difficult, sometimes. I've always felt somewhat responsible for them. Don finds that annoying, and Zeus thinks it's hilarious, especially since he's the one in charge at Olympus. Hera ignores it, mostly."

Persephone frowned slightly. "You think of Hera as your sister?"

"Oh, yes. The best of us, frankly. She could do anything she wanted, but she seems happy to be Zeus's partner and manage the rest of us. I've sometimes wondered whether her talents are sufficiently exercised. But I think she'd let us know if she were unhappy. What is it?"

"Oh, nothing," Persephone said. "I was just thinking, how it's so difficult to know people, even when you're related to them." She paused as they stopped by her car. "Let's always tell each other the truth, okay? No matter what."

"Of course."

119

"White lies are all right," she added. "Like if I don't look good in something, you're allowed to tell me I do."

"You look good in everything," Hades said indignantly.

She laughed, and was still laughing when she pulled his face down to hers. The laughter burbled against his lips in delighted little spurts, and he put his mind to making her stop. She jerked when he nipped at her bottom lip, and dragged him closer, hands fisted in his shirt.

He leaned over her, barely conscious of where they were. His senses were focused on her skin, her scent, the moan she let out when she grabbed one of his hands and placed it on her breast.

He felt like moaning himself, but watched through narrowed eyes as he gently cupped the warm weight. Even through her layers, he could feel the nipple harden against his palm. "Persephone," he said, and her eyes opened.

Her gaze fastened on him.

"What do you want?" he asked. "I won't–you have to tell me."

"You," she said. "Just... all of you. Can I take you home?"

"*Yes,*" he said, and kissed her again.

There was a gasp, and then a nervous giggle behind them, and he surfaced to discover a group of young women had come into the garage.

While he was mauling Persephone against her car door.

His hands froze in place and then jerked away from her body. Persephone had gone bright red.

"Um, are you okay?" one of the girls called uncertainly.

"Yes," Persephone called back. "This is my boyfriend. Sorry, we got carried away."

Boyfriend.

"Oh! Sorry to interrupt!"

"No, thank you for checking!" Persephone hit the button on her keys and slid into the drivers' seat.

Hades took his cue and dodged around to the other side, waving in what he hoped was an appropriate manner at the young women. He got inside and stared at her.

After a suffused moment, Persephone started giggling.

"Your face!" she gasped. "Their faces!"

Hades wasn't ready to laugh yet, but he dared a smile.

Persephone turned her key in the ignition, still chuckling, and took them out into the city. Despite the city planners' mania for their confusing one-way grid, traffic tended to hum along efficiently enough, but Hades had always liked driving at night, when it was peaceful.

Persephone took them past the inner-city limits, through the closest suburbs, and then through the green belt, to the Attica development, where people didn't really own houses, but estates. The entire suburb was essentially a series of private parks. Zeus had once made noises about purchasing something out there, but Hera had asked him if he wanted her to live in the *suburbs* in tones of such horror that he'd retracted almost immediately.

Prompted by that incident, a thought rose to the surface of Hades's mind. It wasn't important, perhaps, but it would keep bugging him until he knew.

"In the interests of honesty," he said. "May I ask you a question?"

"Sure."

"Why did you have your mother call Zeus to get you into the intern program?"

"What?"

"I don't mean that you don't deserve your place," Hades said hastily. "Everyone speaks very highly of your work. I just wondered, were you not sure you could meet the standards?"

Persephone was staring straight ahead. She signaled and pulled over, the car coasting to a controlled stop on the side of the street. A giant spruce waved over them, its shadow flickering over her face.

Hades's stomach fell through the floor. "I'm sorry," he said. "I've offended you. Please forget that I asked."

"You haven't offended me," she said, the words wooden. "The answer is, I didn't ask my mother to call. You're not just assuming she did, are you? Someone told you she had."

"I—yes."

"Someone who would know for sure? Someone you trust?"

Hades thought back to that conversation in the elevator. Had he assumed or misunderstood something? Had Hera? But no, she'd said, definitively, that Demeter had called Zeus, and Hera didn't make mistakes like that. "Yes."

"I see." Persephone turned to look at him. Her face was stiff, her features wooden, frozen between pain and anger. "In fact, I specifically asked her not to do that. And she promised she wouldn't."

"I'm sorry," Hades said. He didn't know what else he could do. "I didn't know. I didn't think—"

"I thought I'd earned it," Persephone, her voice wobbling. She gulped, and it became a sob.

Hades got his arms around her as best he could in the confined space, and she collapsed against his chest. He was saying things, tender, nonsense phrases, apologies and assurances, while she shook against him and he stroked the golden silk of her hair.

When the storm of tears abated, she gently unentangled herself and gave him a wobbly smile. "Thank you," she said. "I think–would you mind? I think I'd better drop you home."

"Not really the right mood," Hades agreed, and was rewarded with a shaky laugh.

"No," she said. "And I need to talk to my mother." She blew out a breath, and turned the car engine back on. Her three-point-turn was a thing of beauty, but Hades was too worried to appreciate it.

"Tell me something," she said, after the silence had gone on too long. "Something about your brothers, a fun story."

Hades racked his brain. "Oh, well," he began, and launched into the story of Don's first horse-riding lesson. Zeus told it much better, with a devilish twinkle and impressive brio, but he got through it all right, and Persephone responded with an anecdote about her and Hecate's college days, and by the time she dropped him off outside his townhouse, he was no longer feeling sick to his stomach.

Sexually frustrated, and very worried about Persephone, but he could handle both of those.

"I'll text you," she said, and kissed him goodnight.

There was a little flicker of the heat that had ignited between them before–not a conflagration, but enough to keep him warm as he let himself in.

Don was halfway up a stepstool in the entrance hall, taking measurements. "How'd it go?" he asked absently.

Hades hesitated. Good? Bad? Both? "I'm not sure," he said, and headed up the stairs, ignoring the questions his brother flung at his back.

Chapter Five

Persephone watched Hades close his door.

She was oddly calm. The crying had leeched something out of her, and she felt as if she were floating serenely in the middle of a maelstrom. Rage and shame and frustration were surging all around her, but they couldn't touch her yet.

She texted Hecate, but didn't expect a reply. Hecate was working late nights reviewing precedents for an upcoming case, and she often put her phone in a drawer in order to focus.

She had a text from Terry. It read, in total: :??:

Persephone didn't have enough capacity to worry about this. :Tell you tomorrow. Nothing shady, I promise. Can you keep it on the DL?:

Terry: :okayyyyy:

Persephone: :Thanks [heart emoji]:

She tossed her phone in her bag and drove home. Each thought seemed to sink into her conscious awareness with a hard clarity, like perfect round stones dropping into a clear pool.

Persephone had asked her mother not to make a call.

Demeter had promised she wouldn't.

Demeter had broken her promise.

Persephone had not earned her place at Olympus.

Her mother had lied.

Her mother had known that Persephone was lying, all unaware.

Her mother had let her lie.

Persephone parked outside the guest house, and only then realized that she'd driven home on auto-pilot. Not a good habit to get into, but she couldn't bring herself to care.

It was just before nine pm, and Demeter hadn't mentioned any plans. She'd still be up.

The main house foyer was a sweeping expanse of polished wooden floors and tasteful floral still lifes. Demeter didn't really live in the front of the house, but in the cozier spaces at the back, where she could indulge her love for cottagecore and French Country decor. The shift from graceful and austere to a thousand and one knickknacks and doilies was abrupt.

Persephone glared at a china cabinet full of pewter rabbits and charming porcelain shepherdesses, and wanted to kick the whole thing to bits.

"Mom!" she called, heading up the back stairs to the bedroom. "Are you up?"

"Darling, of course!" Demeter appeared on the small mezzanine, wrapped in her red silk robe. Her face had been wiped clean of makeup, and her hair was back in two loose braids. "What is it?" she asked, as Persephone mounted the stairs. "Darling, what's wrong? Did the date go badly? Do we need to call the police?"

"No," Persephone said, through clenched teeth. "He was a total gentleman, and I would be right now banging his brains out, if you hadn't *completely* ruined the mood."

She had never, even in the sulkiest days of her teenage rebellion, said anything that crude to her mother. Demeter actually recoiled, her hand fluttering at her heart.

"Persephone Kore Erinyes!"

"Mom! You lied to me! I asked you not to call Zeus to get me into the program, and you did!"

Persephone saw the moment when her mother contemplated denying it. Instead, Demeter rose to her full height and glared at her. "And what if I did? I did it for you!"

"I asked you not to. I specifically asked, and you *promised*, Mom!"

"Oh, darling."

Tears prickled at Persephone's eyes. "No, Mom! You knew it was important to me. I've been telling everyone I earned my place, and I didn't even know it was a lie! Now I'll never know if I was good enough."

"Darling," Demeter said softly. "Darling, the terrible truth is... you weren't."

The words had physical weight. Persephone staggered backwards.

Demeter pressed her advantage, her eyes melting pools of sympathy. "Your work experience was minimal, your grades were average... I mean, you have a fine arts degree, for heaven's sake. Your character references were lovely, but nobody could be honestly superlative about your work ethic, now could they? Anyone could see you weren't going to make it into Olympus."

"I-- Other programs wanted me."

"Oh, other programs," Demeter said, dismissing them with a flick of her wrist. "But you had your heart set on Olympus. So, yes, I picked up the phone. I got you your heart's desire. I always have, and I always will."

"Mom," Persephone said, but her voice broke on the word. She was crying again, all her fury and resolve disappearing like mist scorched by the sun. "That's not–you knew—"

"There now, darling," Demeter said, and she gathered Persephone into her arms.

Too exhausted to fight, Persephone let her do it. She couldn't help but compare the embrace to Hades's. He'd said sweet, encouraging things under his breath, so softly that she wasn't even sure he'd registered them. He'd called her brave, brilliant, capable and vibrant.

She didn't feel like any of those things now.

Demeter was kindly, implacably going through the reasons why what she'd done was an act of love, a real favor to her helpless little girl. Why, when you thought about it, Persephone should be grateful, not sad. And she should be grateful she'd found out, too, because now that she knew she wasn't good enough for that intern position, she could give up the job that made her work so late and spend so much time away from the mother who loved her.

"What?" Persephone mumbled.

"Now, don't worry about a thing," Demeter said, stroking her hair. "I'll call tomorrow, hm?" She gave a tinkling little laugh. "I can't help but feel a little guilty for putting you in this terrible job in the first place. It's only right I should get you out of it."

Persephone put her hands on her mother's shoulders and held her at arm's length. "Mom," she said quietly. "I'm not quitting my job."

Anger flickered in Demeter's eyes before she rearranged her features. "Don't be silly, darling. Of course you are."

"I'm not. Whether you got the chance for me, or I earned it myself, I still have it. I'm going to use it."

"But, sweetheart, it's so bad for you. Can't you see that?"

"It's the best opportunity I've ever had."

"Oh," Demeter said, and now her eyes were angry. "Better than the opportunity of being my daughter, is it?"

"Mom, of course not. You know I didn't mean it that way."

"Well, I'm sure I don't know what you mean, Persephone! You're so moody all the time, and this job has absolutely ruined your home life. And even when you have a night off, you want to spend it on a date instead of with me!"

"I'm allowed to date, Mom. People date."

"And need I remind you that this job resulted in you being actually assaulted, Persephone? In you being made an absolute laughing stock, all over the internet, in front of all my friends?" She threw her hands into the air and turned dramatically away. "Well, you can do what you like! I've never stopped you. But I can't stand by and watch you destroy your own life. It's too much to ask of me, Persephone. It's too much!"

Persephone watched her. The cool, distant calm was washing over her again. It wasn't separate from the anger, she was dimly beginning to recognize. It was an anger so great that it made everything still and quiet. "So, what now?" she asked. "I'm not quitting, Mom. What do you plan to do?"

"If you're going to choose this job over me—"

"I'm not," Persephone said firmly. "I'm choosing my desire to work over your desire that I quit."

"Don't interrupt me! Persephone, you know I've never asked much from you. I've given you everything!"

"Yes," Persephone acknowledged. "You have."

Demeter seemed taken aback by the calmness with which she said it, but the tracks were already laid, and she couldn't change course now. Persephone watched with mild interest as she worked herself up again.

"You've forced me to this, Persephone, be very clear on that. If you will persist in ignoring my wishes and advice, if you reject my love and care, then you reject all of it. If you won't listen to reason, I will cut you off." Demeter's mouth was a straight line, her eyes stabbing at her recalcitrant daughter. "Do you hear me?"

"I hear you," Persephone said. The calm was turning into a terrible numbness, her tongue slow and heavy in her mouth.

"No allowance, no credit card," Demeter said. "No guest house. If you want so badly to be independent, then you should learn exactly what that means. I think you'll quickly learn to appreciate me!" She folded her arms and lifted her chin, triumphant.

Persephone was supposed to cry again.

She turned on her heel, and heard the unrehearsed shock of Demeter's gasp.

"Where are you going?" her mother shrieked after her.

Persephone shrugged, and tossed the reply over her shoulder: "To pack."

***

Hades looked at his phone, put his phone down, picked it up again, turned it face down on his desk, and let his face sink into his hands.

He'd texted Persephone the night before: :Did you get home all right? Are you okay?:

He'd got three dots for a long time, then, :Yes. Too much to say over text. Lunch tomorrow?:

:Sure! Kaeko's?:.

She'd agreed with a thumbs-up emoji.

Since then–since 11:03pm the night before—nothing.

It wasn't as if he didn't have work to do. Daphne had sent him the final paperwork for the month's severance packages, he had to run a random check on Accounting, Odysseus had suggested two new capital expenditure working groups (where did the man find the energy, and how could Hades steal some?), and the next board meeting was coming up.

Plus, Zeus's latest expenses had come in–extremely late and first sent to an email address that didn't exist–and there were entirely *new* unexplained items in the reimbursement list.

But none of that mattered, because Persephone was hurting. He kept telling himself to stop freaking out, but it wasn't working. Every ten minutes, he had to go through his list of reasons not to panic.

One, Persephone was working in Kitchens. Her day had probably started before his, and she'd be too busy to text. He was lucky she'd seen the texts he'd sent before bed.

Two, he absolutely could not get in touch with her via work channels. That would make a mockery of the boundaries they'd so carefully established.

Three, if she wanted help, she'd ask. Until then, offering unprompted assistance would be an insult to the independence she clearly prized. That crying fit hadn't come out of nowhere; she'd wept as if a dam were breaking.

He found himself wishing that he'd asked a few more questions about Demeter Erinyes while he was talking to Hera. Hera hadn't seemed as if she disliked the woman—but neither had her voice warmed nearly imperceptibly, the way it did when she discussed her few real friends.

He couldn't ask now. That would also be interfering.

Hades looked at his phone, put it down, groaned, and opened his draft email inbox.

There was one thing she'd asked him to do, and he'd do it, no matter how uncomfortable it made him.

He stared at the draft he'd been tinkering with for two hours. He'd spent nearly twenty minutes on the greeting alone—"Dear Mark" was far too familiar for a man he barely spoke to, "Attn: Mr. Hermes" far too formal for a fellow department head—and he was afraid this was the best he was going to get.

Mark,

I am interested in entering a romantic relationship with another Olympus employee (NOT in my direct chain of command). As suggested in the Employee Relationships, Disputes and Mediation Policy (2018), we would both like to meet (jointly if possible, severally if necessary) with a Human Resources representative to discuss any potential conflicts of interest or issues that might arise.

Given my position within the company, I would prefer that you be the HR representative if possible. If not, please advise who might be best suited to a discussion of this nature.

Best regards,

Hades Kronion.

The email was ugly and awkward and had nothing in common with the warm and lovely woman who'd so happily laughed against his mouth the night before. But she'd asked him to arrange the meeting. At least, when he met her for lunch, he could tell her that was done.

He deleted "Best" as too casual and his surname as too formal, and hit send.

The undo button blinked at him for a few tantalizing seconds, and then it vanished and he sighed, relaxing his tensed hands.

All right. It was nearly noon. Time to get some work done.

Hestia insisted on her staff having an actual lunch break ("tired cooks make terrible mistakes"), before or after the big rush in the dining room. Persephone, as an intern, got the worst slot, at 3pm, but she'd have forty minutes. Hades had carefully selected a Japanese-style cafe just a five-minute walk from Olympus–far enough that no one from work would go there casually, but not so far that she wouldn't have time for a real break.

He was already seated when she came in, their table covered in a selection of sandwiches and cake.

"Oh, wow," she said, and smiled. "This looks too pretty to eat."

Hades pretended to reach for the slice of strawberry cake, and Persephone grabbed it, stabbing her fork at him threateningly.

"So," she said, once she'd made her way through the tiny rectangles of salmon and cucumber sandwiches. "Last night."

Hades put his own utensils down and listened intently while Persephone related her conversation with her mother. Her voice was flat, but her recitation was precise; Demeter's barbed words had clearly stuck fast. "And then I called Hecate," she concluded. "She picked me up, and I'm crashing on her couch." She sighed. "I thought I wasn't in a fit condition to drive, but I should have worked something out. Now I don't have a car."

Hades blinked. "Your car belongs to your mother?"

"It was a gift," Persephone said. "The kind of gift where she bought it and gave me the keys. I never got around to registering it in my name. I don't think she'd try to repossess it if I had it, but I guarantee I won't be allowed to go back to get it. Not unless I go back and beg." There was a gleam in her eye that promised that wasn't happening.

She absently popped another sandwich in her mouth and chewed thoughtfully before swallowing. "She's threatened to cut me off before. But she's never gone through with it. Hecate says it was because I never pushed her so far, and I deserve a medal for making it out." Persephone looked up at him, her eyes rueful. "I'm sorry. This must sound completely crazy to you."

Hades cleared his throat. "Not at all. Someday soon, I'll tell you about my father."

"I'd like that," Persephone said. Her eyes refocused, determined. "I'm going to make it stick, though. And I'm not going to crash on Hecate's couch forever, either. I've got the rest of this quarter's allowance, and the last two months' paychecks, and that'll be enough to set me up in an apartment. Then I'll have to live within my means." She nodded firmly. "And once Mom sees that I can be an adult, maybe she'll stop treating me like a child."

Hades had his doubts about that, but now wasn't the time to voice them. "That sounds very admirable," he said. "I'm glad you have a plan." The urge to offer his resources was a faint thing, easily ignored. But his skills, that would surely be all right. "I've constructed a budget or two, in my time. Do let me know if you think that would be helpful."

Persephone blew out a breath. "Honestly? That would be great. I don't have any idea how to do that."

Hades nodded, and dropped to the next item on his mental agenda. "I've emailed Mark Hermes, but I haven't heard back about the meeting yet. Hopefully this week."

"Oh," Persephone said, looking dismayed.

He wasn't looking forward to the meeting either, and he'd carefully considered what might be a more enjoyable occasion, at least for her. "Also, my sister-in-law throws a New Year's Eve party every year. I was wondering if you'd like to accompany me."

"Your sister-in-law. Hera Kronion."

"If I have another sister-in-law, Don hasn't told me about her yet," Hades said. He tried to keep his voice light, but could hear the anxiety starting to bleed in.

"I don't think I should," Persephone said. She was staring at her hands, but she lifted her gaze to look at him. She looked strained and unhappy, and Hades wanted to reach out and ease her pain. But her body language didn't welcome that, and he stomped firmly on his own desperate need to comfort.

"I understand," he said. "It's a big deal, meeting the family. Formally, I mean. I mean, you've met all of them, except Don, and—"

"That's not it. Well, not really." Persephone visibly braced herself. "I don't think we should see each other anymore. Romantically, I mean."

Hades's body physically reacted before his racing mind could catch up. He felt the words like a knife, and, far too late, tried to keep the pain off his face.

Persephone's own face twisted. "I like you," she said. "I mean, I really like you. We've been on one date and it shouldn't hurt this much to let go, but I think I have to."

"Can you tell me why?" Hades asked. He was distantly proud that his voice didn't tremble. Somewhere, in the back of his head, a voice was screaming at him, telling him not to let her go, to do whatever it took to hold onto her.

"I was really proud of myself for getting this internship," she said. "I thought I'd earned it. But then I found out that I hadn't."

"You've earned it," Hades said forcefully. "You work as hard as any of the interns. You're as worthy as any of them, and everyone knows it."

"But that's it," she said, and he could hear the tears she wasn't letting fall. "I don't think they do know it. And I've moved out. I want to be independent, and make my own way."

"... And you can't do it with me," Hades said, as the problem became clear. "Because if we're together, people will think your successes aren't yours. They'll assume I pulled strings or called in favors."

"I know you wouldn't do that. But what if people try to reach you through me? What if they give me opportunities I don't deserve because they want a favor from you?" She took a deep, shuddering breath. "I've never been on my own. I don't know what I'm worth, alone. But I think I need to find out."

"I understand," Hades said. He carefully picked up her hand. Her fingers clutched at his convulsively. "Persephone? I really do understand." And he did. How could he condemn her for resisting nepotism when he'd always despised it? How could he be anything but admiring of her determination to claim an independence she'd never had?

Oh, but it hurt. It hurt.

"I'm sorry," she whispered.

"Me too," he said. "I hope–this is presumptuous, and perhaps it brings about the same problem, but I hope you can consider me a new friend?"

Her smile flashed relief at him. "Yes. Friends is okay. I would like–" she gestured around them. "I can be a coffee friend, a lunch friend. But not a dinner and a show friend."

"I'd prefer to skip the shows, anyway," Hades said gravely.

Persephone laughed, and gently withdrew her fingers from his hand. "To be honest, if we meet at night, I might not be able to keep my hands off you," she admitted.

Hades met her eyes, and felt desire spark between them. "Likewise," he said, his voice sure and low.

Persephone broke the eye contact, and he coughed, both of them all too aware of the sensual electricity. "And," she said, and fiddled with her fork. "It might not be forever. The just friends thing. But I don't want to make any promises I can't keep."

Hades tried not to entertain the sudden hope. She'd *just* told him she couldn't make promises. "I'd better get back to the office," he said instead.

"Me too," Persephone said, and signaled the quietly hovering waitress.

Hades felt mild alarm. He hadn't stinted on the order. "I'll, uh, I'll get the check."

"You hardly ate anything," Persephone protested.

"But I ordered everything before you got here, so you didn't have a chance to fit it into your budget. That means I pay."

"All right," Persephone said doubtfully. "But next time it's on me."

Hades made a mental note to find cheap, good eating places near Olympus. They walked back in near-silence, making only idle observations on the chill in the air and the holiday decorations in the store windows. He was very conscious of her hand swinging beside his, but he couldn't take it now. He couldn't touch her or kiss her cheek, much less her lush and willing mouth.

Being near her as just-a-friend was going to be torture. For a moment, Hades doubted he was strong enough to withstand it. Then he reminded himself he was an intelligent adult, not a horny teenager, and he could either keep it in his pants or take care of business himself.

It was in this frame of mind that he said goodbye in the lobby, rounded the corner to take the stairs down to the basement, and bumped right into Mark Hermes.

"Ah, just the man I wanted to see," Mark said, and clapped him on the shoulder. "I got your email, and thought I'd better come and have a chat in person, hm?"

Hades stared at him, appalled.

Mark lowered his voice. "I saw you coming in. I take it that Ms. Erinyes is the other party?"

"No," Hades said. "Not–I mean she was, but not anymore. We can cancel the meeting."

"Ah?" Mark said. For a moment he looked almost disappointed, which made no sense, because Hades had just taken a difficult task off his to-do list.

"We both decided to be friends for now," Hades said, because it sounded better than "she dumped me for reasons I have to respect before we really started going out."

"Ah, I understand," Mark said. "Well. Do tell me if things change, hm?"

"I'll do that," Hades said, and brushed past him to make his descent.

***

Persephone finished scrubbing the last stove top, took off her rubber gloves, and stretched backwards. Her spine cracked.

"I actually heard that," Thalia said. She sounded impressed, but spoiled the effect by yawning.

"It'll happen to you too, youngster," Persephone told her.

Hestia, with the instincts that made her such a respected terror in her domain, wandered in from her office at that point. She inspected the stoves and floors and took a couple of pans down from their hooks for a random cleanliness check.

"Good," she said. "Go home."

In the tiny Kitchens locker room, Thalia untied her apron and tossed it in the laundry pile, but paused as she was putting her coat on. "Some of us are going out for drinks," she said. "Do you want to come?"

Thalia had been making friendly overtures since the disastrous night at the party, and Persephone had resolved to accept the next one, but her whole body ached. The kitchen work had been a relief, that afternoon, while she tried not to think about Hades's face and the terrible pain he'd shown before his iron self-control kicked in.

It didn't make any logical sense. Persephone shouldn't have had the power to cause him that kind of pain. Walking away from their relationship shouldn't have felt like she was ripping off an arm. It was very clear that they were both in way too deep.

And her mother's lies had made it impossible for them to explore those deep waters together.

"Raincheck," she told Thalia. "I, um, I moved out of my mother's place. I have to do some apartment hunting."

"Oh, gotcha!" Thalia gave her a sympathetic look. "Good luck."

"Good luck?" Terry inquired, appearing in the doorway. He'd gone very masculine today, with polished black brogues and a snappy suit. Working with Penny in Wardrobe obviously suited him.

"Persephone's looking for a place to live," Thalia said, while Persephone eyed Terry warily. She hadn't forgotten her promise to tell him everything later. She just wasn't sure how to do that, now there wasn't much to tell.

"Is she?" Terry said easily. "I might know someone looking. Thalia, love, the others are already there. You head off while I find that info for Persephone."

Thalia exited in a swirl of scarves and Terry leaned against the doorframe.

"Do you really have a lead on a place?" Persephone asked.

"Sure," he said, not moving. "I'll trade, secret for secret."

Persephone rolled her eyes. "It's not a secret. I was on a date, okay? That's allowed."

Terry's eyebrow arched at her snappish tone. "And it went badly?"

"It went great," Persephone said. She remembered Hades' lean frame, pushing her back against the car door, the certainty in his eyes as he'd moved his hand over her breast. "Really great. Until I had to go home and have a giant fight with my mother, and she kicked me out of the house."

Terry's eyes widened, and Persephone snapped. At this point, she didn't much care whether he passed it round all of the interns or put notices in the elevators. "Turns out, my mother did make a call to Zeus to get me into the program," she said recklessly. "All of you were right. I didn't get here on my own merits. I took someone else's place, someone who actually deserved it. Go on, tell me you told me so."

"I would never," Terry said. He'd dropped the insouciant stance against the wall. "You didn't know?"

"Of course not. I went home and yelled at my mom, and she told me it was for my own good, and now that I'd found out I could quit and be her good little girl forever, and when I said I wasn't quitting–" She gulped in air. It was suddenly too hard to keep going.

"She kicked you out."

"Yeah." Persephone gestured wildly at him. "So if you actually do know someone looking for a roommate, or a one-bedroom that's up for lease, or something that means I don't wear out my welcome on my best friend's couch, I would really appreciate it, please and thank you."

"I--yes, of course." Terry groped for their phone, nearly dropping it. "A friend of mine–someone in the play, actually–is leaving for a six-month engagement in Vegas, and they need someone to sublet."

"Great. Awesome."

There was a beat, then Terry looked up. "Um, so the date..."

"Oh, fuck," Persephone said. "Yeah. The only date I'm likely to get, because I blew that up too." She huffed out a breath. "I was really-- I really like him, okay? But the last thing I need is to go from people thinking my mommy gets me everything to them thinking my boyfriend does." She made a fending off gesture at Terry, who had stepped closer, their face sympathetic. "Don't, just don't."

"I was only going to say, you don't need to care about what people think," Terry said.

"Sure. Okay. But I do." She shrugged angrily. "So. That's it."

"Come for a drink with us," Terry urged.

"No, my friend Hecate's picking me up."

"Well, can I walk you out?" Terry winced. "I'm sorry. I feel bad for misjudging you, so I'm doing the thing where I try to make amends without checking if you want them. My therapist says it's a work in progress."

"Hah," Persephone said. "Well, give me your therapist's number too. And yeah, you can walk me out." She grimaced. "I'm not really mad at *you*."

"I get it. You had a tough day."

"Yeah." Persephone shrugged into her coat and yanked her hat over her hair. "How's Wardrobe?"

"Penny is the best," Terry said, jumping on the change of subject with obvious relief. He burbled about Penny's style, her taste, and her wicked sense of humor all the way downstairs and through the lobby, barely pausing to say goodbye to the guards as they walked past the security desk.

Hecate was parked right outside the building in the pick-up zone, leaning on her car door. She was wearing her black heavy silk trench coat, open over a black turtleneck mini-dress, and knee-length spike-heeled boots. Her skin was marble-pale, her lips were scarlet, and she looked like a Snow White who had decided to throw out the puffy medieval dresses and become a centerfold for Sexy Business Wear Weekly instead.

Terry actually stumbled.

Persephone grinned. "Come and say hi," she said, and ruthlessly steered him towards Hecate, whose smile had acquired the attentive air of a cat scenting prey.

"Hecate, she/her," she purred, holding her hand out.

"Terry, he/she/they," Terry said, obviously dazed. For a moment, Persephone thought they were actually going to kiss Hecate's hand, but at the last moment they turned it into a firm shake.

Hecate let her fingers linger before slipping them free, a trick she'd tried to explain to Persephone a few times, and then looked enquiringly at Persephone. "Are we giving Terry a ride?"

"No, he's going to meet some friends for drinks," Persephone said, forestalling Terry's half-formed protest.

"Pity," Hecate murmured. "Then I'll hope to see more of you later."

"Likewise," Terry said. They'd recovered a lot faster than most people did when first exposed to Hecate on the prowl, and Persephone spotted the spark of genuine interest in Hecate before she hooded her eyes and slid into the driver's seat.

"Bye, Terry!" Persephone called cheerfully. "Thanks for the apartment lead!"

"Yum," Hecate said, expertly navigating them into the flow of traffic. "Do they grow many of those at Olympus?"

"One or two. Thank you for the ride."

"No problem."

"You really didn't need to."

"You really didn't need to decode public transport today. It's not a problem. I told Minerva I had a family emergency and took my work home for the night."

"Oh," Persephone said. "Well, I don't want you to think you need to lie to your boss for me."

"It wasn't a lie," Hecate said brusquely. "What was that about an apartment lead?"

Persephone explained while Hecate drove to her building, a tall steel-and-glass monstrosity that suited Hecate's taste for clean lines. She spent far too much of her associate's pay on the rent, she'd explained to Persephone, in what Persephone thought was probably a hint about how much she should expect to pay for something much shabbier.

Hecate ordered dinner for both of them, ignored Persephone's attempt to pay her half, and went to her room to get some work done, while Persephone sat cross-legged on the couch and tried to make lists of everything she needed. A place to live, first, and then some basic furniture to go in it. Kitchen appliances and utensils, and thank goodness she knew at least the basics of cooking.

Her packing the night before had been haphazard at best; she'd grabbed art supplies first, and then most of her work-suitable clothes, but she had only two pairs of shoes and not enough underwear to even see out the week. She was going to have to fit a shopping trip in somehow. She was probably going to have to figure out new shopping places, too--high-end department stores and designer boutiques were certainly out of her price range now.

The food arrived, and Hecate came out to help eat it and pour them both glasses of wine. Persephone broached the shopping problem.

"Drug stores sell underwear," Hecate said. "We can go after dinner."

Persephone blinked. "Really?"

"Mm-hm." Hecate sipped her wine. "Did you bring any bras? That's gonna get expensive for you."

Persephone bit her lip. "Only three."

"Three is fine, if you rotate them. Try and save up for another couple for when they wear out."

"Okay," Persephone said, and put 'two bras' on the list. She was mildly shocked by the idea of having to *save* for bras, but Hecate was right–at her cup and band size, even a simple bra could be pricey. "You mean off the rack, right?"

She looked up when the silence stretched, and saw that Hecate was regarding her with an odd mixture of concern and amusement. It was mostly amusement in her voice when she said, "Yes, Persephone, I mean off the rack."

Persephone put her pen down carefully. "Sorry. I must seem like an idiot."

"Just a bit clueless," Hecate said, with bracing honesty. "It's going to take you some time to get used to this. You know you can stay here as long as you want, right? Maybe you should raincheck getting a new place and make sure you can afford necessities for now."

"No," Persephone said, more forcefully than she meant to. Fortunately, Hecate never minded force. "I mean– I feel like if I don't keep my momentum up, I'll get yanked back. Depending on you isn't the same as depending on my mom, but it's still dependence."

"I get it." Hecate rotated her head, stretching out the muscles at the back of her neck. The oversized t-shirt she was wearing hung loosely on her delicate collarbones. "But if you can't make rent, if you're out of groceries--please, promise you'll call me first. It's not a sign of failure if you need help. Almost everyone needs a safety net at some point."

"You didn't," Persephone said. They'd tiptoed around this, so far. Hecate's mother had kicked her out as a teenager, the summer before she started college. Demeter had at least waited until Persephone was an adult with a degree, earning a basic wage.

Hecate looked at her, and Persephone could see the shadow of that tormented freshman year in her eyes. "I did need a safety net," she said. "And I had one. I had you."

"It was my mother's money," Persephone said, trying to dismiss it. She didn't want Hecate feeling *grateful* to her.

"You spent it on me," Hecate said. "And don't think I didn't notice all those pizzas you were 'too full' to finish, or the 'I saw this and thought of you' clothing gifts you always managed to lose the receipt for."

"It's not the same," Persephone said indignantly. "I did it because we were friends, and friends look after each—"

She fell silent. Hecate smirked.

"Okay, fine," Persephone mumbled. "If I need help, I'll let you know. But I'm still moving out as soon as I can."

"Roger that," Hecate said, and put her empty box of crab rangoon on the coffee table. "You done? Let's go get those undies."

Chapter Six

I t snowed on New Year's Eve.

Hades lingered in the lobby of Hera and Zeus's building, watching the giant flakes tumble down through the glass doors.

It was immature and grossly sentimental to indulge in melancholy when he was heading to a party on which his sister-in-law had lavished considerable money and effort. Outside the glowing penthouse that awaited him, would be people who had nothing at all, much less caviar, champagne, and a family who cared about them. Don was up there; that alone was worthy of celebration.

He should go up right now, and make conversation. He should talk to his brothers, congratulate Hera on her skills, and try his level best to chat with the elegant single women she'd no doubt invited on his behalf. Instead, he slipped out his phone and texted the person he actually wanted to be spending time with.

Hades: :Happy New Year's Eve :

Persephone responded two minutes later with a selfie of her sitting cross-legged on her bed, an empty pizza box sitting on a pink and yellow towel spread in front of her. She was wearing an oversized sweatshirt and leggings, her hair was tumbling over her shoulders, and she had perched a sparkly cone-shaped party hat on her head. Behind her, Hecate lay curled into a ball, hands tucked under her chin like a child, apparently already asleep.

Persephone: :gonna be a real rager:

Hades laughed, and put his phone away, feeling better. Over the last couple of weeks they'd managed two just-friends coffee dates, where Persephone had told him about her new apartment, and he'd told her about Don's increasingly outrageous changes to his own guest bedroom, and his attempts to alter the more public spaces too. She'd laughed at his photos, but carefully avoided asking to see the redecoration in person, just as he'd carefully avoided inviting her. The attraction between them hadn't died, but if neither of them tried to deny it, they also avoided acknowledging it.

The doorman waved Hades up without question, and Hades gritted his teeth for the elevator ride. Twelve stories wasn't thirty, and the heritage building didn't allow for the floor-to-ceiling glass he hated so much in Zeus's office, but the swoop in his stomach at the sudden motion was the same. He predicted that he was going to get a lot of exercise from May, climbing the eight floors to his new office.

Persephone would be three quarters of the way through her internship by then. Maybe she'd accept a permanent position at Olympus, or maybe she'd use the experience and confidence to get a design position somewhere else. About half of the interns who made it through the full program ended up at Olympus, but the rest, Odysseus had told him, didn't have trouble finding work afterwards. Titan Publishing was always particularly eager to poach ex-Olympus personnel—and vice versa.

And maybe, with a real job in hand, and a real salary to match (well, a real publishing salary, for what that was worth) Persephone would consider herself sufficiently independent to revisit the idea of being "just friends" with him.

Or maybe she'd fall in love with one of the other interns, like the intimidatingly well-dressed Terry. Terry had helped Persephone find her apartment. Hades had spotted them eating lunch in the dining room together several times. Odysseus had told him that Terry was, at 23, the second oldest intern. Odysseus said that Penny had said Terry was one of the best Wardrobe interns she'd ever had, and if their heart hadn't been so set on Photography she would have snapped them up to be a accessories stylist. Odysseus had also noted that Penny said Terry had a good sense of humor and was "very sweet."

Hades had the cloudy sensation that he should probably stop Odysseus from saying quite so much on the subject of Terry, but he was a weak fool who couldn't order his subordinates around, and was also desperately curious, emphasis on the desperate.

The elevator doors opened, and he stepped out into a burst of warmth and chatter. Hera didn't overtly theme her New Year's Eve event, but the gold and black color scheme and geometric decorations suggested an Art Deco revival. When a young man offered him a tray of miniature mint juleps, that was enough to convince him. He wandered into the spacious living room, where the sideboard had been replaced by a well-attended bar. Zeus was engaged in uproarious laughter with a group of business associates, but spotted Hades immediately and beckoned him over.

"Hades!" Zeus boomed. From his flushed face, he'd had a few of those tiny cocktails already. "Always late to the party! Don got here hours ago! Where's your date?"

"I'm solo tonight," Hades said, and nodded non-committally at Zeus's friends. He recognized a few of them from Zeus's college days–sports buddies and secret society fellows, no doubt, plus the odd dark horse who'd turned into a tech or media mogul. Zeus's business skills weren't anything shabby, but his ability to befriend people who might be useful later was unparalleled.

"Take my date if you like," one of them said now. "She's been complaining lately that *I* talk too much. I told her, baby, only one of us looks pretty enough to stay quiet, and she lost it. It was a compliment!"

"Mm," Hades said, while the men around him laughed uproariously. Zeus was laughing too. "Where's Hera? I should say hello."

"Dining room?" Zeus said.

Hera wasn't in the dining room. She wasn't on the balcony, which he surveyed without actually stepping onto. She definitely wasn't in the kitchen, which was full of very efficient catering staff moving at top speed, and so busy that he backed out muttering apologies for the disturbance. Cradling his empty mint julep glass, and feeling a bit like a thief, he wandered down the hallway and caught the quiet murmuring of voices from the open door of Hera's office.

Zeus called it "the library," and they did store most of the bookshelves in there, but it was where Hera did much of her events planning and charity organization, and it was a light, airy space, with a touch of the ocean in the blue walls and white furnishings. Hera was sitting at her desk in front of a large, open book, while Don stood behind her, looking over her shoulder.

"And you could try something like this, to bring in color and a garden effect," she was saying. "Though these palm trees are too kitschy. Hades likes botanicals, I think, but not the tropics."

Absorbed, neither of them had noticed Hades pausing in the doorway. Hera was focusing on the book, and Don... Don was focusing on Hera.

She couldn't see him, but the way he was looking at her, with a kind of open hopelessness, immediately told Hades something he had never wanted to have confirmed.

He averted his eyes and coughed slightly, giving them a few fleeting moments to notice he was there. When he looked up, Hera had snatched the book guiltily to her chest. Don didn't look guilty at all; he had produced one of his most devilish grins.

"Busted," he said.

"Oh, damn," Hera said peevishly, and laid the book down. "Don was going to get the painters in while you went on retreat."

"I said talk to me if you were making any drastic changes," Hades protested, and Don and Hera both waved that away.

"We could always paint over it if you hated it," Hera said.

"Which he won't," Don told her. "He'll pretend he does, and then say it would be too much trouble to get painted over, so it might as well stay."

Hades rolled his eyes. "What exactly were you planning?"

Hera showed him the cover: it was a glossy art book called *Walls of Wonder*, full of indoor murals.

"Murals," Hades said, trying to envisage the blank white walls of his home festooned with giant, attention-grabbing shapes and colors. It was difficult to imagine. He had his degrees neatly framed in his study, and some black and white streetscapes in his living room, which went nicely with his light grey lounge set. Don had rearranged the bedrooms, brought in some startling new pieces of furniture, and snuck plants into spots all through the house, but so far he'd left the walls alone. "I think I have to put my foot down on murals."

"I wasn't going to cover your house in them," Don said impatiently. "That would look tacky. I want to put something up the stairwell walls, so it looks less like an institutional corridor and more like a place where someone with a personality actually lives."

"Thanks," Hades said dryly, and sat down in a small armchair. "Don, where did this yen for renovation even come from? Do they do a lot of decorating on cargo ships?"

"I think it's good that Don's expanding his interests," Hera said.

"He's expanding them all over my house," Hades said, but it was a mild protest. Don did seem genuinely enthusiastic, and more importantly, the more interested he was in remodeling Hades's home, the longer he'd stick around. Maybe even long enough to acquire a home of his own. "Can we compromise on a one-color statement wall in the stairwell? Navy might be nice."

Hera shook her head, and Don said, "Definitely not navy, do you want to feel like you live in a cave?"

"But a mural?" Hades said. He held his hands out for the book, and started looking through it. The palm trees, definitely not. Some of the geometric prints looked rather nice, but when he said so, Hera pressed her lips together and Don was emphatic on the evils of minimalism. There was one, more muted, that looked like a stylized dark pine forest rising out of the mist, and he paused on it.

"I told you," Hera said, looking smug.

"Maybe something like this," Hades said, over Don's groan, and touched the page. It reminded him of something, the way the branches appeared out of the mists. It took him a moment, but then he had it.

Persephone's tattoos, rising out of her clothes.

He hadn't seen all of them, of course (not *nearly* enough of them) but he'd liked that combination of black outline and watercolor flowing over the lines, exuberantly failing to be contained. He'd liked the vibrancy and the sense of motion, as if these flowers weren't static, but alive and well on her skin.

He was almost positive that he didn't just like them because it was *her* skin.

"I might know an artist," he said.

"*You* know an artist?" Don said, unflatteringly shocked, but Hera cocked an eyebrow at him.

"I'll think about it," he said, both to Don and that look on Hera's face. "No guarantees."

"What the hell are you all doing?" Zeus demanded, appearing in the doorway. "I'm on my own out there!"

"You love being the center of attention," Don said, but Hera jumped to her feet and went to her husband, kissing him on the cheek.

"Let's go out," she said, and Hades very carefully didn't look at Don watching them leave together.

"All right," Don said, after a moment. "It's the last night of the year, we're both going stag, and Hera, wonderful hostess that she is, has provided her guests with a metric ton of booze. Let's get drunk."

"Deal," Hades said, and pulled out his phone. "One second, though." He texted Persephone, promising himself it would be the last time that night: :Do you take commissions? I have a project you might like.:

***

Persephone had hesitated before saying yes to painting the mural. She could certainly use the money–her first electricity bill had come as an unpleasant shock—and Hades had offered a generous amount for the work. It wasn't exactly an employer/employee arrangement, either–friends had paid her for artwork before. But the reason she *wanted* to say yes wasn't the money–it was the chance to see Hades's home and how he lived. That seemed too tempting to be an entirely good idea.

But she did need the money. And she could do the work. And he seemed touchingly certain that *her* art was what it needed.

In the event, when she arrived on the Saturday morning after New Year's Eve, he wasn't there, having gone in to the office. His housekeeper let her in and showed her the stairwell, told her that if she needed anything she'd be in the kitchen, and left her to it.

Persephone's first impression of Hades's home was that it didn't suit him at *all*. All right, to an outsider, the sleek lines and monochrome color scheme screamed "somber workaholic," and he was certainly a precise and tidy person, from his clipped beard to his well-polished shoes. But Hades was also warm and earnest, with a wry sense of humor. There was nothing warm in the living room, and absolutely nothing had a sense of humor.

He'd texted her a picture from a book of murals, showing pine trees rising from mist, as a starting point. That would at least be something living, something that showed there was more beneath the glossy surface. But she thought pine trees might be too stark, the color scheme too dark for the space.

She flipped her sketchbook open, sat cross-legged on the dark grey carpet at the foot of the stairs, and got to work.

Sometime later, she was shocked out of her creative fugue by a male voice saying, meditatively, "I like the one with the squirrel."

"Gah!" Persephone responded, and pitched forward, catching herself against the lip of the bottom step. She shuffled around on her butt, flinching as her joints creaked, and accepted the hand that was held out to her.

Don Kronion pulled her to her feet with no visible effort, which was not something she experienced often. She was a fairly heavy person, but he'd shifted her as if he carried heavier loads every day, and didn't notice. "Hi," he said. "You're Persephone, the woman who's not dating my brother." His face was impassive; it was impossible to tell whether this was a judgment for or against her.

Persephone eyed him, trying to look equally expressionless. "And you're Don. His brother."

He grinned at her. "Wow. That was pretty impressive. I could actually hear you leaving out all the adjectives before 'brother.'"

"Such as?"

"Runaway. Irresponsible. Lazy."

"He's never said anything like that," Persephone said indignantly.

"No?"

"No. Mostly he calls you a would-be packrat who's discovered a new way to torment him through home furnishings." She looked doubtfully around the living room. "Though it doesn't look like you've done much here."

"He's being stubborn about the public spaces," Don said. "You should see what I've done to his bedroom." He gestured at her sketchbook before she could react to the innuendo–if it was innuendo. "Can I see?"

"I should probably show the client first," she said, just as the front door opened.

"We're in here!" Don called, without taking his eyes off her, and, after a startled moment, Hades appeared in the living room.

He'd taken his shoes off at the door, and the sight of his stocking feet hit her unexpectedly hard. As his slightly anxious eyes sought her face, she felt blood rush to her cheeks.

"Hm," Don said. He'd watched her reaction, blatantly appraising.

Hades didn't notice. "Is something wrong?" he asked her. "I thought you were planning to leave at noon."

Before he'd planned to come home, avoiding exactly this meeting. Persephone checked her phone. It was nearly 2pm.

"I lost track of time," she said, faintly appalled. She hadn't been absorbed in her art in that way for months. It was like sinking into a deep, still pool where only the work existed, flickering images and sure strokes. Now that she'd surfaced, her body was bringing a number of aches and pains to her attention.

"I'll pay you for the extra hours," Hades said immediately.

"Oh, no need," Persephone said.

Don muttered something under his breath, and Hades looked at him inquiringly.

"I said, stay for lunch!" Don said, smiling widely.

"Oh, I—"

"Only if you'd like to," Hades said, and she acquiesced.

"I'll tell Theresa," Don announced, and slipped adroitly from the room, leaving the two of them alone.

The air thickened.

Hades cleared his throat. "Are those the plans? May I see?"

"Oh! Sure! They're just ideas for now, but here." Persephone handed him the sketchbook, valiantly ignoring the way his fingers trembled as they brushed hers. Her own hands weren't the steadiest, come to that. She shoved them in her jeans pockets and firmly told herself to chill, already. They were just friends. She had very good reasons to stay that way for now, and he agreed with her.

The fact that she wanted to jump his bones in the worst way was irrelevant.

Hades wasn't flicking through the sketches, waiting for something spectacular to jump out at him. He was going slowly, absorbing every detail, showing an appreciation of her work that was rare, and extremely gratifying. She forgot herself enough to crowd over his shoulder, answering his occasional question, smiling at his obvious delight. She'd begun with something similar to the pine trees in mist, outlining in charcoal and using her colored pencils to add quick swatches of color. She'd moved away from the initial image as she worked, getting gradually more detailed, adding more life.

He turned to the last sketch, the one Don had seen, and stopped dead.

The pine trees were gone. Instead, she'd covered the outline of the stairwell with cypress varieties, from deep gold to dark green, making the most of the contrast between spreading, weeping limbs and the dense thickets of compact boughs. The ground beneath them was bare, with hints of green moss and yellow lichen. She'd added animal life in quick lines–an electric blue jay, an orange-breasted robin, two tiny humming-birds hovering in the highest corner, the fanned tail of a sooty grouse searching for seeds, and the squirrel that Don had liked, perched on a branch halfway up the stairs, boldly staring at the viewer.

Going up or down the stairs would be like ascending or descending a slope covered in verdant life. Gaps in the branches revealed a deep blue sky, and a hint of ocean below, but the sense of height was lightened by the close cluster of trees. No one could fall from here–the branches would hold them safe.

Hades looked from the picture to her face, his lips softly parting with wonder. "It's perfect," he said. "I didn't know you could do this. I didn't know anyone could do this."

Their faces were so close. They were sharing the same air, breathing in unison. His eyes drifted to her lips.

Persephone stepped away. She didn't want to. She wanted to tug him up those barren white stairs to his bedroom, but she stepped back anyway, and saw her withdrawal mirrored in Hades's face as he remembered all of those very good reasons they weren't doing this.

"Close call," she said, her voice shakier than she would have liked. "I think I'd better not stay for lunch."

Hades nodded ruefully, and held out her sketchbook. They were careful not to touch, this time.

"Coffee on Thursday?" he suggested.

"The retreat," Persephone reminded him. There might be time for coffee on the Olympus retreat, but she'd been warned that the interns, although allowed to go, were primarily there to look after the guest speakers and run errands for whatever their supervisors simply couldn't do without for four days, and were to consider themselves permanently on-call. Not the ideal situation for a just-friends date.

"Oh, damn it, yes. Well. The week after, then."

"Absolutely. In the meantime, I'll work with these designs and email you some possibilities."

"I want the last one," he said, with no hesitation.

"I'll need to come back," she said, gesturing at the stairwell. "To get measurements and so on." She'd meant to do that today–her measuring tape, bought new for this project, was a lump in her back pocket–but if she stayed here long enough to measure the walls, she was going to lose her head and also her clothes.

"Yes," he said, gazing at her.

Persephone had the distinct impression he hadn't quite heard what she was saying, but the longer she stood here, the harder it was going to be to leave. "Okay," she said. "I'll... email you. Text me later?"

He nodded, and escorted her towards the front door. Don poked his head out of the kitchen while Persephone was putting on her coat, and then came all the way into the hallway, frowning. "Theresa's roasted a chicken," he said.

"It smells amazing," Persephone told him, with absolute honesty. "But I, um, I gotta—"

"She has a weekend to get back to," Hades said. His voice held a hint of brotherly frustration, but mostly he was still drinking her up with his eyes. Persephone was pretty sure her own face was doing something similar. She turned with a real effort of will and fumbled for the door handle.

Outside, the cold air was a welcome slap in the face, a reminder that if she wanted to get warm and stay warm, she needed to keep her mind on the job. Both jobs. She tugged her coat around herself more tightly, and trudged to the nearest bus stop.

He'd thought her work was perfect.

And she really, really wanted to see what his bedroom looked like.

***

Zeus was a good driver, Hades reminded himself. He was a little fast sometimes, but he had good reflexes and an instinct for even unfamiliar roads. And the road to the ski retreat wasn't unfamiliar; Zeus drove it several times a year, even if he only had his big brother in the backseat for one of those annual occasions.

The problem was the view out the window.

It was like the evil twin of the cypress forest on a hill Persephone's sketches had conjured. Her trees had stood under a bright sky, and they'd rise up around the viewer in a secure embrace. These trees were far below, crouching under a grey sky and burdened with snow. The road was edged with icy brown sludge, and it dropped away, into a sheer expanse he could not look at. It would have been smarter to sit behind Hera, so that he could firmly put his back to the view. Instead, he'd put himself behind Zeus, so that he could talk to Hera, reasoning that this would help him distract himself, without also distracting Zeus.

And Hera was doing her part, half-turned in her seat, discussing the performance of The Firebird they'd been to last week. The problem was that, in looking at her, he kept catching glimpses of the desolation behind her. After one particularly hair-raising turn, Hera evidently decided to bring out the nuclear option of distraction.

"And how are things going with Persephone?" she asked. "I was disappointed you didn't invite her to New Year's Eve."

"What's this?" Zeus demanded. "Persephone Erinyes? Demeter's little girl?" He chortled. "Hades, you dog!"

"She's not a little girl," Hades told his brother, then, to Hera: "I did invite her. She declined."

"Playing hard to get?" Zeus inquired. Hera tapped his shoulder lightly. "Ah, well, glad to see you're putting yourself out there."

"Yes, Don told me about your peculiar arrangement," Hera said. She was frowning slightly. "How long do you think this 'just friends' thing can last?"

"That depends," Hades said.

"On what?"

"On a lot of things, Hera. On her. On me. On if she gets a job that makes her feel less reliant. On if she meets someone else in the meantime."

Hera's eyes sharpened. "Or if you do?"

"Yes," Hades said, and knew it was a beat too late. Hera knew him too well. She knew that he wasn't looking for other candidates. He was waiting for this one to declare herself, or to permanently decline.

It was pathetic to be in love with a woman who you'd gone on one date with, and who you'd kissed only a precious handful of times, a woman who couldn't promise you more than friendship–but there it was. He loved Persephone. He'd looked at the sketches she'd made, at the transformation she wanted to bring to his home, and he'd known it was true. She'd left before he could do something stupid, like confess.

"If you got friend-zoned, it's over," Zeus said. "Look, just let me know if you want me to be your wingman. Any time."

It was an honest, generous offer from a busy man, which somehow made it even more terrifying. Hades sought for a change of subject and took refuge in work: "I heard from my contact in the tax department.

She can't confirm anything, but I got the impression that we're probably getting audited this year."

"Bummer. Well, you've got it handled, I'm sure."

"Oh, certainly, our records are fine." He paused, reminded. "Except for that expenses discrepancy from your office. Have you got any further with that?"

There was a pause, punctuated only by the hissing roar of wheels on wet road. "I don't know if you've noticed," Zeus said, his voice distinctly annoyed. "But I'm running a whole damn company up there. I don't have time to do detective work on my employees' coffee runs."

The sum was considerably larger than a few missing receipts for coffee, but the principle mattered far more than the amount.

"Well, I could send someone from my office to do forensics," Hades began, trying to figure out who. He couldn't spare Odysseus. Daphne would be the next logical choice, since she got on with nearly everybody she met, but Jonathan was the most relentless.

"We don't have time for someone else nosing around either. Just fold the expense into something else."

"I can't do that!" Hades said, genuinely shocked. Did Zeus not actually realize that would be illegal? "Without proof that it's not a legitimate business expense, I can't guarantee that the tax department won't—"

Zeus threw up one hand, a gesture that was particularly unnerving on someone driving up a steep and winding mountain road.

"Fine! Don't reimburse me." He glanced at Hera. "Sorry, darling. We'll have to tighten our belts."

"Belts are in right now," Hera said mildly. She wasn't taking sides, but she winced a little as Zeus sped up.

Hades flinched as Zeus took them sharply around a turn. "Zeus, someone in your office could be stealing. Don't you care?"

"My people wouldn't do that," Zeus said, his voice icing over. "And I don't appreciate your lack of trust in them. Maybe *your* people made a mistake."

"I checked the report myself," Hades said stiffly. The car lurched around another corner, and his hand leapt up to the side window handle before he could stop himself.

Predictably, Zeus took offence. "What's the matter?" he demanded. "Don't like the way I drive?"

Hades tried to calm his breathing. "It's a little fast for the conditions, don't you think?"

"Oh, I see. This is your heights thing."

"Zeus," Hera said, a note of warning in her voice.

"Oh, come on, Hera. I'm sick of coddling him and pretending we don't notice. Just admit it, Hades."

"Admit what?" Hades said. His jaw was clenching. It wasn't wise to bait Zeus, but he couldn't help it. Revealing this weakness when his brother was in this mood was impossible.

"You're scared of heights, man. Like a little kid." The scorn in Zeus's voice was palpable.

"I'm not *scared*," Hades said, aware both that this was a lie, and that he sounded like a little kid. When Zeus was like this, he was far too much like their father.

"Oh, really?" Zeus asked, and flung them into another turn.

Hades was forced against the window, and made the mistake of looking out.

The void sucked at him. He let out a squeezed noise, and tightened his grip on the handle.

"Stop it," Hera said.

"No, Hera! If he's not scared, then it's not a problem, right?" Zeus abruptly slowed down, and Hades sucked in a breath, but then the car edged up to the side of the road, crawling close to the cliff and he realized the torture wasn't over. Hades pressed himself against his window, as far from the edge as he could get. "Stop," he managed. His stomach was churning. His skin was clammy.

"Stop what?" Zeus asked, and sped up again.

Hades let out another noise, and Hera said something sharp, but he couldn't make it out over the pounding in his ears as Zeus took them up the side of the mountain, all speed and curves, and the void, the void below them, eager to devour. Zeus was shouting, at him, at Hera, and Hera was shouting back.

Hera hated losing control. Hades squeezed his eyes shut.

A horn blared, and his eyes popped open to see another car sweeping past them, coming down the mountain. The driver's face was livid with anger. Zeus braked sharply.

"You could kill us," Hera said, into the silence, rage sunk into every syllable. "Get out. I'm driving."

Zeus's jaw set, and he looked as if he might object, but he grunted something and got out. The slam of his door rocked the car.

Hera twisted to look at Hades. Her face creased in sympathy. "It won't be long," she promised.

And it wasn't long. Hera drove slowly and very carefully, while Hades tried to control his breathing and Zeus fumed in the passenger seat, but it was still only a few minutes more to the ski resort. Hera parked neatly in the space that had been set aside for them, and sighed.

"Hey," Zeus said, his voice more tentative. "I just—"

"No," Hera said. "I'll talk to you later." She got out and opened Hades's door. He'd been trying to control his breathing and relax his grip on the window handle. His fingers were stiff, the knuckles aching from the tension.

Hera didn't try to help him out, exactly–she just placed herself so that if he needed to, say, fall in a clumsy heap, she'd be there to catch him. As it was, his knees buckled a little, but he managed to stay upright.

"My bags," he began, but she shook her head.

"I'll deal with them. Let's get you to your room."

His room, with walls, and drapes he could close over the windows. "Yes," he said, and walked with her.

As the terror subsided, he was starting to feel embarrassed. They'd come up later than most of the employees, who had traveled on chartered buses, but the retreat work day didn't start until noon, so there were plenty of Olympus employees clustered in the lobby. They lounged in the large leather sofas and put large mugs on the scarred wooden tables to watch the wife of their CEO walk in, arm-in-arm with the CFO, who was clearly not well.

"One moment," Hera said, and went to deal with the concierge. She was back barely a minute later, with his room keycard and directions. She stepped towards the elevator, and hesitated.

"Can we take the stairs?" he said, hearing his voice crack, and despising himself for it.

"Of course," Hera said, and climbed with him, all six flights, without saying a word or asking a question. He appreciated the restraint, but she was clearly seething, and the intensity of her presence wasn't restful. It was a relief when she left him outside his room with a murmur about sending up his things.

The room was more properly a suite, with a small living area and a separate bedroom. It was warm and comfortable, tending heavily towards the same hunting lodge aesthetic that marked the lobby, but with discreetly upmarket textiles. There were blankets everywhere–two on the king-sized oak bed, one thrown on a plush armchair, and another couple visible on open shelves below the wardrobe. Hades grabbed the one from the armchair and wrapped it around his shoulders, sinking into the chair.

He kicked off his shoes, dragged his hands down his face, and tried to come to terms with the first full panic attack he'd had since his father's death. From experience, he knew that it would take an hour or so for the physical symptoms to subside, and even longer before he felt settled again. He started his old breathing exercises, counting slowly as his lungs expanded and deflated, and had managed a tenuous calm by the time the knock came at the door.

His bags. He stood up and hobbled to the door, automatically pulling his wallet out for a tip.

It wasn't his bags.

Persephone was lifting her fist for another knock when he opened the door. She looked like she'd run up those eight flights, her hair disordered, and her breath coming quickly. She paused as he appeared, then flung herself at him.

"Persephone," he said. He looked, he knew, like an absolute wreck. He couldn't make his hands stop shaking, and he felt both sweaty and chilled, even in the climate-controlled room. If he'd had any pride left, he would have felt embarrassed to have her see him in this state.

As it was, he simply opened his arms, and let the blanket slip from his shoulders as she wrapped herself around him. She kicked the door closed behind them and squeezed tightly before loosening her grip a little to lean back and look at his face.

"Hera told me what happened," she said, and he could feel her anger underneath the words she strove to make calm. "Are you—well, clearly you're not okay. Come sit down."

Neither of the armchairs would fit both of them at the same time, and Persephone showed absolutely no inclination to let go of him. Instead, they stumbled into the bedroom and onto the bed in an awkward waltz, and she arranged him to her liking, propped up against the head of the bed, with her arm securely around his waist and his around her shoulders. She leaned forward long enough to snag a blanket and drag it up over their hips, and then rested her head against his shoulder.

He pressed his face into her hair, and felt tears prick his eyes at the jasmine-and-mint scent of her. This was so right. It was absolutely, un-deniably, where they were meant to be. She wasn't a cure–nobody could be a panacea for the misfired neurochemicals going wild in his brain–but her soft warmth and steady presence was so infinitely soothing that he could feel some of the tension in his shoulders and belly relax.

"Should Hera not have told me?" she said anxiously. "I know you like to be private."

"Not with you," he said, and she nestled a little closer against him. "Tell me something good?"

"Sure," she said readily, and started talking about setting up the lecture space for the guest speakers. She didn't demand, or appear to expect any response from him, and as she went on, he felt his eyes drifting closed.

"I'm going to sleep," he realized, and he must have mumbled it out loud, because she pulled the blanket up to their shoulders and gently encouraged him back into the pillows. He was mildly concerned that this meant she was leaving, but the gentle heat of her body didn't shift away.

"Sleep," he heard her say, her hand drifting lightly down the back of his neck, and he pulled her tightly against him and obeyed.

Chapter Seven

P ersephone wondered if it might be appropriate to take off her bra.

It would definitely be more comfortable. Hades had been sleeping for nearly an hour, the exhausted sleep of a man driven to his limits and finding safety at last. He was tucked up behind her, his long limbs tangled around hers, and his breath puffed gently against the back of her neck. It was a pleasantly frustrating sensation.

Hera had found her in the main restaurant, where Mr. Hermes had commandeered all the interns and gotten them setting up the space for the guest speakers, clearing the tables and turning the big room into a lecture theatre. Terry had unwisely revealed that they'd done lighting for college theater, and promptly been hauled over to the tech desk. Persephone had been setting out chairs when Hera stormed in and pointed at her.

"I'm stealing this one," she'd told Mr. Hermes, in tones of such authority that no one had pointed out that Hera Kronion wasn't the boss of anyone at Olympus.

Mr. Hermes *had* looked like he might have wanted to protest, but he'd taken a closer look at Hera and nodded, sending Persephone over with a jerk of his chin.

"What can I do for you?" Persephone asked, and then as she got closer, and got a good look at Hera's face: "What's wrong?" Surely Hera didn't have any reason to look at her like that, with mingled sympathy and fury, as if she were breaking bad news about a terrible accident.

Persephone staggered between steps. What if there'd been a terrible accident?

"Hades is not hurt," Hera said, and Persephone's heart kicked painfully back into life. Hera read her look of relief as easily as she'd read the fear, and added, more subdued: "Not exactly hurt. But he is not well. Will you come?"

"*Yes,*" Persephone said, without thinking about how it would look to Mr. Hermes, or the other interns, or Hera herself. "Where is he?"

Hera led her back through the lobby and to the elevators. "You know Hades has a heights phobia?"

No beating around the bush here. "Yes."

"Well." Hera fidgeted with the button of her Versace coat, and Persephone realized that the woman was *embarrassed*. "My husband... chose to challenge that fear on the drive up."

"He *what?*" Persephone demanded.

Hera's eyes flashed. "I will be discussing that with him," she said.

"That's disgusting!"

"I don't disagree," Hera said, but there was a warning in her voice, a careful reminder of the boundaries between boss's wife and... What did Hera think Persephone was, to Hades?

Persephone was abruptly aware that she was acting with a little more emotion than could be reasonably expected of a distant workmate or casual friend. She didn't think she could stop. "How is Hades now?" she asked.

"He had a panic attack," Hera said bluntly. "I imagine he's still feeling the after-affects. I would have stayed with him, but I am not..." She let the words drift, obviously struggling to find the right phrase. "Comforting. It occurred to me that you might be." She stepped out of the elevator and gestured towards the door.

Comforting. It wasn't flattering–it made her sound like a bowl of mashed potatoes or a fuzzy toy. But maybe that was what Hades needed. She walked past Hera, sparing her a nod, and knocked on the door.

Hades had looked like a man who had seen death. Persephone immediately stopped caring about whether she was mashed potatoes, and hugged him. The way he clung to her, as if he didn't intend to let go, had made it very clear that this had been the right move.

They hadn't talked much. Hades had drifted off quickly.

So she'd been able to think.

Clearly, the just friends thing wasn't working, because her own stupid heart kept betraying her. She wanted Hades. She wanted to be with Hades.

But her desire to be independent was also very real. Being with Hades would probably mean she'd lose the camaraderie she'd built with her fellow interns. She'd definitely have to deal with people's perception of her as a spoiled rich kid, a nepo baby taking advantage of her connections in the worst possible way.

And on top of that it wasn't as if the rest of her life was easy right now.

Demeter texted her a lot. Persephone had stopped answering her calls after the second screaming match, but she couldn't bring herself to cut contact off completely and block her mother's number. It was a step too far. But scrolling through the texts made for depressing reading. There were pleas, threats, and promises that if Persephone came back, everything would be different. There was a long rant that Persephone had only ever loved her mother for her money, and now that was gone it was clear what a selfish little tramp she was, followed almost immediately by a pitiful description of how lonely Demeter was, rattling around the house all by herself.

Persephone texted back when she thought she could handle it. Hecate wanted her to stop, she knew, but Persephone couldn't help but think the right combination of words or the most reasonable argument might get through to Demeter. So far, not so much.

In addition to the emotional turmoil, it was so much harder to live on her paycheck than she'd thought it would be. It was hard to remember that she couldn't buy whatever she wanted, whenever she wanted it. She'd never thought of herself as extravagant, but now she had to consider every cost, plan her shopping list in advance, and work around public transport timetables. Every minor issue–ripped hose, a light left on all day, a sick day–became an anxiety-inducing expense. It wasn't just the money. It was all the time and energy it took to deal with having less money.

Everything was messy, everything was tangled up, and she couldn't find any way to unravel the knots.

But one thing had become clear, as she lay here, wrapped in Hades's arms.

She did care about what people thought of her. It was unfortunate, but true.

But she cared about this more.

And, that decided, she was definitely going to do something about the way her underwire was poking into her boobs. She wriggled one arm backwards, between their bodies, an angle she wasn't sure she could maintain for long, and scrabbled at the band.

"Mm?" Hades mumbled.

"Don't worry," she whispered. "I'm just getting rid of my bra."

"Mm," Hades responded, apparently happy with this sentiment. His arms shifted, giving her a little more room and--oh, actually, he'd given himself more room. His hands went unerringly to her breasts, cupping them through her sweater.

Persephone's body reacted immediately. She arched her back, pressing herself into his hands, unable to suppress the moan that surged from her throat. He'd been breathing on her neck for an hour, and now, as his breathing quickened and became harsher, she felt that gentle tease flash into prickling heat, surging down her spine and pooling in her belly.

She twisted, turning to face him, flinging one leg over his hips to drag him closer. His eyes were still half-closed, a lazy smile on his face as he tipped her mouth up to his.

There was no hesitancy in his kiss. He licked into her with absolute confidence, his hands sliding down her back to grab her ass in a steady grip. Persephone groaned into his mouth.

"Clothes, clothes, off," she said frantically, and went for his sweater, a soft cashmere that was unbelievably luxurious against her over-sensitized skin. Hades gasped as she tugged, and she saw his eyes widen as, she belatedly realized, he fully woke up.

"Persephone?" he said, voice rough. "Is this real?"

"I sure hope so," she said, letting go of the sweater hem. Even with the layers of clothing between them, she could feel that at least one part of Hades was very awake, pressing against her full belly, but she needed all of him to be on board. "It's okay if you want to stop. Do you need a second?"

She could see him putting everything together, remembering the circumstances that had put them in this bed. His hands slid up to her soft waist, holding her like a precious thing, rather than the grope she'd eagerly welcomed a moment before. "I want to keep going," he said, his eyes burning into hers. "But I think... you need to know what it means to me if we do."

Persephone tilted her head in inquiry. She was finding it hard to breathe.

"I think I love you," he said, looking utterly miserable. "I'm sorry. I know it's inconvenient, and far too early. But it's the truth. I love you, and I don't think I can be just a friend you slept with once. If we do this, I'm all in."

He was so honest. He was so brave. She owed him nothing less than the truth.

"I can't say it back yet," she said, and grabbed his arm when he flinched away. "No, wait. I want you, and I like you a lot, and I want to be your girlfriend. Is that enough for now?"

When he rolled her onto her back and kissed her again, Persephone figured the answer was yes.

***

Hades felt as if he were floating, even as he pressed Persephone into the bed. She wanted to be his girlfriend. She couldn't say she loved him *yet*, but even that implied she thought she could one day.

"You're so beautiful," he blurted, and raised up on his elbows to stare at her. She smiled up at him and wound her hands around his neck.

"Hades," she said, her tone even and sensible. "If you don't get naked and inside me within the next five minutes, I may die."

"Excuse me," he said, and rose up long enough to yank his sweater and shirt off over his head, ignoring the button popping in the sleeve cuff. Persephone was making short work of her own outer layers, though she was finding it difficult to wriggle out of her jeans.

"Can I get a hand?' she asked.

"Certainly," Hades said, and tugged firmly. The jeans peeled down her long legs, and he tossed them. She was displayed beneath him, dimpled flesh and flushed skin, the wide, generous expanse of her offered up to his devouring eyes. The only thing she was wearing now was a dark green bra and panties set, her nipples showing clearly through the thin silk.

The flowers flowed down her arms, bold and beautiful on her golden skin.

"Beautiful," he said again, and ducked to take a nipple into his mouth. She cried out as he licked her through the silk, her hands grasping eagerly at his shoulders. His own hand swept up the curve of her inner thigh, soft, hot flesh giving slightly as he stroked.

"Yes, touch me," she said as he opened her thighs and stroked between her legs, feeling the damp fabric. She was wet for him. His cock twitched at that sure indication of her desire.

"I believe the lady said naked," he said, and knelt upright, his hands going to his belt.

"Oh, allow me," Persephone said, and sat up. Her clever fingers undid the belt and pushed down the zipper, then curved confidently around his cock. She swept her thumb over the head and he thrust helplessly into her grip.

She grinned at him, plush lips widening.

He reached down and undid her bra, and she let go of him to slide it off, letting out a little sigh of relief. The bra had left red marks across her breasts, and he made an urgent noise in his throat as he reached for them, wanting to soothe the tortured skin. He traced his fingers across the incredible softness of her areolae, then gently stroked the puckered nipples.

Persephone made a sound partway between a groan and a cry, and pulled him back down on top of her. "I said five minutes," she panted in his ear, and in a flurry of activity the rest of their clothes were gone, and she was laid out beneath him again, but this time fully naked and glorious, open to his devouring mouth and careful hands.

He had his wallet, thank all things holy, and the single condom within it. He shared a worried thought that it might have expired, but the second he'd checked and found it all right, Persephone took the packet from his hand, ripped it open, and rolled it down his cock.

"Open for me," he murmured in her ear, and she lifted her knees, her ankles locking across his back. Hades smiled dizzily down at her, still half-wondering if this was a fantasy, and slid smoothly into place. Her full thighs embraced him, warm and welcoming.

Hades was self-conscious in public settings, but he'd never been shy about sex. In his experience, if someone wanted you in their bed, the best way to reciprocate was with unabashed enthusiasm. Persephone was certainly responding, her mouth falling as he fucked her in sure, smooth strokes.

He licked a line down the soft skin of her throat, and heard her gasp. "Is this good?"

"Yes," she said, her voice stuttering on the word as he thrust. "More."

"Can you come like this? I want you to come, Persephone."

"Oh," she said, her eyes flying open. "I can... here." He helped her turn over, until she was on her knees, one forearm braced against the bed. She reached down and slipped her other hand between her legs, and he grabbed the base of his cock, urging it to calm down, because watching her fingers slide on either side of her clit was the most erotic thing he'd ever seen.

Her back was a riot of color, leaves unfurling from the divot of her spine above her hips, stalks spiraling out from the folds along her ribs until they exploded into exuberant blooms across her shoulder blades, those red, red poppies caressing the back of her neck.

"Were you waiting for an invitation?" she asked, her breathing fast.

"Just enjoying the view," he said, and pressed in behind her, his fingers sinking into her ass. The angle let him drive even deeper with every slow stroke. He smiled as she panted and gasped.

"Don't tease," she said, almost begging.

He stroked one hand over her back, tracing the tattoos.

"Did these hurt?" he asked.

"Yes," Persephone said. She was writhing beneath him, her free hand clutching at the bedspread.

"Did you like it?"

"A little. Yes. More, Hades, please."

He firmly gripped her incredible hips and increased his speed, driving into her over and over. "This is so good, Persephone, so fucking good," he panted. "Come for me, please, I want to feel you come."

She cried out, her hand moving frantically between her legs, and he felt her walls clench around him in fluttering convulsions. He followed her down as her knees gave way, holding himself up one handed while he thrust into her once, twice, three times.

The orgasm was blindingly good, whiting out his vision. He blinked back to full consciousness a moment later, sprawled bonelessly on top of his squirming lover, sweaty, and sated, and very, very happy.

"Holy shit," Persephone said, after a long, breathless moment. "Damn."

Hades chuckled, and kissed the back of her neck.

"Seriously, I was expecting great things but *damn*. Five out of five stars, would most definitely bang again."

"That was more or less the idea," he said, and withdrew regretfully, getting rid of the condom while Persephone stretched and watched him, flatteringly wide-eyed. She was utterly unselfconscious in her nudity.

"Now I need a nap," she said, and then frowned. "What's the time?"

For a moment, it had been just the two of them, together alone. Now, with the reminder of times and schedules, the world came crashing back in.

Her phone had been in her jeans pocket. He recalled it sliding out when he tugged her pants off, but it took them both some moments of searching before he found it under the bed, further hidden by a fallen pillow.

He glanced at it, and couldn't help noticing the notifications screen was full of texts from "Mom." Another one flashed up, beginning: :If you care at all you should:. He handed her the phone without comment.

"Thanks," Persephone said absently, and poked at it. "Crap. I have to get going. What are your plans?"

Hades considered the question. The retreat structure aimed to provide both business and pleasure. This morning aside, the mornings were for dedicated team-building exercises in departments. Weather permitting, employees were then free to take full advantage of the resort facilities until late afternoon, when the keynote speeches took place, followed by a buffet dinner and, usually, some competitive drinking. Zeus always rounded off the last evening with his own speech.

Tonight, Hades was supposed to be giving everybody an update on the state of the company's finances, suitably glossed for the layperson. As ever, he'd sweated over writing it, running several versions past Odysseus's discerning eye. As ever, he was gloomily aware that very few people would listen at all, and those who did would be bored stiff, by his delivery as much as the content.

The speech was pointless, a burden on everyone in the room, including him. He'd done it, year after year, because Zeus had told him it was necessary.

Hades felt remarkably uninclined to do what Zeus told him.

"I think I'm going to take the day off," he said. "Would you like to join me this evening? Or–" he hesitated, but she had said *girlfriend* "--or move your things in here?" He patted the enormous bed. "Lots of room."

Persephone chewed her lip, but her voice was decisive. "Yes," she said. "It'll save Thalia from listening to me snore."

"Does that mean I have to listen to you snore?" Hades asked, mock-afraid.

Persephone rolled on top of him and buried her hands in his hair, lifting his mouth to hers for a long, remarkably filthy kiss. "Don't worry," she whispered in his ear. "By the time I'm done with you, you won't be able to stay awake to hear it."

***

Privately, Persephone felt that Hades's stunned reaction to that announcement would have been an excellent exit line—or, failing that, a great time to introduce round two.

However, there was no way she could show up to her duties looking and smelling like she'd just been thoroughly fucked. She claimed first shower, declining–with regret—Hades's offer to join her, and quickly washed up.

She couldn't so easily wash away the memories. Even as she hurried down to the restaurant, she remembered the ease with which he'd drawn an orgasm from her and the obvious joy he'd taken in her body. Persephone liked her body, and always had, but she'd had a few unfortunate encounters with men who, however attracted to her they actually were, acted as if acknowledging that attraction in bed would be failing some kind of test.

Hades had behaved as if he couldn't get enough of her. He'd taken everything she had to give, and come back for more.

I love you. I'm sorry.

She took one final moment to make sure her sweater was on the right way and that her hair wasn't any messier than usual, and walked through the restaurant doors. The interns were sitting and lying on the new-ly-erected speaker's stage, evidently taking a break. Persephone didn't feel guilty for going to Hades's aid, nor for the mind-shattering sex that had followed, but she did feel a little bad that the other interns had had to do her work as well as their own.

"Is everything all right?" Thalia asked, sitting up from her prone position. "I thought you were going to faint when Hera nabbed you."

There was a murmur of agreement from the other interns, and Persephone realized that they'd actually been worried for her.

"Um," she said. She hadn't thought about how to explain this, and now she was going to have to. It wasn't fair to let them worry, and she definitely didn't intend to keep the relationship a secret. That way accusations lay. "There was kind of an accident on the way up, and she wanted to let me know and see if I could check in with Hades."

Terry's spine straightened, their face sharpening with interest. Everybody else just looked bemused.

"Hades Kronion?" Thalia asked. "Why?"

"Well, he's um. He's my boyfriend."

Carlos actually gasped. Thalia blinked very fast. She could see the exchanged glances and stares from the other interns. Only Terry met her eyes, and nodded slightly. "It's very recent," she said, rushing on. "And it doesn't affect anything to do with the program. It's just. Yeah. Sorry, I left you guys doing all the setup."

"Is he okay?" Carlos asked, sounding genuinely concerned.

"He's doing better," Persephone said, deciding on the spur of the moment that vague reassurances were the best option. If they wanted to think she'd spent the last two hours feeding Hades hot soup and putting bandages on his booboos, she was okay with that. "But he's taking it easy for the rest of the day. He's skipping his speech tonight."

"Ah, then you will all be spared one of the more refined tortures of the Olympus retreat experience," said a plummy British voice, and

Persephone winced as Mr. Hermes emerged out of the curtained-off backstage space, where he'd clearly been listening the whole time. "No offence intended to your boyfriend, Ms. Erinyes, but no one can make a profit-loss statement very exciting." He clapped his hands together sharply. "Now! If I may have your attention, please."

Everyone tried to look attentive.

"As you're aware, the Olympus intern program usually moves you through departments in two to three week stretches, before placing you in a department of your choice for the final six months of your internship." He paused, then, satisfied there were no questions, went on. "This year, several department heads have requested more stability. Provided your reports continue to be positive, you will all receive the allocation you requested at the beginning of April. However, after this retreat, you will be placed with one department, and one only, until the end of March."

Persephone could see the dismay on other interns' faces. Part of the appeal of the Olympus program–part of what made it special–was the way you were moved around so often. You met people all over the business, and gained an understanding of what made such a complex machine operate, instead of being stuck in one place. Persephone wasn't the only intern who'd had a negative report from a department head, but it didn't matter so much when you'd be moving on to another department, and another boss who might have more use for your particular skills.

"I have endeavored to consider your preferences and skills, as outlined in your applications," Mr. Hermes said. His voice was a little sharp, but Persephone couldn't tell if he was annoyed with his interns, or with the change to the program. "Think of it as a chance to develop a secondary specialty, hm? After all, if your preferred department doesn't have any job openings, you may well wish to have a back-up, come September."

That was a better argument, Persephone thought. She *wanted* to be in the Art department, but she'd been looking forward to Wardrobe and Carlos had said PR was a lot more fun than it might appear. And maybe Photography was a possibility, too. Celebrity photographers did most of the big model shoots, but the in-house Photography team got to do almost everything else. They visited homes for the architecture and design publications and did a lot of filming for Olympus's various digital offerings. Persephone had specialized in Illustration and Design in college, but she'd taken some photography and film classes, and although she wouldn't be doing any of the real work, she'd at least know what people were talking about.

She could see her growing excitement reflected in the eyes of those around her.

"Good," Mr. Hermes said. "See Debbie for your assignments, and then you're on leave until this evening. Ms. Erinyes, a quick word, please."

Terry gave her a sympathetic look, but everybody else seemed to have forgotten the scandalous details of Persephone's love life in the excitement of learning their new intern positions. Persephone followed Mr. Hermes to the hotel's business center, where a sad, thoroughly outdated desktop computer sat beside a dusty inkjet printer.

"First," Mr. Hermes said, "I need to ask if you have been in any way coerced into a relationship with Mr. Kronion."

Persephone flinched, but she'd expected the question at some point. "No."

"Have you been promised anything?" he pressed. "Any kind of position or reward?"

"Absolutely not," Persephone said firmly. "I really like Hades. I want to date him, for him, not for anything he could do for me. In fact..." She hesitated.

Mr. Hermes spread his hands in invitation to continue.

"I don't *want* any favors," she said. "I know people are going to think that, and I hate it. I've spent the last month *not* dating him because of it. And now that seems like a stupid waste of time, but I still... I really want to succeed, Mr. Hermes, and I want it to be because I deserve it. Not because of who I'm sleeping with, or who my mom is."

"I understand," Mr. Hermes said. "And, if I may add, I'm glad to hear it. Unfortunately, given that, you may dislike what I'm about to say. Mr. Kronion—Mr. *Zeus* Kronion–has personally requested that you join his office staff, interning with his assistants."

Persephone stared at him.

"I don't know the details, but he seemed... hm. He acted as if it was the solution to something."

"Hades didn't ask him to do that," Persephone said, with absolute certainty. Maybe Hera had suggested it? Persephone had thought she was more perceptive than that. "Do I have to? I mean... if I don't say yes, am I fired?"

Mr. Hermes paused. "You can decline," he said carefully. "I would be willing to offer you another position. But refusal might be taken poorly. Very few interns are ever permitted to work for Zeus directly. The last was three years ago, and she had a double degree in journalism and business management."

183

Persephone tried to think. If she said no, she'd offend Zeus Kronion, who probably thought he was doing her a massive favor. She couldn't see herself getting a real job at Olympus after turning him down; who'd want to be the department head who hired the kid Zeus was pissed at? She'd look like a drama queen, and far more trouble than she was worth.

But if she said yes, no matter how Mr. Hermes spun it, everybody's worst assumptions about her would be confirmed. It was so clearly a position she didn't deserve. She didn't even have any administration experience.

Which was worse: drama queen or nepo baby?

"But afterwards, I get to go to the Art department?" she asked.

"Yes," Mr. Hermes said. "Does that mean you'll take the head office position?" He looked sympathetic, but also uncomfortable. Persephone was bitterly aware that it was his job to protect the company, not her. She was probably lucky that he'd bothered to check if her relationship was on the level. Lots of HR managers would have preferred not to know, rather than deal with the potentially messy aftermath. And pleasing Zeus was clearly better for the company, regardless of what it did to the reputation of a lowly intern.

It abruptly occurred to Persephone that even if she'd wanted to, she couldn't just say no to both options and leave. She had no money. She needed every cent of her measly paycheck to pay her rent and keep the lights on. If she lost this internship, she'd be in real trouble.

The phone in her pocket, with the unanswered, unopened messages from her mother, felt oppressively heavy.

"Yes," she said, as steadily as she could. "I'll accept the head office position."

"Good," Mr. Hermes said. He was obviously relieved. She tried not to blame him for it.

The other interns had scattered. No one had waited for her, not even Terry. Persephone considered her options and went to the room she was sharing with Thalia.

She hadn't paid much attention to the room before. Now that she was looking at it closely, the difference between Hades's top-floor suite and this twin bed arrangement, with its functional but spartan bathroom, was kind of obvious. She firmly suppressed her guilt. Thalia would be happier being able to spread over the whole room, and she would be happier with Hades. Net benefit for everyone.

She hadn't done much unpacking, so it was easy to grab her few hanging clothes from the wardrobe and take her toiletries case from the bathroom. Thalia banged into the room just as Persephone was wondering whether she should text her, or leave a note.

"Oh, hey," Thalia said, looking curiously at the upright suitcase. "Going somewhere?"

Persephone flushed. "Um, Hades has his own room, so..."

"*Got* it," Thalia said, winking. "Hey, no skin off my nose. Maybe I'll find someone to entertain me. And guess what!"

"What?"

"I got Wardrobe!" Thalia actually jumped a little, like an excited child. "Three months with the most gorgeous clothes in the world! I hear that they do a clear out ever season and it's first come, first served, interns included. Terry says Penny is by far the best boss they've ever had, too, so that's great."

"That *is* great," Persephone said warmly. "What did Terry get?"

"Kitchens. They're pretending to bitch about it, but you just know they're dying for a chance to see all that food photography up close. Did you know that they have a whole bookshelf of cookbooks? They don't even cook much. They just like the art."

Persephone didn't know. Terry had never invited her to their apartment.

Thalia sat down on the bed, still bouncing a little, and looked expectantly at Persephone.

"Not nearly as exciting," Persephone said. "I'll be doing boring admin and PA stuff."

"Oh, bummer. Admin where?"

Persephone knew that she'd paused just a little too long. Thalia's face was already beginning to change when she said: "Um, up in the top office."

"The top office," Thalia said carefully. "Zeus's office."

"Yes," Persephone said, and then, almost desperately: "Thalia, I didn't ask for it! I don't want any favors, you know that."

Thalia clasped her hands together, obviously steeling herself for something. "I know that you keep *saying* you don't want any favors. But you still get them."

Persephone's eyes stung. "Working in Zeus's office isn't a benefit."

"Sure," Thalia said. "Well. You keep telling yourself that, while you move into your boyfriend's room. Your boyfriend, who just happens to be Zeus's brother."

Persephone opened her mouth, not sure if she was going to apologize or shout, but the other girl was already grimacing.

"I'm sorry," Thalia said, holding up her hand. "That was gross and mean, and I didn't mean it. Who you sleep with isn't any of my business.

I know you're not a gold-digger, and I'm like, happy, that you found someone. But don't you see how much you get, without even trying?" She sounded exhausted.

Persephone thought about Hecate taking her to the drugstore to buy underwear and winced. "I see some of it. I'm trying to see more."

Thalia's face twisted, and for a nightmare moment Persephone thought she was going to cry. Then her expression smoothed out, calm and implacable, a mask between them as impenetrable as a wall. "Okay. Well. I guess you're trying." She looked over Persephone's shoulder, deliberately not making eye contact. "Look, I don't, like, hate you or anything. You're clearly a nice person. But I've had to work so fucking hard just to get a shot at this, and you keep getting these amazing opportunities you don't even *appreciate—*"

"Yeah," Persephone said. "I get it. I'm gonna go, okay? I'll see you later?"

"Sure," Thalia said, but she still wouldn't look Persephone in the eye.

Persephone dragged her bags up to Hades's room and used the keycard he'd slipped into the back pocket of her jeans. She tried to remember how fun it had been when he'd taken such obvious pleasure in taking the opportunity to squeeze her ass.

But it was hard, when the world seemed determined to immediately punish her for their union.

Well, sorry, Thalia, and damn you, Mr. Hermes, and screw you to her mother, and an especially big fuck off to Zeus Kronion, who had managed to terrify Hades into a panic attack *and* mess up her relationship with her workmates in the space of a single morning.

She was Persephone Erinyes, and she was going to show them all she was worthy.

Chapter Eight

Hades couldn't remember the last time he'd taken a real vacation. Despite Odysseus's complaints, he didn't work all weekend, every weekend. He'd tried to make more of an effort to be social over the last couple of months, and while he still didn't plan to join Penny's table-top role-playing group, he'd managed dinner and drinks with her and Odysseus a few times, and even taken his godson Mackie for an exhilarating—and exhausting—visit to the trampoline park. Mackie was energetic, wily and determined to get his own way; exactly the kind of child Odysseus deserved. Hades would have felt sorry for Penny, but Mackie was as enthralled with her as Odysseus was, and much more likely to follow her instructions.

So Hades wasn't *completely* devoid of social interaction or opportunities for relaxation, but nevertheless, an actual vacation, even if it was technically a work trip, felt like a gift. He'd texted Zeus a curt notice that he wouldn't be speaking that night, and emailed Odysseus his speech and some instructions.

Then he'd considered what to do with this unexpected day off.

Snow sports, given their propensity to mountains and high vistas, were not his ideal recreational activity, so he'd started with the resort spa. After a long soak in the hot mineral water pool and a firm massage that had kneaded some of the tension out of his spine, he'd headed outside to one of the other restaurants on site, where he'd had a late, leisurely lunch, and plotted some activities for the evening, when Persephone could join him.

Now, blatantly ignoring the bustle of Olympus employees filing into the hotel restaurant for the speeches, he returned to his room to put those plans into practice.

Persephone's bags were placed by his. The coffee-maker was set up, ready to be switched on. He opened a drawer at random, and found that she'd already claimed it for her clothes. The jasmine-and-mint scent floated out, and it was as if it bypassed his sense of smell to clutch directly at his heart.

She'd left a note on his pillow.

Can't wait for tonight!

Yours, P.

She'd moved herself into his room with no hesitation. Despite her valid misgivings, she'd chosen him, and if he knew anything about Persephone Erinyes, he knew that once she'd chosen a goal, she'd pursue it.

Yours, P.

Hades folded the note and slipped it carefully into his pocket. Then he sauntered down to the lobby bar, ordered a whiskey, and asked the bartender if she could recommend a good book to read on his phone.

She folded her arms, not in defense, but as if it were a question that needed some thought. "What do you like to read?"

"I hardly know," he admitted. "I haven't done any leisure reading in a long time."

The bar was nearly empty, and the bartender obviously bored, but he was still astonished by how much time she was willing to devote to the purpose. They ascertained that he didn't like most serious literary fiction or anything too outlandishly speculative. He vaguely remembered enjoying mysteries and thrillers, if they weren't too bloody.

"No vampires, then," she said, looking disappointed, and then recommended a detective series she described as "seaside cozy yacht club murders."

Hades, who had met quite a few people at yacht clubs that he'd suspected someone would very much like to murder, agreed that this sounded interesting.

And so it proved. He was halfway through the sensible amateur detective's quest to prove her ex-husband couldn't have murdered one of his closest friends when the rush of sound alerted him to the fact that the Olympus staff had been set free for the evening.

He paid his tab, and wrote in a tip he thought was appropriate for the bartender's exemplary service.

She glanced at it, and then did a double take. "Are you sure?" she blurted. "That's ten times the cost of your drink."

"Yes, that seems about right," Hades said. "Thank you very much; I'm enjoying the book immensely."

He turned as Olympians flooded into the bar. Zeus was at their head.

"First drink on me!" he boomed cheerfully, as he did every year, and the employees cheered and crowded the bar. Hades tried to slip out before Zeus saw him, but it was in vain. Zeus strode over and took his brother's shoulders in both hands, either ignoring or not noticing Hades's flinch.

Zeus did, at least, drop his volume. "How are you feeling?" he asked. "Don't worry, Hera read me the riot act." He did a theatrical shudder, then gave Hades a searching look. "Things all right with Persephone, then?"

That wasn't an apology, and there was nothing Hades wanted to discuss less with his brother than Persephone. Unfortunately, the head of Finance dating a much lower-ranked employee was something that his *boss* would certainly know about soon. You could even argue that he had a right to the information.

"We're officially seeing each other," he said, and didn't smile when Zeus laughed and smacked him heartily on the back.

"Good, good! I did a little something for her, as a favor to you." He winked at Hades. "But I'll let her tell you about it."

Hades felt the muscles in his face freeze. "What did you do?"

"It's a surprise," Zeus said, and winked again.

Hades stared at him. Was it possible that Zeus thought he was being *generous*? That whatever bizarre 'favor' he'd decided upon was his way of making amends?

It was horribly likely.

"See you later," Hades said and escaped the bar.

Persephone had got to their suite first, which hadn't been in the plan. Damn Zeus for distracting him anyway.

When he came in, she was poking curiously at the charcuterie plate he'd ordered and eyeing the champagne chilling in its ice bucket.

"Is this for me?" she asked.

Hades pretended offense. "Excuse me, it's for both of us."

"Okay, but dibs on the olives." She smiled at him, but he could see the weariness in her eyes. "How are you?"

"Oh, fine," Hades said, and held his hand out to demonstrate that it wasn't shaking. "I had a very relaxing day. Listen, Zeus said he'd done something for you..."

"He's put me in his office," Persephone said simply. "I'm interning directly under him for the next three months."

"That stupid fuck," Hades said immediately.

Persephone burst into laughter. He stared at her in consternation as her giggles acquired a slight edge of hysteria, but she waved him away and sank into one of the armchairs on a last burble of hilarity. "That was more or less what I wanted to say," she said, gazing at him fondly. "But instead I had to say yes, of course."

"This is my fault."

"No, it's Zeus's fault. And anyway, I got the feeling he thinks he's being nice to you by being nice to me?"

"That, or it's the closest he can get to an apology," Hades said. He sat at her feet and leaned back against her knees. Her fingers combed through his hair, scratching lightly at his scalp. "I can try to get you out of it, but..."

"That really would be you doing me favors," Persephone said. "I thought about it, afterwards. But I said yes, and I have to stick by it. Is he that hard to work for?"

"I don't really know. It's like a little kingdom of its own up there. He took a while to settle on the people he wanted, but once he did, they've stayed. Low turnover is a good sign. I do know that his senior assistants are paid nearly as well as I am."

"Well, that doesn't sound too bad. It's just how it looks." Persephone sighed. "I keep telling myself it's only three months."

"And you'll be up so *high*," Hades said, envisioning the open, glass-walled rooms of Zeus's floor.

Persephone laughed again. "I'll come down for you," she promised, leaning down to hug him.

Hades turned in her arms and kissed her, aware of both the growing interest of his cock, and the hard surface under him. A younger self might have tugged Persephone's pants down and knelt between her thighs, ignoring incipient knee pain in order to explore her glorious cleft with fingers and tongue.

Hades, older and wiser, snagged a cushion and slid it under his knees before he got to work.

***

Persephone stared blankly at the ceiling, her blood still surging in her ears.

"Are you all right?" Hades asked, a note of satisfied amusement in his voice.

"No," she said. "I've died. I'm dead. How did you do that?"

He laughed, sounding very smug. "Mostly consistent pressure and following explicit directions. Thank you for that, by the way."

He sat back on his heels, as Persephone dazedly dropped her heels back to the floor. He'd had her thighs resting on his shoulders–not to mention clamped around his head–for that last, dramatic explosion, nearly tugging her right off the edge of the chair. She'd felt completely exposed and nearly delirious with desire, the words spilling out of her mouth unheeded as she'd begged him not to stop, not to slow down, to stay there, there, there...

He'd obviously paid attention.

"I need another shower," she said and shucked the rest of her clothes. "You want to join me?"

"Absolutely," Hades said, but when they walked hand in hand to the bathroom, Persephone took one look at the deep spa tub, and the array of bath products lined up beside it, and changed her mind. The products hadn't been there this morning. Hades had obviously gone out and acquired these things for her–for them.

She noted the bottle of silicone-based lube–marked "Waterproof!" in clear letters–and grinned, starting the bath.

Twenty minutes later, when their gentle kissing turned serious, she urged him to sit on the end of the bath, bracing against the wall behind him. She picked up the bottle and slowly drizzled the lube over her breasts.

"Really?" Hades blurted, and if she hadn't already wanted to do this, his expression of stunned awe would have thrown it several places up her willing-to-try list.

"You've never done this before?" she asked, as she gently moulded her breasts around his erection. He thrust automatically, sliding neatly along her well-padded cleavage. The water sloshed around her, warm and inviting, bearing some of their weight.

"No," he said, throwing his head back. "Never like this, never with— It's so good, Persephone. So good, so good."

Persephone hummed encouragingly. This wasn't doing much for any of her erogenous zones, but she'd had her turn earlier. Hades's cries as he thrust against her generous flesh, and the choked noise he made as he came, eyes actually rolling back into his head, were rewarding in their own right. She dipped back into the water to clean up, and he followed, embracing her with great enthusiasm and not much precision, and sloshing a lot of water out of the tub.

"I think I need to renovate my bathroom next," he said, once he'd got his breath back enough to talk.

Persephone grinned at him. "Well, we should check this one out more before you make any hasty changes. We've got three more nights before we head home. Do you think that'll be enough time to run proper testing?"

"Probably not, but I'll give it my best shot," Hades said solemnly, and kissed the tip of her nose. It was so sweet and unexpected that she hugged him. More water splashed out.

"Okay, if we stay in here much longer we're going to get shriveled," Persephone decided. They clambered out, with more laughter and some slippery groping, and Persephone claimed the olives. They laughed through dinner, before she took Hades to bed, and made good on her claim that she'd exhaust him too much to hear her snore.

He snored a little himself but, warm and held, she found it hard to mind.

***

The next three days went past very swiftly. Persephone ignored Thalia as much as possible, did what she was told by Mr. Hermes and his terrifying HR assistants, and participated in all the events the interns were allowed to attend.

Terry sat beside her on the bus home. It was probably a statement of something, and she tried not to be too pathetically grateful for it. The intern group chat she was part of had gone very quiet. When she asked, her voice pitched low, Terry confirmed that the others had started a new one, so they could complain without worrying she'd tell tales.

"They're not bitching *about* you in there," they assured her, and then more doubtfully, "Unless there's a third one I'm not in..."

Persephone sighed. "I wish they could trust me."

"Well, I trust you," they said staunchly. "And, honestly, I think most of them *want* to. It's just, if they're wrong, and you mention something, even accidentally..."

"I get it," Persephone said wearily.

It was nearly midnight by the time they got back to the city. Persephone waited at the stop for the last bus of the night, the one that would take her home to her tiny, definitely illegally sublet apartment. The contrast between the last four nights of luxury and the drafty fourth-floor walk-up were not lost on her. But she and Hades needed a night away from each other—to recover, as much as anything else.

She snuggled into her bed, yawned widely, and fell instantly asleep.

She was woken, far too early, by her phone.

"Hecate?"

"Yes. Persephone—"

Persephone yawned. She'd texted Hecate about the change in her relationship status from the mountain and had received some complex memes that she thought worked out to be congratulatory. But they needed to meet to go over everything in detail. "Couldn't the play-by-play wait until a decent hour?"

There was a brief pause. "Oh, yes. I'm happy for you. But that's not why I'm calling. I have a late email from my boss, wondering why I hadn't thought to mention to her a potential conflict of interest in the Pontus case."

Persephone woke all the way up. "What?"

Hecate's voice gained more bite. "You see, Minerva got a phone call from a concerned major philanthropist. She was worried that Minerva wasn't aware of the close connection between myself and the *guy we're suing*, since I am, what was the phrase, practically the adopted sister of his god-daughter."

"Oh no."

"Oh yes, Persephone. Your mother called my boss to accuse me of deliberate misconduct, because according to her, you had already warned me of the connection. Which was news to me, because, to be the best of my recollection, you've never mentioned it,"

Persephone felt an unpleasant lurch in her chest. "I didn't–she said I should talk to you a couple of months ago, but I didn't think it mattered."

"You didn't think it mattered," Hecate repeated. Her voice was deliberately bland, using the speaker's own words to invite further elaboration. It was her lawyer voice, and she'd never used it on Persephone before.

"I didn't–there's *no* connection! You're not my adopted sister, and Miles Pontus isn't my godfather. I barely know the guy! Mom is conducting some kind of feud with Solaria Ceto, and she doesn't want her group to win the case, that's all."

"Well, fascinating as this insight into the petty squabbles of the permanently bored and idly vicious is, I would have appreciated a *fucking heads-up.*"

"Hecate, I'm so sorry. But you can't really be in trouble? There's no conflict of interest, right?"

"Of course there's no fucking conflict of interest!" Hecate was practically howling into the phone. Persephone flinched away, holding the phone further from her ear as if she could distance herself from what her friend was saying. "But my boss can't ignore the claim, especially because she had no notice from me that it might come up, because *I didn't know.* I have to be investigated and cleared before I get back on the case, and that's going to be a note in my performance review, and *that* affects my ability to make partner on schedule! How could you not warn me?"

"I'm sorry!" Persephone repeated, almost wailing. "I didn't know she was going to do that!"

"You didn't--Persephone, your mother is a vindictive narcissist who thinks I stole her favorite punching bag! Of course she was going to target me."

"I'm not a *punching* bag," Persephone said, the words tearing out of her. "And my mother can be a little self-involved, but she's not a *narcissist.*"

"Oh, come on, Persephone! She treats everyone around her as objects that either help or harm her, she has no notion that other people have internal lives worthy of respect—"

"Hecate, shut up!"

But Hecate kept going, her own voice rising. "And she views her child as an extension of herself! She thinks you only exist to please her! She doesn't think you're *real.*"

"Shut up!" Persephone screamed. There were tears rolling down her cheeks. "You're not a doctor, you're not a psychiatrist, you don't know what you're talking about!"

"I don't have a medical degree, that's true, but I have watched that woman steal your life for *years* and—"

"My mother loves me!" Persephone inhaled. She knew what would make Hecate stop, and in her panic and fear, she said it: "You're just jealous that yours *doesn't love you.*"

There was a faint noise that might have been a gasp, before the phone went dead.

Persephone threw it across the room and curled into her sheets, sobbing.

***

Having spent the entire weekend crafting dozens of apology texts to Hecate which she'd deleted before sending, breaking her budget on wine and ice cream she definitely couldn't afford, and ruining a date night by crying inconsolably while Hades tried to console her, Persephone was not in the best frame of mind to start her new position as Zeus's intern.

Poorly slept, and more than a little hungover, Persephone knew that she didn't look her best, but Zeus's senior personal assistants responded to her presence by actually recoiling. They were a man and a woman, both tall, thin Nordic types, with immaculate blond hair and icy blue eyes. They were wearing labels Persephone recognized from when she hadn't had to check the price of clothes before she bought them.

Had that really been just five weeks ago? She stifled a whisper of regret for the bespoke tailored suit she'd been too tired to press last night, and held her hand out. "Hi," she said. "I'm Persephone."

"I'm Polly, and that's Artie," the man said, pointing. He wiped his hand on his immaculate turtleneck after he shook, making no effort to conceal the gesture.

Artie simply ignored Persephone's offered hand altogether, her lips pursed as she made a head-to-toe examination of her outfit. "Have we abandoned the intern dress code?" she asked Polly.

"I don't *think* so," Polly said doubtfully, making his own assessment.

"Okay!" Persephone said brightly. She was not in the mood to be bullied by snobs. Her wide-legged slacks and cropped blazer were last year's winter-wear, instead of the absolutely on-trend clothes the other two were wearing, but they were clean, well-made, office-appropriate, and absolutely within the boundaries of the dress code. "So where do you want me? I should warn you that I have no experience in office administration."

Artie openly rolled her eyes. "You'll be in the *back* office," she said, pointing at the corridor that led away from Zeus's glass-enclosed domain to the closed-in part of the floor. "Past the meeting rooms. The sign says 'intern.'"

"Great," Persephone said. "And what do you want me doing first?"

"You can do the dishes," Polly said. "Third door on the left. We kind of let them build up, sorry." His smirk made it clear the apology was entirely insincere.

"Oh, no problem," Persephone said, deciding on the spot that she was going to take everything they said at face value. "I'll get on that right away!" She managed to insert a little extra energy into her walk, and from the slightly perturbed silence behind her, chalked that one up as a victory.

The intern office was dingy and small, and the dishes in the little kitchenette were as bad as she'd feared, at least a week's worth piled up in the sink and beside it. On the tiny table was an opened box of porcelain plates, with a box of cutlery beside it. She discovered more boxes in the cupboards. It looked like Polly and Artie had simply ignored washing, and pulled new dishes out when they needed them.

Which left open the question of who was supposed to wash them when they didn't have an intern to torture.

Persephone sighed, and started clearing the sink.

The mystery of the phantom dishwasher was answered after she'd washed and dried one pile and was working on the next. She heard racing footsteps, followed by Artie's sharp, "You're *late.*"

Moments later, a young man hurried into the kitchenette.

He stared at her.

Persephone stared back. He was quite the most beautiful man she'd ever seen, with wide, dewy brown eyes, unfairly long eyelashes, and smooth, fine-grained skin.

"Um?" he said, and looked helplessly at her.

Persephone wiped her sudsy hands on a dishtowel. "I'm Persephone, the intern," she said.

"Oh. I'm Gary, the receptionist. I usually... do that." He made an aborted gesture towards the sponge in her hand.

"I'm nearly done, but would you like to help dry?"

"Sure," he said eagerly, and accompanied the activity with a long description of the vacation he'd been on, that's why he'd been away and hadn't taken care of the dishes, sorry, Mr. Kronion said he didn't need a receptionist on retreat, so Gary had gone to visit his Nonna and Pop-Pop for a week, and Polly and Artie must have been um, too busy, sorry about the dishes again.

"I'm the intern," Persephone said blandly. "I'm here for the scut-work. Just tell me what to do."

"Oh!" Gary said, as if the idea had just occurred to him. "Oh, well, the trash, maybe? Cleaning Mr. Kronion's desk? Mr. Kronion doesn't let the cleaners in his office. Too much confidential stuff. You can't trust those jerks at Titan."

Persephone remembered Hera showing them party plans acquired by corporate espionage and nodded solemnly.

"Or maybe I should show you and you learn from me," he said, and nodded to himself. "Yes. Okay. This way."

Either Gary had been ruthlessly pranked by the senior assistants, which Persephone was entirely willing to believe, or Zeus was incredibly particular about his office cleaning routine. Gary grabbed a cleaning caddy from a cubby under his reception desk and whisked Persephone through a painstaking tour of which products went where, and how to move polishing cloths *counter-clockwise.* His hands never stopped moving. Neither did his tongue.

In the seating area, the chairs had to be cleaned with the handheld vacuum cleaner, regardless of whether anyone had actually sat in them. Then the cushions had to be fluffed up and placed zip *down.* The polo trophies in the bookshelves were to be dusted with microfiber cloths, and the stylized golden lightning bolt Zeus used for a letter opener should be checked daily in case it needed polishing, and then returned to its stand, which had to be at a thirty-degree angle from the monitor. The monitor itself had a three step cleaning process—lint cloth, screen wipes, and then a polishing cloth of the outside. The keyboard got a spritz of compressed air, and Gary briskly shook the dust out into the desk trashcan before gathering the little bag and dumping it in his caddy. "All right," he said. "Now for the flat surfaces."

Persephone tried to commit it all to memory as best she could, but had actually resorted to taking notes, when Artie appeared in the doorway to the office with an armful of magazines.

"He's on his way," she snapped, laying them out on the coffee table.

"Dang," Gary said, and snatched up the cleaning caddy. He hustled Persephone towards the bookshelves and pressed a hidden button. The bookshelf swung open.

"Quick, in," Gary said, urgently motioning at her.

Persephone obeyed, trying not to laugh at the absurdity. "He has a secret door?" she asked, hearing her voice squeak a little with the effort.

Fortunately, Gary took it as awe. "I know! Cool, right?" he whispered. "Mr. Kronion doesn't like many people in his space first thing in the morning, so if we might get caught in the office, we have to go this way."

The hidden door had opened onto a tiny room, scarcely bigger than a closet. She could hear Zeus' booming voice from the main office, but the actual words were muffled. There was a plain white door opposite the bookshelf entrance. At Gary's gesture, Persephone tried to open it, and frowned when it didn't move.

"Magnetic lock," Gary explained, and fumbled for the keycard on his lanyard. Persephone held out her hand for it, and was surprised when he shook his head. "You don't get one of these until Mr. Kronion says," he said, and tried to squeeze past her to wave it at the lock himself.

The attempt meant that he wasn't just in her personal space; he was actively pressed against her. "Hey!" Persephone said. "Boundaries!"

The rumbling flow of words from the main office paused. Gary froze like a possum in porch lights.

The bookshelf door swung open, and Zeus peered in on them, frowning. Artie was standing behind him, a tablet in her hand. "Gary," he began, and then he spotted Persephone, and his face cleared. "Persephone! Hello!"

"Hello, Mr. Kronion," she said politely.

He laughed genially. "Now, I've told you, you've got to call me Zeus." The words were playful. Gary stared at her, white-faced.

"Come on out of there, you two," he said, and stood back to let them pass.

"Sorry about this," she told Zeus. "Gary was showing me the cleaning routine, and I think I slowed him down."

"Cleaning?" Zeus said. "Gary, don't tell me you made Persephone do your dirty work!"

"I asked if I could," Persephone said. "You know, to help out. That's what I'm here for." She smiled, trying to inject some softness into her voice.

"Artie!" Zeus boomed. "Surely we can find something more interesting for Persephone to do!"

"Of course, Mr. Kronion." Artie's words were polite, but her face was a mask of furious disbelief. Persephone didn't feel particularly bad about that, but she was worried about Gary, who was actually trembling, and showed no signs of being able to speak.

"Good, good," Zeus said heartily. "Well, I've got a busy week, but maybe we can get lunch sometime, Persephone, you and me and Hades?"

Was he being malicious, or oblivious? Persephone looked at the big, open face, and genuinely couldn't tell. She surrendered to the inevitable. "Of course, Zeus. That would be nice."

Behind him, Artie jerked her head viciously at the office door, and Gary scurried out. Persephone followed at a more reasonable pace, and heard Zeus's voice continue with the flow of instructions to Artie. She closed the office door and turned to find both Polly and Gary staring at her.

"You know Mr. Kronion?" Polly asked.

Well, she clearly wasn't going to be able to keep it on the down-low, not with Zeus trying his version of friendly charm at her. And she might as well get some satisfaction out of it. "Sure," she said cheerfully. "I'm dating his brother."

Gary dropped the cleaning caddy.

Polly broke the silence that followed the crash. "Let's talk about when you'll take your lunch," he said, with an obvious effort at politeness.

Persephone kept her smile plastered to her face. It was going to be a long three months.

***

Chapter Nine

H ades stared at the mold patterns on Persephone's ceiling and worried. It was true that worry was his natural condition, but he was more than usually concerned.

It had been a month since Persephone's disastrous fight with Hecate, and as far as he could tell, they hadn't spoken to each other since. She was still alienated from most of her fellow interns, and from the little Persephone had said about her current work, she wasn't happy in Zeus' office, either. It didn't sound like she was doing or learning very much there.

He had so far managed to resist asking Zeus to put his girlfriend in another department, offering her direct financial assistance or asking if she wanted to move in to his place. The first would have been an appalling misuse of his position, and the latter two would have been intolerable threats to her precarious independence, however badly he wanted to help. After that first time, he hadn't even said again that he loved her, though it remained shatteringly true. He had no illusions that she'd had to give up a great deal to be with him, and he didn't want to add more pressure. That she liked him very much, enjoyed his company, and contributed enthusiastically to their sex life was more than enough. For now.

He was still worried. He wanted to be a good thing in her life, a joy always and a comfort when she needed it.

But he didn't want to be the *only* good thing.

"I can hear you thinking," Persephone mumbled, her voice sleep-muffled. "Only you can think first thing on a Saturday."

Hades rolled onto his side and kissed her bare shoulder. The dubious springs of the cheap mattress complained. "Good morning."

She flopped onto her back, her eyes hazy. "Good morning. Happy Valentine's Day."

"Happy Valentine's Day," Hades said. He reached under his pillow and pulled out the fuzzy handcuffs he'd stashed there when he first woke up. "If you're awake, I have plans for the first of your presents."

"What a coincidence," Persephone said, her hand wandering down his body. "I had a similar gift planned for you. Shall we use them on you or me first?"

Hades's mind went blank, and his cock jumped in her grip. "Flip a coin for it?" he managed after a moment. Persephone giggled, and they set about making the mattress springs sing.

Later—much later—after Persephone finally unlocked the handcuffs, they sat half-dressed in her tiny kitchen and living area, and he embarked on the second of her Valentine's gifts.

This one, she'd actually requested.

"Most people wouldn't consider this very romantic," Hades noted, as he entered her charitable donations into a spreadsheet.

"Believe me, I'm incredibly turned on," she said, and put a plate of pancakes on the table for him. "I don't know how to do any of this, and I doubt my mother's accountant is going to do my taxes pro bono."

"Now, I believe I was supposed to be teaching you how to do this for yourself?" He looked at her sternly over his reading glasses.

"Oh boy," she said, twirling a lock of hair around her finger and pouting. "I've always been such a bad student."

Hades made a grab and pulled her into his lap, smothering her laugh with his lips. "You'd better pay attention," he said, when he pulled back for air. "There's going to be a quiz later, and the punishments are severe."

He ended up taking the taxes home with him that afternoon, so that he could finish them without further distractions. He had a few concerns over the way her mother had handled her finances, and he wasn't sure how to point them out to Persephone. Perhaps he shouldn't—she seemed happy enough now. And despite her best efforts to play bratty schoolgirl, Persephone *had* learned a few things about claimable expenses, so he was calling it a win.

They had agreed not to buy anything for each other for Valentine's Day—the only gifts were to be things they could do for each other. Mind-blowing sex, tax returns, and pancakes were already making for the best Valentine's Day of his life, but it was the evening he was focused on.

Persephone's final gift wasn't a secret—she'd been working on the stairwell mural for a few weekends now. He'd seen the sketches and linework on the wall, but Don had collaborated with Persephone in keeping the final product a secret, constructing a frame around the work that let the paint dry behind a canvas screen.

His own plans, he'd kept quieter. Over several weeks and many apparently casual conversations, he'd collected observations about Persephone's favorite meals and most-loved dishes. He couldn't take her out to dinner without breaking the rules, but he'd reasoned he was paying his housekeeper anyway. Paying Theresa for a few extra hours to teach him how to cook wouldn't be cheating.

So, with Theresa's help, he'd planned a menu she thought he could manage, and practiced every dish under his housekeeper's expert tutelage until she pronounced herself impressed.

Even Don had taken to stealing bites from his trial runs.

Don was waiting for him in the kitchen, wearing crisp chef whites, complete with hat.

"Okay, what's this?" Hades asked, eyeing him warily. Don in costume was always worthy of some wariness.

Don saluted. "Sous-chef Kronion, reporting for duty, sir!"

Hades put his laptop down on the kitchen island. "And you're here because?" Don had promised to take himself out for the night--where, Hades didn't know and hadn't asked.

Don grinned. "Don't worry. I'm making myself scarce after the grand unveiling. But Persephone asked me to help with taking the frame down and making sure you don't peek beforehand, and I thought, hey, if I can help her, I can help Hades."

"Oh," Hades said. "That's... thank you, Don. That's very thoughtful."

"No problem. I like your Persephone."

"I like her too," Hades admitted.

"At first I wondered if you were having a mid-life crisis, but you two are really good together," Don continued blandly.

"Thanks," Hades said, with more bite. "Shouldn't you be chopping something?"

"Chef! Yes, chef!"

***

Three hours later, the doorbell rang. Hades, hurrying down the stairs after a quick shower and shave was stymied by Don, who opened the door, swept off his hat, and bowed. "Madame," he intoned.

Persephone had become accustomed to Don. She boggled only momentarily at his costume, and then looked over his shoulder to smile at Hades.

Her cheeks were pink, brightened by the cold outside, and she was warmly wrapped in her navy coat and scarf. When she took them off, he stared for a moment, actually dumbfounded.

"You like?" she asked, twirling. "Turns out, some of my nicer dresses were left at the drycleaners when I moved out. They called to ask if I was ever going to pick them up."

She was wearing a high-necked, sleeveless gown that flowed over her breasts, gathered under them, and then fell straight to the floor in hundreds of tiny pleats. The dress started out silvery white near her throat, deepened to yellow, then light green as it descended, and shaded into dark green at the hem. She wore no jewelry; the vivid colors of her bared arms and the long sweep of her hair provided all the decoration the dress required. In it, she was as stunning as the first daffodil of spring.

"I think you made him mute," Don murmured.

"Shh. Hades? You said to dress up." Her voice sounded a note of uncertainty. "Is this too much?"

"You look incredible," Hades said fervently, able to find his voice at last. "You're always beautiful. But. Just. Wow."

210

Persephone beamed at him. "Thank you. You also look very nice, though I'm not going to go into detail with your brother here."

"Please don't," Don said. "Hades, why don't you take this gorgeous vision into the dining room and feed her an appetizer while I take down the frame?"

Hades took Persephone's hand. Mostly, he and Don ate in the kitchen, but for an event like this, the dining room was required. His own tableware was functional and monochrome; not a suitable match for Persephone's brightness. He'd gone to Hera and requested a loan.

Persephone gasped. The table was set for two, with sunflower yellow place mats under deep orange plates. Flowers were out; he couldn't buy them, and there was certainly nothing blooming in his own frozen backyard. But he'd borrowed a deep, golden vase from Hera, and filled it with holly branches, ruthlessly stolen from his neighbor's hedge. The thin black sticks were festooned with bright red berries, glowing in the light of the candles he'd placed around this corner of the table.

The effect, he hoped, was warm and intimate, bright and beautiful. All the things Persephone made him feel.

"Hades," she said softly, and stroked his arm. "I—This is wonderful."

He pulled out her chair and gestured her into it. "For a starter, madam, we offer roasted beet and radicchio salad, with creamed goat cheese and pomegranate seeds, accompanied by a grassy New Zealand sauvignon blanc."

"Ooooh."

Hades collected the giant wooden bowl from the kitchen and brought it to the table, dished them both a generous serving, then poured the wine.

Persephone stabbed a piece of radicchio, captured a cube of beet to go with it, and swirled it through the creamed goat cheese dressing. A few jewel-like pomegranate seeds clung to the bite. Faint banging noises were coming from the stairwell, but all of Hades's attention was on Persephone as she slid the first forkful into her mouth.

Her eyes closed in concentration. She chewed and swallowed, and looked directly at him.

"Hades. Did you cook for me?"

"Yes." Honesty compelled him to add, "Theresa and Don helped me figure it out."

Persephone put her fork down with calm precision. "I love you," she said quietly.

Hades looked at her. She meant it. "I love you, too," he said. There was a deep, spreading warmth in his chest. He picked up Persephone's hand and they stared at each other in mutual bemused joy.

Persephone's phone rang.

"Oh, no," she said, half laughing, half exasperated, and fished it out of her purse. "I forgot to set it to silent. Just a–" She blinked at the screen, and instead of hanging up, answered. "Hello?" she said. "Yes, this is she."

Something was wrong. Persephone had gone very still, and the color was draining out of her face as she listened to the calm murmuring on the phone. "Is she going to be all right?" she asked. "I see. Yes. I'll be there as soon as I can. Thank you."

Hades was already getting up as she stood. "Where are we going?" he asked, striving for calm.

"Caduceus Central Hospital," she said. "My mom fell, or fainted or—theyr'e not sure, but the housekeeper found her on the floor at the bottom of the stairs. I'm still her emergency contact." She spared a miserable glance at the food he'd so painstakingly prepared. "Hades, I'm so sorry."

"Don't even think about it. I'll drive you."

She was hurrying to the door, reaching for scarf and coat. Don emerged from the stairwell, looking equal parts curious and concerned.

"Demeter's had to go to hospital," Hades told him, so that Persephone didn't have to. "Can you turn off the oven?"

"Of course. I hope everything's okay, Persephone."

Persephone didn't respond. Hades wasn't even sure if she'd heard him. She was biting her lip, struggling to belt her coat with shaking fingers. He did it for her, hugged her briefly, but fiercely, and got them both out the door.

***

Caduceus Central was where Hades's father had died, bitter and gasping in his bed. Only Zeus had been there; Hera and Hades had stepped out for a quick cup of coffee and a brief respite from the patient's petty insults.

Afterwards, his doctor had told them it often happened that way. "Family gather, they say goodbye, and then they let go," she'd told them, her voice soothing. "We see it all the time."

If so, it was the first time Hades's father had let go of anything, but he'd tried to believe her.

He fervently hoped, as they hurried into the ER department, that he wasn't delivering Persephone to the same situation.

But Demeter was awake when they got to the room she'd been assigned, propped up and pale among pillows. "My darling," she said weakly, and raised one trembling hand to her daughter.

Persephone clutched it, sank to her knees beside her mother's bed, and burst into tears.

Demeter stroked her hair, smiling benevolently.

Hades felt uneasy about that smile, and not just because this was an uncomfortable way to officially meet your girlfriend's mother.

"Hello," she said, still smiling. "Hades, isn't it? Would you be a dear and fetch us coffee? There's a little lounge just down the hallway, I believe."

Hades went. When he came back, Persephone was in a chair beside the bed. Her eyes were red and puffy, but she'd stopped crying.

"—just don't remember," Demeter was saying mournfully. "One minute, right as rain, the next..." She made a definite gesture with her hand, then winced. "The doctors say I probably didn't fall very far, but I feel terribly bruised and shaken."

"Did they take your blood pressure?" Persephone pressed.

Demeter smiled bravely. "It's a bit low."

"Mom, how low?"

"Darling, I'm fine. Well, I'll be fine." She gave her a long look, her lip trembling. "Honestly, just seeing you makes me feel so much better. I'm sorry to have ruined your evening."

"That doesn't matter," Persephone said instantly.

"Of course not, Demeter," Hades echoed. "We're just glad you'll be all right. Are they keeping you in overnight?"

"Well, they weren't sure about that, but I do feel a little worried about going home by myself..."

"Mom, of course I'm going home with you." Persephone hesitated. "Unless you don't want me there?"

"Darling," Demeter said, her voice quavering. "I'd *love* to have you, but only if you're very sure you don't mind."

"Mom, no."

"Do you still love me?"

"I'll love you forever," Persephone said. It had the cadence of an automatic response.

"More than anybody?" Demeter asked, and her eyes flicked to Hades.

Persephone didn't hesitate. "More than anybody in the whole wide world."

By the time Demeter had been released from medical care and given her prescriptions to take home—mostly lower-dose painkillers, Hades couldn't help noticing—it was nearly midnight. Demeter had the front seat while Persephone perched anxiously behind him as he drove them both to Demeter's house.

He drove very carefully, but Demeter winced at every bounce. Persephone kept up a torrent of bright chatter that was obviously supposed to distract her mother from aches and pains. Hades could almost feel the anxiety welling out of her, as thick and wet as a heavy fog. He waited as she helped her mother into a guest bedroom on the ground floor and came out to him again, her face drawn.

Wordlessly, he opened his arms.

She clung to him for a moment, shaking, and then took a deep breath and stepped back. "Thank you," she said. "I know this wasn't the evening we'd planned. I hope you like the mural."

"I know I will," Hades said. "Is there anything else I can do?"

Persephone hesitated. "I think Mom's more scared than she's letting on," she said reluctantly. "I might have to stay over a few nights, just until she's steady on her feet. If I give you my key and text a list, could you pick up a few things for me tomorrow?"

"Not a problem."

"It won't be that much; I still have a lot here." She attempted a smile. "At least I can get all my bras. You'll like my bras."

"I like everything you wear," Hades said. "You are just planning to stay over a few nights?"

Persephone frowned. "Do you think I should stay longer?"

Hades considered his next words very carefully. "I think you've worked very hard to become independent, and with your mother feeling unwell, it might be harder to maintain that."

Persephone's cheeks flushed. "I know," she said, sounding frustrated. "But what else can I do? She's my mom. I love her."

"More than anybody in the whole wide world," Hades said, smiling.

Persephone's expression lightened. "That's from a picture book she used to read me."

"Well, whatever you need to do, I'm here," Hades said. "I love you. In an entirely different, absolutely non-parental way."

She smiled properly then. "I love you too," she said, and for a moment, that same warm contentment spread between them.

But only for a moment. Then Persephone turned to go back to her mother, and Hades went home alone, in the cold and the dark.

There was no sign of Don when he got in. Hades hung his coat and moved towards the stairs on autopilot. He'd actually forgotten the mural until he saw it.

"Oh," he said, and sat on the bottom step, staring.

The mural wasn't photorealistic, but neither was it cartoony. Persephone had added more detail in some areas, and left others more sketchy and impressionistic, and her use of perspective, as far as he could tell, was impeccable. But it was the color that had brought the cypress forest to life. It felt like every shade of green was present, with touches of gold and white where sunlight glimmered. The jewel-like intensity of the brighter birds stood out against dull brown and grey trunks, textured so expertly that he could imagine the bark under his fingers.

Persephone had taken this cold, dull, functional space and turned into a celebration of flourishing life.

He'd known she was good. He would never have set her up to fail. But this... this was sublime. It wasn't a piece from a talented apprentice still practicing, but the assured work of a skilled artist delighting in her craft.

After a long time, Hades went to bed.

***

Every time Persephone thought about her mother lying on the floor, a cold fist squeezed her heart.

If Jocasta hadn't found her, who knew how long she'd have lain there? How confused and scared Demeter must have been when Jocasta got her awake.

She'd stayed all weekend, and braced herself to have to explain to her mother that she'd have to return to work on Monday.

"Of course, darling," Demeter said. She was propped up in bed, wearing her most spectacular pink silk dressing gown.

Persephone had been expecting more opposition.

"But you'll be home tonight, won't you?" Demeter had added anxiously, and relieved at the lack of conflict, Persephone had reassured her that she would.

At first she'd tried to insist upon paying her own way, but Demeter had very reasonably pointed out that Persephone was staying as a favor to her mother, and it made no sense for her to find time for groceries when Jocasta would be putting in a delivery order anyway. And then it didn't make sense not to stay and help use up the groceries, and the next night her mother had been a little wobbly, and before Persephone was entirely aware of how it had happened, it was Saturday morning again, and she was back to the guesthouse, waking up in her old bed.

Hades had been unwavering supportive. He'd brought her lunch on Monday (leftover salad, and cold roast lamb she was very sorry she hadn't been able to eat when it was fresh out of the oven) and taken her out for long coffee breaks at the Japanese café. She had almost nothing to do in Zeus' office, but it was a different story for Hades; she knew the time he was taking for her was cutting into his own tight schedule, in the busiest time of the fiscal year.

No one else at work knew or cared. Her college friends were spread all over the world, and the friends she'd made among the children of her mother's circle were either enjoying themselves in ski resorts much nicer than the one had Olympus rented out, or had decamped to warmer climates. Terry texted her often, and they'd had lunch a few times, but Terry was also very busy and trying to impress Hestia with their food styling skills.

Persephone wanted, very badly, to talk to Hecate. But the shame of what she'd said kept stopping her. It was unforgivable, even if it was true. Perhaps it was unforgivable *because* it was true. Hecate's mother didn't

218

love her fierce, beautiful, brilliant daughter. She might have loved the boy Hecate had known she could never be, but she'd absolutely refused to accept the girl she had. Hecate's mother had thrown her out at seventeen, when Hecate had flatly refused to pretend any more.

Persephone had said the most terrible thing possible, and while she owed Hecate the strongest apology she could make, she was too much of a coward to make it.

Because what if Hecate wouldn't accept it?

What if she'd lost her best friend forever?

Her phone beeped, with a text from Hades: "Art gallery still on? Thought we could go to the Augean after."

"You bet!" she typed back, and did her morning yoga routine, trying to capture a sense of peace. Afterwards, as had quickly become habit, she checked in on Demeter.

Her mother was up at her usual time today and moving around, showing much more ease than she had earlier in the week, though she still flinched if she turned too fast. "Darling!" she said. "I was thinking of making you pancakes for brunch. You used to love pancakes when you were little."

"I still do," Persephone said, smiling. She loved her mother best like this, bright and busy, singing little snatches of jazz classics to herself as she moved around the enormous kitchen. After brunch, Demeter went back upstairs for a nap.

Persephone bundled up, and took her sketchbook and pencils out to the back garden. Hades had been so flatteringly impressed by her mural, and it had given her an idea. Her sublet walls were filthy. It wouldn't cost much to scrub them down and repaint one white, then create a mural of her own–a snowscape, widening out into the distance, to give the tiny apartment the illusion of depth. And if the landlord didn't like it, it would be easy to paint over again.

She sat on a wooden bench and sketched the bare skeletons of trees and bushes, the different shapes that snow made, mounded over dirt or plant life, and the tentative footprints of a cat, crossing the snowy ground on a diagonal path. She was contemplating whether a robin would be a nice splash of color, or just too cutesy, when her phone rang.

It was Aphrodite. Very few people actually called her, but Aphrodite never texted. "Hey," she said breezily, when Persephone answered. "I'm back from that shoot. What are you doing tonight?"

"I'm going to a gallery opening and then dinner with Hades."

"Aw, adorable," Aphrodite cooed. "That's super cute. Okay, I'll hit up someone else. But we are going to hang out soon, right?"

"Sure," Persephone said. Aphrodite had called her a few times since their awkward meeting at the Olympus winter party. Persephone kept waiting for her to get bored, but it did appear that Aphrodite Urania, easily the world's most famous supermodel, wanted to be her friend.

"How's work with the Twins of Bitch?"

Persephone laughed. "One day I'm going to slip and actually call Polly and Artie that, and then I'm fired for sure."

"Please. You're untouchable. What boring, petty bullshit did they find for you this week?"

"I'm still opening Zeus' mail, which occupies, oh, about two hours of a ten-hour work day. But they've realized that with me there, they can take lunch breaks together and leave me to answer the phones. It's at least mildly more interesting. How was St. Moritz?"

"The worst," Aphrodite said instantly. "I don't know if you've ever worn a bikini in snow, but it is *not* fun, and I don't care how good the shots are."

"You know they look amazing, though."

"So? They had to tape my nipples down so they'd stop poking through! I think I got frostbite. Can you get frostbite of the nipples?"

"I think you can get frostbite anywhere."

"Well, if my nipples fall off, I'm definitely going to sue."

"Darling!" Demeter called, from somewhere upstairs.

"Sorry, Aphrodite, I've got to go."

"Okay, well, call me when you're free, okay? I've got a thing in Australia in two weeks, but I'm here until then."

"Darling!"

"Yep, absolutely," Persephone said, and sprinted inside, tossing her art supplies on the kitchen table. "Mom?"

"Up here, darling!"

Demeter was at the very top of the stairs, on the little half-landing with the door to the attic. Persephone climbed up to meet her.

"Mom, what are you doing up here?"

"I thought that since I'm homebound for a little bit, I needed a project, and I remembered that I'd kept meaning to make a collage of your baby photos and give it to you on your twenty-first birthday."

Persephone's twenty-first had been six years ago, but she couldn't help smiling at the thought. "That's sweet, Mom."

"I thought I'd make it a surprise, and then I thought, Persephone will be quite upset if I try to go up to the attic to get baby photos and have another little turn there..."

Persephone laughed. "I'll get them. Do you want to set up in the kitchen? I can bring some collage stuff from the guest house."

"Oh, that's very generous of you, darling! I'll see you down there."

The attic had been meticulously organized by professionals, with labelled shelves and see-through plastic tubs. Persephone found the tub marked 'Baby Memorabilia,' and navigated down the stairs with it. In the kitchen, Demeter was looking through Persephone's sketchbook. Persephone felt the back of her neck prickle, and tried to dismiss it. Her mother was just curious; that wasn't a crime.

"You've got some lovely little sketches of your fellow in here!" Demeter said, as Persephone put the tub on the table. "I've been meaning to ask, isn't he just a little too old for you? What is the age difference?"

"Fifteen years."

"Gracious."

"It isn't a problem," Persephone said firmly. She dampened a cloth for the dust and wiped down the tub.

Demeter, amazingly, appeared to take the hint, and flipped onwards, stopping at the most recent page–the snowscape Persephone had been working on. "Oh, this is nice. Why don't you paint it? Your old easel is around somewhere, and we could get you some new oils."

"It's for a mural," Persephone said, and explained her plans for her apartment. Her mother's frown deepened as she went on.

"Darling," she said, and then hesitated. "No, perhaps I shouldn't."

Persephone pulled the tub lid off. The container was packed with baby clothes, photo albums, old books and battered toys. Affection curled her lips as she tugged out the first album; her mother had kept all these things.

"What is it, Mom?" she asked, with more indulgence than she might have.

Demeter apparently regarded this as encouragement. "I wish you'd move back home," she said plaintively. "I've been so lonely without you, and I just want to put all those hurtful words behind us and move on."

Persephone's hands went still. "I'm okay where I am," she said carefully.

"But it can't have been *easy*, darling."

"No," Persephone agreed. "It hasn't been easy." Weeks of peanut butter sandwiches for lunch, huddling under three blankets because the heat was inadequate, falling asleep on the bus; none of it had been easy. But she could do it. She'd learned she could do it. And, what was more, she'd watched Hades carefully refrain from offering to help her out when he could probably buy her entire building. He thought she could do it. And Hecate had thought so too, before...

She wrenched her attention back to her mother. "I think a little distance has been good for us, Mom."

Demeter's lip trembled. "Will you at least think about it?"

"Sure," Persephone agreed. She could think about it, for a few more seconds, before dismissing the idea. And since they were already having an awkward conversation, and no one had shouted or cried yet, she essayed a further step. "Mom, did you try to get Hecate in trouble at her work?"

"Hm? Oh, your little friend." Demeter pulled a photo album from the tub. "Well, I was worried, you know, because Miles Pontus said she was still on that case, and I thought dear Minerva must not know about their connection."

"They don't have a connection, Mom. I told you."

"But you said you'd speak to your Hecate, darling, so that she could check. Did I misremember that?"

"No," Persephone admitted. She had said that.

"So when Minerva said she didn't know what I was talking about—she's so direct, isn't she?—I got a little flustered and maybe said some things that weren't quite right." Demeter smiled lovingly at her. "But Minerva said she would take care of all that. Has she?"

Persephone bit her lip. Even if Hecate wasn't ready to hear an apology, Persephone should at least check to make sure she'd been cleared of any wrongdoing.

"—darling?"

"Sorry, Mom, I didn't catch that. I was thinking about something else."

"My little scatterbrain," Demeter said, laughing fondly. "I asked if you were still planning to go to the gallery this evening." She opened the photo album. "Oh, it's so good to have you home."

***

"I'm sorry," Persephone's voice said. "But I really don't think I should leave her."

"Of course," Hades said. "I hope she feels better soon."

Persephone exhaled. She sounded a little annoyed, which Hades took as an encouraging sign. "She says she feels dizzy and nauseated, but she doesn't want to get checked out at urgent care. Honestly, I think she's probably okay, but she did throw up, and she hates that."

"Do you need anything?"

"Oh, no! You should still go to the thing. Didn't you say Hera would be there?"

The artist was somebody Hera was championing, and Hades had said he'd go when he first received the invitation. Personally, he wasn't sure if he was a fan of abstract sculpture, but Persephone had sounded very enthusiastic about it.

"Are you sure?"

"Yes! Tell me all about it tomorrow."

So, Hades put on the blue shirt Hera had given him, for the pleasure of seeing her smile at it, and ordered a car to the gallery. If Persephone had accompanied him, he would have driven, but for some reason he felt as if he might indulge in the complimentary beverages tonight.

Hera was there, but far too busy for him. She was standing small and self-assured beside the artist, who was clearly mentally clinging to her as a sailor would a life-raft in a storm-tossed sea.

While he waited for her to be free, Hades wandered around the gallery, trying to act like a normal person.

He hadn't forgotten how awkward it was to be at something alone, how much he struggled to make polite conversation or engage in small talk, but it was abruptly clear just how much Persephone had made that easier over the six weeks of their acknowledged relationship. She was so effortlessly light, with an easy way of talking and an interest in other people's lives that seemed natural and sincere. People wanted to be around her, because she made them feel good.

She made *him* feel good.

Caught up in thoughts of her, he didn't notice who was at the next piece until he was standing beside her.

"Hello," Hecate said cautiously, and darted a glance around.

Hades thought he could hazard a guess at who she was looking for. "It's just me tonight."

"Oh," Hecate said.

"Persephone's with her mother."

Hecate blinked three times before she spoke. "She's what?"

"Last Saturday, her mother fainted, or fell, or something–she was found unconscious at the foot of the stairs. The doctors say she wasn't badly hurt, but Persephone moved back to take care of her—"

"That *bitch*," Hecate said, perhaps a bit too loudly. Several people nearby glanced up at them.

"Pardon?"

"Demeter faked it," Hecate said, with absolute certainty. "Or if it did happen, it wasn't nearly as bad as she says it was. Persephone's been at her mother's place for how long?"

"A week today."

"Oh, please. For a fainting spell?"

"She relapsed this evening," Hades said. He hesitated a bare moment before plunging ahead, voicing the suspicion he hadn't tried to articulate before. "Just before Persephone had planned to come out with me. I thought it might be a coincidence, but I couldn't help wondering—"

"No," Hecate said immediately. "That's exactly what she does. If anyone starts becoming important to Persephone, Demeter tries to cut them out, or goes for the charm offensive to bring them onto her side."

"But *why*?"

"Persephone's world should only have room for Demeter in it. That's how she thinks." Hecate gave him a measuring look. "If she's cutting you out, it's a compliment. It means she thinks you're a threat."

"She got sick the first time on Valentine's Day," Hades said. "Right before dinner."

"Wow. She thinks you're a *serious* threat." Hecate gave him an ironic salute. "Congratulations."

"Which did Demeter try on you? Charm or isolation?"

"Both," Hecate said shortly, and snagged a long-stemmed wine glass from a passing server.

"This really isn't any of my business," Hades said. "But is there any way you and Persephone might be able to reconcile?"

"It's not any of your business," Hecate said, and sipped her wine.

Hades waited.

"I hope so," Hecate said. Her voice shook, very slightly. "Look. To be completely honest, I came here tonight because I thought Persephone might be here. But if it's me or her mother, I think Persephone's going to choose her mother. It's not even—well, it's her choice, but it also isn't. She's been manipulated into choosing that way her entire life. I was so proud of her for moving out. I *knew* I was pushing her on that phone call, but I was so mad, and I couldn't stop."

"And you thought you were right."

"I am right." She grimaced. "Do you know that Persephone doesn't even have a trust fund? I mean, she's essentially a trust fund kid, but she doesn't have the actual *fund*, with all the legal protections that involves."

"I know," Hades said grimly. "I've been preparing her tax return. I discovered that when Persephone said she had an allowance, she meant exactly that. Paid quarterly."

"Did you point out how that conditioned her towards dependence?"

Hades hesitated. "I wasn't sure how to. And she seemed to be more independent anyway, and then Demeter fainted, and it wasn't the right time to bring it up, so..." He let his voice fade out. Hecate was nodding a long, a knowing look in her eye. "Ah. I see."

"Demeter tried to bribe me," Hecate said. "In sophomore year, when it was clear she couldn't get rid of me the other way. She took me out for a drink alone, just us girls, and told me that the Erinyes Foundation had a new scholarship I'd be perfect for. It would fully cover undergrad, plus law school. She sweetly assured me that it came with a generous yearly living stipend. A very generous stipend. More than I get paid right now, in fact."

Hades raised his eyebrows. "What was the catch?"

"The scholarship was only available for a student studying abroad."

"She tried to get you out of the *country*?"

"Yep. I told her that I was happy where I was, thanks." She sighed. "Honestly, for a moment, I was tempted. I was so tired of the hustle. But then I pictured abandoning Persephone to her—and living without Persephone in my life—and I just couldn't do it. That's when the sweetness stopped. She told me that I was a grasping little bitch who was ruining her daughter's life, and if I knew what was good for me, I'd take the money and go." The words came out with bite, obviously quoted verbatim.

Hades felt sick. "Does Persephone know?"

"No. At the time, Demeter would have denied the whole thing, and there was no way Persephone could have believed me. And then, it was something that had happened too long ago, and Demeter could explain it away–I'd misunderstood a generous offer from the concerned parent of my friend, or something like that. When Persephone finally moved out, I thought, well, I could tell her now, and she'd believe me, but it would just hurt her for no reason. Let it lie." She gestured at him. "Like the allowance."

"I think you should tell her," Hades said urgently. "I can tell her about the allowance, but not the bribe, because that's yours to tell. But it doesn't feel right that I know and she doesn't. And she's with Demeter again, and I think it's going to be hard to leave."

Hecate grimaced. "I would have told her, if I'd thought she'd go back." She finished her glass and squared her shoulders. "All right. Yes, I will. If Persephone lets me get it out."

"I think she will. I know she misses you very much."

Hecate was looking at him curiously. "So, what's your deal? I guess if you're in it this far, you must like her a lot."

"I love her," Hades said. It was the first time he'd said it to anyone else. Hecate stood still for a moment, then nodded.

"She's very lovable," she said quietly.

"Oh. Did you...? Persephone never said—"

Hecate cackled. "Your *face*. No. Never. She's straight, and I'm not into her that way." She patted him on the arm. It felt like an enormous gesture of approval, from such a self-contained woman. "Any tips for how I should get in touch?"

"She's very bored at work," Hades told her. "If nothing else, she'd welcome the distraction of a phone call."

Chapter Ten

I f Persephone thought about it the right way, Artie and Polly leaving her to watch the phones while they took lunch breaks was a compliment.

Clearly, they hadn't trusted Gary with the task; they barely trusted him to guide people in from the floor's reception space. The junior assistant was apparently some important designer's nephew; literal nepotism at work. He was so beautiful that no one could claim he didn't look the part of stylish magazine receptionist, but a year under the tender care of the senior assistants had eroded whatever self-confidence he'd started with–and Persephone didn't think it had been a lot.

After Zeus' cavalier revelation of her relationship with his brother, the senior assistants had obviously decided that Persephone's presence here was just as unearned, but by the same token, she was too close to the top to seriously bully. Polly had made some limp attempts at sucking up to Persephone before he got bored. Artie barely spoke to her at all, but had an impressive repertoire of disdainful looks and barely audible sighs.

Persephone had made a game of doing whatever she was asked to do with cheerful enthusiasm, mostly because it clearly infuriated Artie beyond reason.

They were truly horrible people, but she couldn't fault their work ethic, nor their loyalty to their boss. Answering the phones was easily the busiest she got all day, and that wasn't even a twentieth of their job. She'd personally witnessed Polly confirm the details of a weekend trip for Zeus and Hera at the same time that he was answering an email about a postponed board meeting *and* haranguing a travel photographer who hadn't paid attention to the impact of the international date line on his deadline.

Polly popped his head into the back room she'd been relegated to. "We're leaving," he announced.

Persephone waited. The other petty joy she had was making them tell her what they wanted, rather than trying to anticipate their instructions. Gary made a wreck of himself attempting to divine their desires, but it had taken only a few smirks and eye-rolls at her obvious stupidity before she perfected her perky smile and waited.

"Cover the phones," Polly said.

"You bet!" Persephone said, bouncing to her feet and following him to the outer office. The sacred door was closed, and Zeus was out somewhere. This was a bonus; she might be able to hide again before he came back and tried to make conversation.

Artie was already waiting impatiently at the door, her short blonde hair topped with a dark plum-colored beret. Persephone had to give her points for style, but her ears were going to get cold.

The phone rang before the door had even closed behind them.

"Zeus Kronion's office," she said.

"Oh, hi, Persephone, Odysseus here. Zeus around?"

Persephone perked up. Odysseus was fun. "It's just me at the moment."

"Okay, can you take a note? Expenses report query, please respond, very urgent."

"Got it," she said, and was mildly disappointed when he said goodbye, clearly too busy to chat. Everybody was busy except for her. She flipped her sketchbook open and started refining her snowscape, based around what she remembered of the kitchen wall dimensions in her sublet. She had to get back there soon, at least to pick up mail. Ugh, there were probably still dishes in her sink.

The phone rang again.

"Zeus Kronion's office."

"Get your boss on the line for me right now," a woman's voice demanded.

Persephone's hackles rose. "I'm afraid he's not in at the moment," she said, in her best imitation of Artie's freezing tones.

"Don't give me that bullshit, Artie. The payment's late again and I'm sick of it."

"Um, if this is about a freelance contract, I can redirect you to Finance—"

The woman snorted. "Oh, I would *love* to talk to Finance. Stop fucking around and put me through to Zeus."

"He's not here."

"Artie, do I need to call my lawyer?"

"I'm not Artie," Persephone said desperately.

There was a slight pause, while the unseen woman recalibrated. "Who is this?"

"I'm Persephone. I'm the intern."

"Ah. I'm sorry for snapping at you, Persephone. I thought I was talking to Artie."

"Oh, we all want to snap at Artie," Persephone said, before she could help herself.

The other woman laughed. "Well, could you please ask her to call me back?"

"Of course. Who shall I say was calling?"

Another brief silence. "Semele," the woman said. "Ask her to call Semele. You're an intern? In Zeus' office?"

"Yes."

"I—" Semele hesitated. "Look after yourself, okay?" she said. The words sounded reluctant, as if she wasn't sure she should say them.

"Um, sure, but—"

Semele hung up.

Persephone put the phone back in its cradle very slowly, but the second she did, the phone rang again. She scribbled CALL SEMELE while she picked up with the other hand.

"Zeus Kronion's office," she said, adding hastily, "Persephone speaking."

"It's Hestia from Kitchens. Has Zeus made the call on the 'Spectacular Caketacular' versus 'Five Wonderful Ways With Pasta' features?"

"I'll get that message to him as soon as he's back in the office."

"Good." The phone went dead. Hestia wasn't much for small talk.

When the senior assistants returned, thirty busy minutes later, Persephone went back to her little room. There was absolutely nothing for her to do, so she flipped open her sketchbooks, and realized, with annoyance and some dread, that she'd written "Call Semele" in the corner of her snowscape, not on the official message slip. Fessing up was going to result in an inevitable review of her failings.

For a moment, she contemplated pretending to be as incompetent as they thought her, and "forgetting" to pass it on.

But Semele had sounded both furious and desperate. Persephone hadn't liked the implications of that demand for "payment," nor the warning to her, as an intern in Zeus' office.

Hades had referred to his brother's affairs just once, in a way that indicated he didn't in the least approve of Zeus' infidelity, but also considered it firmly relegated to the past.

But she couldn't think of many reasons why Zeus would be paying a woman money, avoiding her calls, and behaving in a way where calling a lawyer was a credible threat.

She sighed, picked up the sketchbook, and walked down the little corridor to the main office, mentally rehearsing an apology that would appear sincere, while also appearing totally incurious about who Semele was and why she was calling.

The acoustics of the massive, glass-walled space of the main office meant that she could hear Artie and Polly before she saw them, concealed as she was by the corridor walls.

"—think of that blue thing?" Polly asked.

Persephone looked down at her blue woolen skater dress and paused.

"Even Hades could do better," Artie replied.

Abstractly, Persephone admired Artie's ability to insult two people in five words, even as she considered her response.

"I don't get it," Polly said. "Like, her face is *okay*, but hello, that hair? So messy, and not in the good way."

Ouch. Persephone was about to conclude that eavesdroppers never heard good of themselves and interrupt, when Polly's voice became sly and insinuating. The inherent appeal of a secret froze her in place.

"But I guess these things run in the family."

"What do you mean?" Artie asked. The sudden snap in her voice would have warned Persephone, but Polly must have thought he was immune.

"You know. The Kronions and their interns."

There was a pause. Persephone could exactly imagine the withering stare Artie was delivering; she'd been on the receiving end of it a few times.

"It was just a joke," Polly said sulkily.

"If you have time to joke, you have time to organize the dry cleaning," Artie told him.

"That's Gary's job!"

"Not today."

Polly muttered something, his voice growing louder, and Persephone realized too late what that meant. He appeared at the end of the corridor and saw her.

His look of shock slid into his habitual disdainful expression. "What is it?"

"Um, I accidentally wrote one of the messages in my notebook..."

He rolled his eyes. "What is it?"

"It's for Artie. 'Call Semele.'"

Polly's face froze. Behind him, Artie appeared, looming at the end of the corridor.

"Did she say anything else?" she demanded.

Persephone made a lightning-fast decision. "No, sorry. She called, I told her you were out, she asked you to call back. I'm so sorry I didn't write it on a message slip, but Hestia called right afterwards, and—"

"That's all right," Artie said, and if the senior assistants' conversation hadn't been enough of a warning that something was wrong, this ready forgiveness would have clinched it. Artie seemed to realize that herself. "I *was* going to give you a new responsibility," she said cuttingly. "But maybe you're not ready yet."

Polly darted a look at her. "I think she's ready," he said tentatively. "It was just a small mistake, Artie."

Persephone tried to look both eager and properly remorseful.

"Hm. All right. Get here at 6 a.m. tomorrow, and Polly will show you the opening routine. If he thinks you can handle it, you can do the office opening from now on." Artie said it as if it were a special treat, not something that guaranteed Persephone would be hauling her ass out of bed at 5 a.m. every work day. But at least they'd stopped talking about Semele.

"The message," Artie said, extending her hand.

Persephone tore out the page with the snowscape and handed it over.

Artie snatched it. "Go take your lunch," she said abruptly, and Persephone fled for the elevators, all too aware of the seething silence behind her.

***

Hades was up to his ears in reviews when Cherry announced he had a visitor.

"I wasn't expecting anyone," he said absently, and straightened when his girlfriend slipped in, smiling. "Oh! Did I forget a lunch date?"

"Nope, but I was hoping I could kidnap you for a quick coffee?"

"Um," Hades said, looking at his to-do list, and then at Persephone's face. On second thought, she looked more worried than hopeful. Perhaps a new problem with Demeter? "Sure."

"Thanks. I know you're busy. This'll be twenty minutes, tops."

Despite the time limit, she took them out of the Olympus building. Hades's feeling of unease grew.

"I got a very strange phone call today," Persephone said.

"Hecate?" Hades asked, wincing. If Hecate's story about the bribe hadn't been believed...

Persephone frowned. "No," she said simply, and told him what had happened. Her voice was very neutral as she recounted the story, but her hands clenched nervously around her cup.

Hades felt his stomach slowly cramp as Persephone went on, looking apologetic as she relayed a nasty aside about "the Kronions and their interns."

"And then Artie told me to go to lunch and I got the hell out of there," she concluded. "I didn't know if I should tell anyone but it seemed too big to keep to myself." She grimaced. "I'm just now thinking that I should have gone to Mr. Hermes, not you. Sorry."

"No," Hades said automatically, and then realized she was right. Suspected misconduct should be reported to HR, not the Head of Finance. Still, he was glad she hadn't done it. Mark Hermes was, he thought, a man with some integrity, but even he might find it hard to investigate possible wrongdoing by his boss without worrying about the consequences to himself.

Hades wasn't vulnerable to the same pressures. He owned twenty percent of Olympus. And unlike Mark, he owed loyalty to Hera as much as to Zeus and the company. "I'll— will you trust me to look into it? I promise, if this is a real issue, I won't cover it up. But I need to make sure."

Persephone looked relieved. "Yes. I trust you."

Something melted a little in his chest, but he was still feeling chilly.

When Hades returned to his office, he stared unseeingly at his computer monitors. What would be the best course of action?

Asking Zeus about it would be both the easiest path, and completely unproductive. If it wasn't an affair, Zeus would deny it and be furious at the suggestion. If it was an affair, he would *also* deny it and be furious at the suggestion. Either way, he'd want to know where Hades had got the information, and that could drop Persephone right in the middle of a problem that was neither her fault nor hers to resolve.

He hit his intercom. "Cherry? Could you please ask Odysseus to see me?"

A few minutes later, Odysseus walked in.

"Close the door and sit down," Hades said.

Odysseus complied. "What's up? Don't tell me you're canceling the move."

"No." Hades paused, considering. "The intern Zeus had in his office a few years ago. Do you recall her name?"

"Semele Cadmida," Odysseus said readily. "I remember, because I was betting on her to stay, but she left the program early."

"Do you remember why?"

"I don't think I ever heard." He tilted his head at Hades. "What's up?"

Hades blew out a breath. "Can I ask you for a favor? Mostly as a friend, but for the company too."

To his credit, Odysseus did try to damp down his obviously avid curiosity. "You can."

"Are you still friends with that private detective?"

"Meg? She's more Penny's friend than mine, but sure."

"I need to hire her to look into Semele Cadmida," Hades said. "Particularly, any illicit connection she might have, or might have had, with Zeus."

"Oh, shit," Odysseus said, leaning back. He thought about it for a second, and added, "Oh, *shit*. Three years ago–that's *after* Hera and Zeus remarried, with that no-adultery instant divorce prenup. You don't think that Zeus—"

"Maybe," Hades said. He felt disloyal for even thinking it, but Persephone's ability to read people was excellent, and if she thought there was something strange going on with this Semele, she was almost certainly right. "And she might be blackmailing him. I don't know anything for sure, and I need more information before I can act. But if something did happen, she was in his direct line of command, which I happen to know is absolutely against the Olympus Code of Conduct."

"And she left early," Odysseus said grimly. "Hell."

"And you can't tell anyone else about this yet," Hades said. "Not even Penny."

"Yeah. Yeah, okay." Odysseus rubbed his chin. "How are you doing with all this?"

"I thought he'd changed," Hades said flatly. He had a very vivid picture in his head of Hera, kissing her husband's cheek on New Year's Eve and walking out to entertain their guests. The perfect unit. The ideal couple, at last. "I don't know if I believe this is what it sounds like. But I do need to know."

The rest of the afternoon passed in a blur. By 4 p.m. it was clear that he wasn't going to be able to focus. The reviews were vitally important, and he couldn't approach them with anything but a clear head and minute attention to detail, neither of which he could summon.

Hades Kronion, for the first time in a very long time, considered whether he might actually leave the building before the end of the work day.

Six months ago, he wouldn't even have entertained the idea. Six months ago, he wouldn't have had anything to leave *for*. But increasingly, he was aware that his work hours–the hours he'd thought of as normal, six months ago–were impinging upon other things he wanted to do with his time. He wanted to read the new yacht club murder mystery sitting beside his bed. He wanted to test a new fish recipe on Don before he tried it on Persephone. If he worked less, he'd have more time for babysitting Mackie, that terror, while his parents took a much-needed break. He'd be able to get a massage like the one he'd had at the ski resort, or consider what he wanted to do with his barren backyard, or pose properly for Persephone, who kept threatening to draw him like one of her French girls. He could make sure that he had time for Hera–which he was worried she would definitely need, and wouldn't be able to ask for.

He'd have time for dates with Persephone.

Sex with Persephone.

Walks and talks and silence with Persephone.

He stood up and turned off his monitor.

"Cherry?" he said, hitting the intercom button. "I'm heading out early, and you should too."

"Um," his assistant replied, sounding bemused. Was it that unthinkable? "Sure, boss, but Persephone's here to see you."

For the second time today? Hades's anxiety spiked.

Persephone walked in.

He'd seen her joyful and tearful, annoyed and amused, excited and tired. Until this moment, he realized, he'd never seen her truly angry.

She was incandescent and indomitable, all the soft warmth of her face and body transformed to intimidating mass. This wasn't a woman who tried to carefully negotiate her way through the world; this was a woman who walked through walls without noticing, who felt the ground shake underfoot with the surety of her stride. Her coat was unbuttoned, and it flared around her like the wings of some predatory bird.

He wanted to throw himself at her feet and give worship.

"It was Hecate this time," she said, each world snapped off. "She told me about my mother trying to bribe her."

Hades nodded, not sure whether he should offer support or apology. Evidently, he didn't need to speak at all.

Persephone looked directly at him. "I need to go to my mother's place, pack, and leave. Will you come with me? I might need moral support, and I can't guarantee I'll be safe to drive."

"Yes," Hades said. "Let's go."

***

She called me a grasping little bitch.

The words, in Hecate's voice, circled around and around in Persephone's head, like a shark readying for the kill.

Hecate was Persephone's first best friend, her *only* real friend. Demeter had tried to remove her.

I don't know if she faked being sick, but don't you find the timing convenient?

She'd had a few straying suspicions, the longer the visit dragged on, the more her mother pressed for Persephone to move back, and for "everything to go back to normal".

Persephone couldn't do that normal anymore. The more time she spent away from it, the less normal it seemed.

"Persephone?"

The voice broke into the maelstrom of thoughts, and she blinked hard. They were parked outside the guest house. Her hands were in her lap, tightly gripping each other. She unclamped them with effort, and hit the seatbelt catch. Her mouth tasted sour and metallic.

"Do you want me to come inside?" Hades asked cautiously.

"Yes," Persephone said, then remembered to add, "please".

The guest house door was open, with Jocasta's little trolley of house-cleaning supplies outside it.

Persephone stalked inside. "Jocasta?"

The housekeeper appeared, wiping her hands on her apron. She was a thin, nervous-looking woman in her early fifties, her long black hair tied back in a severe knot. She visibly startled when she saw Persephone's face. "Miss Persephone?"

Why was everyone acting like she was something scary? "Jocasta, can you tell me about how you found my mom?"

"Oh. Well, I came in to the main foyer from the kitchen, and she was lying on the floor."

Persephone frowned. That had the flavor of a rote response. "Are you sure she was unconscious?"

Jocasta's eyes shifted. "I called her name, and she didn't move at first. Then she opened her eyes."

"Well, did you hear anything, like a body falling? Was there a scream?" Jocasta backed away without answering, her eyes wide.

"Persephone," Hades murmured. "You're coming on pretty strong."

Persephone had been advancing on Jocasta without noticing it. She suppressed a growl of irritation and settled her weight on the back of her heels. Then she smiled.

From the horror that crossed Jocasta's face, it wasn't a reassuring smile.

"Jocasta. Do you think Mom faked it?"

Jocasta took a deep breath. "Miss Persephone, I like my job. Your mother's been very good to me over the years, and I'm not interested in looking for another position."

Persephone sighed. "I understand."

"Are you... what's happening?"

"I'm leaving again," Persephone said baldly. "Probably for good. It's about something else, something not connected, but I just... wanted to know. To be sure I was making the right decision. But it's okay. I understand."

Jocasta hesitated. Then she darted up to Persephone, face intent. "She was lying on the floor," she said, her words tumbling over each other. "She acted just like I said when I went to her. But I *saw her lie down*."

She was gone before Persephone could react, the rattle of her trolley wheels announcing her departure in the sudden stillness.

"Well," Persephone said, after a long minute. She was fighting to keep her voice level. "That kind of says it all, doesn't it?"

"What do you need?" Hades asked.

Persephone's cheeks felt weird when she smiled, kind of stretched and painful. "I'm going to make you carry things."

Living on her wages had made her appreciate how important–and expensive–things could be, and she didn't intend to leave much behind. It was maybe stealing; her mother had bought a lot of her possessions for her. But Persephone wasn't worried about that, this time. She moved fast, tumbling everything into whatever receptacle came to hand—plastic tub, trash bags, her handbag collection—and handed them to Hades to ferry out to the car. She took clothes and jewelry, art supplies and kitchen utensils, grimly pleased about the prospect of replacing her cheap and flimsy pans. She stripped the bedding and folded it into a soft pile, tossing her pillows on top. It would be a significant thread count improvement.

"We're running out of room," Hades said, when he returned from stowing her sheets.

Persephone surveyed the room. "Pity we can't take the mattress. It's much better than mine."

"Did you want to talk to your mother?"

"No. I'll call her later. Or maybe email." She snagged two pairs of heels and marched out.

Her mother was coming down the path from the main house, the plastic tub of childhood memorabilia in her hands. "What are you doing?" she all-but-shrieked.

"Leaving," Persephone said, heading for the car.

"What? Why?"

"I'll send you an email once I've had a chance to process, Mom."

Demeter dropped the tub on the path and placed her hands on hips, chest heaving. "No, you tell me right now!"

"Mom, I need space. I'll be in touch."

"How dare you! I've given you everything!"

Persephone turned on her. Demeter actually stepped back. "Yes, you gave me everything," she snarled. "But what did you take from me, Mom?"

"I don't—"

"You tried to bribe Hecate away from me in sophomore year," she said. "What were you hoping? That I'd give up college and come back?"

In spite of herself, a part of her still hoped for an explanation, or at least a show of remorse. A reason that she wouldn't have to go through with this.

But Demeter reared like a snake. "That girl is a *terrible* influence!"

"She's probably the only reason I'm still sane. You tried to ruin her reputation at work! You lied to me about Olympus! What else have you lied about, Mom?"

Demeter burst into tears. "Darling, I love you! I'm your mother!"

"What happened to Mike, Mom?" It was a guess. Mike had been her most interesting college boyfriend; not serious, but something that could have become so. He'd broken up with her with no warning. At the time, Demeter had been so kind, so soothing.

"What has he told you?" Demeter snarled.

Persephone felt something heavy close around her heart. "Nothing," she said dully. "He never told me anything at all, so I guess he stayed bought. Mom, you need help."

"Then help me!" Demeter screamed. "Help me! Stay! If you loved me, you'd stay! You promised to love me forever, more than anybody in the whole wide world. You can't just walk away!"

245

"I do love you, Mom. But I have to love myself too." She wasn't sure if Demeter had even heard her. Her mother had turned on Hades, who had been waiting silently.

"You! You're stealing her!"

"Persephone isn't a thing. No one could steal her," Hades said, looking revolted.

"You're disgusting! An old predator, preying on my poor daughter!"

"We're leaving," Persephone said, and caught Hades' eye.

He nodded, and reached for the driver's door handle. Demeter screamed as if she were being murdered, a long, high shriek, and began to throw things at him as he got in.

The missiles closest at hand were Persephone's childhood toys and books. Persephone wasn't sure why her mother had even brought those with her. Perhaps she'd planned some sentimental appeal. But now, while Persephone darted to her side of the car and got inside, Demeter pelted Hades with them. A teddy bear bounced off his shoulders; a wooden truck caught his arm and dropped into the car. A book flew through the car door, its pages fluttering wildly. Hades ducked, and it nearly caught Persephone in the face.

He slammed the car door. "Are you–" he began, turning to her.

"Just drive," she said.

The last glimpse she had of her mother, Demeter was still standing in the middle of the path, screaming and stamping her feet.

***

Hades seemed to know exactly what she needed. He took her to her place, not his, and helped her unload the car. When he asked if she wanted him to stay the night, she nodded. The heavy angry feeling was ebbing, leaving her shaken and exhausted.

Later, she stood in the shower and let the hot water course over her head and neck, soothing the tension in her shoulders. When she climbed into bed, Hades was reading the picture book Demeter had flung at him.

"That was my favorite book," she said, and curled up next to him. He automatically put his arm around her shoulders and tugged her in. "Maybe not so much now. There's a bit where the baby mouse says he'll love the mother mouse more than anyone else in the whole wide world. Mom used to get me to say it to her too."

Hades frowned. "That's not what it says."

"What do you mean?"

He held the book open.

On the page, a mouse in an apron was hugging a much smaller mouse with a red hat. Persephone read the words, her voice trembling. "'Will you love me forever?' asked Baby Squeak. 'I'll love you forever,' said Mama Mouse. 'More than anybody?' asked Baby Squeak. Mama Mouse hugged Baby Squeak very, very hard. 'More than anybody in the whole wide world,' she said."

Hades was staring at her. "Did she swap it?"

"She always read it to me," Persephone said. "I thought that was the way the story went."

"How old were you?"

"Three or four."

"That's..." Hades shook his head. "I don't know what to say about that."

Persephone leaned her head on his shoulder. "She's really sick, isn't she?" she said sadly. "Mentally ill, I mean."

"I think she might be," Hades said. "But you can't help her get well, sweetheart. Not if she won't recognize that she needs help at all."

The endearment almost made her tear up again. She took a deep breath instead, and snuggled a little closer. Hades' open appreciation of cuddle time was one of the many things she liked about him.

"I haven't told you much about my father," Hades said. "He died nearly twenty years ago, but he was... I don't know. I think you'd call him toxic. Certainly, he poisoned everything he touched."

"What about your mom?"

Hades considered it. "She was tired," he said finally. "She had been very beautiful—Zeus has some of her looks. I think she might have been kind, if she hadn't been so worn down. She died when I was in high school, and I remember being sad, but also feeling as if I were mourning someone who had already been a ghost. The three of us were raised mostly by nannies and boarding schools."

Persephone made a noise, and he patted her blanket-covered thigh. "Honestly, that part was all right," he assured her. "We were looked after, and sometimes loved. It wasn't by our parents, but it helped, I think, to know that some people cared about us. Even if they were paid to do it.

"Dad didn't have much interest in us until college. I was the eldest, and I was good at math and finance, but no threat. He wanted me to work for him, but I told him I wanted to work somewhere else, so that I could build up experience until I was good enough for Olympus. He liked that, the idea that I was making myself worthy enough for him. Don... Don didn't follow the plan. Dad cut him off immediately, completely. He wouldn't let us say his name."

"And Zeus?"

"The golden child," Hades said. He sighed. "My boy Zeus, my son Zeus–always the possessive first, then the name. My little Zeus the sports star, beloved by his college societies, respected by his professors, a hit with the ladies… Dad claimed all those successes for himself. But he was getting restless, I think, worried about whether Zeus might outshine him. I wonder, sometimes. If he hadn't died, Dad might have ended up clashing with Zeus too."

Persephone could hear, in the lack of specific detail, that it must have been much worse than this bare summary could cover. She could picture a younger Hades, always worried, always avoiding his father's notice, always looking out for the neglected middle brother and the beautiful baby his father wanted to claim the credit for. Quietly, carefully, in the background, doing his best for all of them.

She must have been silent too long. Hades' hand tightened on her knee. "I didn't mean… I wasn't trying to outdo your story with mine."

She slipped her hand over his and entwined his fingers with her own. "I know. You were telling me that you get it. And that I can get over it."

"Maybe not over it," Hades said. "But past it. I'm more or less past it. You will be too."

"Do you think Mom will get help?"

"I don't know. I do know that will be up to her. And I think she does love you. Maybe she'll try."

"Maybe," Persephone said doubtfully. She yawned, and wriggled a little more under the covers. "Don't let me sleep through my alarm."

"I won't," Hades said.

He always did what he said he would. It was one of the things she loved about him.

Chapter Eleven

It wasn't that Hades had forgotten about the mysterious Semele and her interactions with his youngest brother. He'd just been somewhat occupied. After Demeter's dramatic parting from her daughter, he hadn't been shocked by the deluge of emails to both his work and personal accounts, demanding that he answer for his (unspecified) crimes and return her daughter. Nor was it a particular surprise when Hera called him a few days after Persephone's second exit.

"Demeter called," she said. "Told me you were a menace and that you'd corrupted her darling girl. Then she pleaded for my help in getting Persephone away from your evil clutches."

"I'm sorry."

"I told her to get therapy and hung up," Hera said. "But she'll call others, and her money talks. Keep your head down."

He *was* surprised when Demeter arrived on his doorstep that Friday evening, catching him just as he was getting home from work. Her hair was loose and uncombed, her eyes enormous in her haggard, make-up free face.

"Give me back my daughter," she said, her voice harsh.

"Persephone's not here," Hades said. He walked past her, feeling a prickle between his shoulder blades, and fumbled for his keys.

She trailed him to the foot of the steps, literally wringing her hands. "Liar!"

"I don't lock her in the basement," Hades said wearily. He was keeping her in his peripheral vision as he got the door unlocked. He didn't think she'd attack him on his own front steps, but then he hadn't expected her to literally throw toys at him, either. "Whether you like it or not, Persephone is 27 years old and she makes her own choices."

"Where is she, then?" she demanded.

"At her apartment, I imagine." In fact, Hecate and Persephone were planning to go dancing, but he wasn't telling Demeter that. For all he knew, she'd go to every club downtown looking for them. "And if your daughter hasn't told you where she lives, I certainly won't. Go home, Demeter. And stop calling all your friends. You're going to run out of them if you keep behaving like this."

"Persephone *is* my home! Tell her that! Tell her she's killing me!"

"No," Hades said. He was running out of his already limited patience. "I won't be passing on any messages for you. Get off my property, Demeter. If you do this again, I'll issue a trespass notice. And if you harass Persephone, I'll make sure you're arrested."

Demeter snarled, and he braced, hoping that he wouldn't have to lay hands on Persephone's mother.

Behind him, the door swung open. Don's imposing bulk filled the frame. "You heard him," he said. The affable, devil-may-care brother had vanished. This was a serious man, physically powerful and very strong. "Get out."

Demeter looked at him, and Hades saw the cold calculation under the histrionic mask. Without a word, she left.

"Mommie dearest?" Don asked, standing aside.

251

Hades walked inside, and discovered that he was shaking. "Yes."

Don shook his head. "How did someone as good as Persephone come from her?"

"How did someone as good as you come from Dad?" Hades said. He'd meant it as a flippant remark, but it came out with real passion.

Don stared at him.

"I mean it," Hades said. "I avoided attention, and Zeus aimed to impress, but you refused to give in to Dad. You're entirely your own man. I can't tell you how much I respect that."

"You can't just say stuff like this, bro," Don said bemusedly.

"Why not?"

"People might start to think we're emotionally healthy adults. I can't live up to that kind of reputation." Moving abruptly, he caught Hades in a rib-squeezing hug, and let him go just as suddenly. "Right, I'm making dinner."

So, when Odysseus called him early Saturday morning, Hades' first impulse was to worry that Demeter had found a way to harass him too.

But Odysseus had other things on his mind. "I got a report back about that matter you asked me to look into," he said. "I think we should meet to discuss the findings. Somewhere that isn't work."

"Not here," Hades said, listening to Don crash around in the kitchen.

"No," Odysseus agreed. "Not my place either." He paused. "The Happy Isles will be open."

"A bar? At 8am?"

"They do brunch," Odysseus said, undeterred. "And you might need a drink."

Hades got there early, and asked for a corner booth. He opted for coffee, rather than a drink, but was too nervous to order food. His stomach was uneasy enough.

Odysseus came in wearing jeans and an Archers band T-shirt, looking every bit the suburban dad. There was even a fresh ketchup stain on the front.

"Mackie objected to me leaving," he said, sitting down. "Unfortunately, he was eating scrambled eggs at the time, and he threw them at me."

"You put ketchup on his scrambled eggs?"

"We put ketchup on literally everything, including peanut butter and jelly sandwiches. It's the only way he'll eat." He yawned, and scratched his unshaven chin. "So. The report."

Hades felt his stomach drop. "Yes. It's bad?"

Odysseus rocked his hand back and forth. "Well, the good news is, I found out where Zeus's extra expenses claims are going."

Hades tasted something bitter in his mouth. "That's an expensive affair," he said. And if Zeus was using company money to fund his sexual escapades, that was a double breach of trust. How was he going to tell Hera?

"I don't think it's a current affair," Odysseus said. Silently, he laid the pictures out.

The pictures were obviously candid shots, with blurry background figures. Semele was a beautiful, dark-haired woman with pink cheeks and a stunning smile. In some of the shots she was outside a strip mall, striding towards her car with grocery bags hanging from her elbows; in others, at a playground.

Also at the playground was a little boy, holding her hand, or climbing into her lap as she sat chatting to another woman. He was about two years old, at a guess, with his mother's pink cheeks.

He also had blue eyes, and a wealth of soft golden curls, fanning around his head like a halo. There were baby pictures of Zeus, sitting between the serious, dark-haired young Hades, and the restless Don, that looked exactly the same.

A resemblance alone wasn't definite proof of anything. But Hades knew.

"It's not blackmail for an affair," Odysseus said. "It's child support."

Hades took off his reading glasses, polished the lenses, and set them on the booth table. He felt very old, and very tired. "She started as an intern three and a half years ago."

"Yes. Best guess is that there was an affair then, and the boy was the result. As far as Meg can tell, Zeus hasn't been seen with her since."

"That's still two years after he and Hera remarried. After he swore up and down that he'd never betray her again." He slammed his fist into the desk. "That incredible asshole. His *intern*. Has he been embezzling from the company this whole time?" It was hard to know which outrage to focus on first, but the money, at least, fell firmly within his purview as CFO.

Odysseus shook his head. "I double checked the accounts. Nothing's unusual until last July. We didn't notice for a couple of months after that—his assistants did a good job concealing the first few payments."

"So why wasn't he paying her before then?"

Odysseus shrugged. "Times are hard for journalists. The newspaper Semele works for was folded into a bigger one, and she was laid off last May. Parents are gone, no support—"

"So Semele goes to Zeus. She could have chased him for parental payments at any time. Why did she wait?"

"That, you'd have to ask her."

Hades groaned and rubbed the bridge of his nose. After a moment, he realized that the silence was expectant.

"Wait," he said. "You mean, really, ask her?"

"It turns out that it's quite hard to spy on an investigative journalist," Odysseus said breezily. "Meg got caught."

"Oh no."

"If it helps, Meg was really embarrassed about it. She didn't reveal who'd hired her, of course, but Semele said that if Meg's employer wanted to discuss the matter, she'd agree to a meeting."

"I can't–" Hades began, and then realized that, in fact, he had to. Whatever secrets this woman was holding, whatever mysteries needed to be revealed here, he couldn't back away from talking to her. His stomach shriveled at the thought.

Odysseus regarded him. "May I make a suggestion?"

"Please."

"Persephone knows something's up. She's spoken to Semele once already. And she's good with people. Take her with you."

"That's... it's not consistent with her job description."

Odysseus gave him a level look. "Hades, I know you want to do the right thing by Olympus. But you'd better start thinking of this as a family affair, too." He tapped one photo of the golden-haired little boy, smiling up at his mother. She gazed at him calmly. "This is your nephew. His name is Dio."

"Dio," Hades repeated. He pulled the photo closer. Dio, his nephew. "How old is he?"

"Two and a half," Odysseus said.

Only a few months younger than Mackie. Was this one a holy terror too? Or was he a biddable child? Hades peered at the photo, at the glint of mischief in Dio's eyes, at the blurry motion of his hand as he pointed at something his mother needed to see. No, Dio wasn't biddable. "Can you set up the meeting with Semele? Tell her... tell her that I'm sorry for the intrusion, and that I mean her and Dio no harm."

"I can do that," Odysseus said. He started picking up the photos, sliding them back into the envelope. He held out his hand for the one Hades was holding, then hesitated. "Do you want to keep that one?"

Hades stared at the small face, and sighed. "No," he said, and handed it over. "I haven't earned the right to it yet."

Odysseus's face was full of sympathy, but for once, he opted for silence.

***

Persephone had no idea what you wore on a weekend afternoon date to meet the mother of your boyfriend's brother's secret child.

"Black," Hecate advised, from where she was sitting in the middle of Persephone's bed, surrounded by discarded outfit choices. She was, naturally, wearing black herself; a black long-sleeved t-shirt and silk lounging pants, barely distinguishable from the pajamas she'd worn for their sleepover the night before.

Persephone threw a scarf at her. "All my black is ballgowns!"

"Yeah, but you look great in Valentino," Hecate said, undeterred. "Okay. Not orange or yellow, because that's way too cheerful for the circumstances. Not red, because she might think you're calling her a scarlet woman."

"Ew. I would never."

"Obviously, but she doesn't know you. Hm. Muted shades or small patterns. That ought to cut down your options."

It did neatly eliminate most of Persephone's wardrobe. She dithered, and then opted for forest green leggings with the same blue skater dress Polly had scoffed at. "Yes?" she asked, posing.

Hecate applauded. Persephone wasn't quite sure how she managed to clap sardonically, but her friend had many talents.

Spontaneously, Persephone hugged her. "I'm so glad you're here," she said. "I'm so glad you forgave me."

Hecate waved this away. "Well, you apologized so nicely," she said.

The apology had been on both sides, though Persephone had much more to apologize for. There'd been tears, and hugs, and a bottle of cheap white wine, and then they'd settled back into their usual back-and-forth. Persephone had shared all the details about Hades that she'd been saving for weeks, and Hecate had given her all the work gossip she'd been missing. Hecate was back on her case at Eule and Spindle, and thought Miles Pontus would settle out of court for an appropriately enormous sum.

It was possible to go back to normal with Hecate, because Hecate had a clear understanding of what normal *was*.

The same wasn't true of Demeter.–

Persephone had dutifully sent her mother the email she'd promised, explaining that she needed time and space to process ("And therapy," Hecate said, but that was going to have to wait until she could afford it) and that she would reach out to Demeter when she was ready to talk. In the meantime, she requested that Demeter not contact her.

And because Persephone absolutely couldn't trust Demeter to respect that request, she'd blocked her on every avenue she could think of, the second she'd hit send. Even so, there were a few social media accounts she hadn't remembered that her mother had found, and some pleas had been forwarded to her email accounts anyway. One message had been very close to a suicide threat, and Persephone had agonized over whether she should respond.

But if she had replied, all her mother would learn was that Persephone would engage if she threatened to harm herself, and that's what she'd do again next time. Demeter had to learn that she *couldn't* make Persephone engage, and that would take time. It might take forever.

Persephone hoped not.

When Hades had called, asking if she'd come with him to this meeting, she'd almost declined. Dealing with her own family's fucked up relationships seemed more than enough for now. But he'd sounded so terrified at the prospect of going alone. And Hecate, unavoidably eavesdropping in the tiny apartment, had broken into the conversation and told her to do it.

"Remember that you can't tell anyone," she warned Hecate.

Hecate rolled her eyes. "I basically already swore a blood-oath to Hades. Why are you two worried I might gossip? I keep multi-million dollar secrets every day."

"Well, this might be one of those too," Persephone said. "But I think Hades is mostly feeling guilty that Hera doesn't know, and you do. He wants to make absolutely certain before he puts her through this again."

"What time are you meeting him?" Hecate asked.

Persephone consulted her phone and gasped. "Two minutes ago. Come on, hurry up!"

Hecate complied with as much enthusiasm as a cat being nudged out of a sunbeam, but Persephone had them both out the door and down the four flights of stairs in moments. Hades' car was idling across the street. He was frowning at his phone, but his face lightened when he saw her.

Hecate waved at him, and he waved back, looking pleased to see her too.

"I like him," Hecate said decisively.

"Me too," Persephone said, aware that she was smiling too broadly.

"If he breaks your heart, I'll sue him into bankruptcy," Hecate said, in the exact same tone.

"Aren't you supposed to promise to help me bury him in the backyard?"

"Digging?" Hecate said. "With *these* nails?" She gave Persephone a hug and sauntered off.

Persephone walked across the road and slid into the passenger seat, kissing Hades as she arrived. "How are you?"

"Terrified," he said. "Angry. Sad. Happy that you're here."

"It'll be... well, not fine. But it'll be what it is. And then you'll have a better idea of what you need to do next."

He took a deep breath and blew it out. "Okay," he said. "Next steps."

***

Semele was a short, slender woman, with glossy, long dark hair. Hades had invited her to set the meeting time and place, and she'd responded by inviting them to her apartment, meeting them at the door.

She nodded when Hades introduced himself, but appeared puzzled by Persephone. Her son was nowhere to be seen, but his presence was everywhere; a sippy cup on the kitchen bench, a playmat in a patch of sunlight on the floor, a collection of stuffed dinosaurs corralled into a line on a low shelf.

Semele's apartment was about the same size as Persephone's, but unlike hers, was meticulously tidy, with a slim laptop and a notepad the only things on her kitchen table. Persephone thought of the sketches, brushes, and used coffee cups on her own table, and tried not to wince.

Semele didn't offer them coffee. She sat at the table, her hands folded in her lap, and waited.

"Thank you for suggesting this meeting," Hades said.

"Did I have much choice?" Her voice was a beautiful, throaty alto, with a trace of an accent Persephone didn't recognize.

Hades flinched. "Yes," he said miserably. "I'm sorry if—I didn't mean to frighten you with my investigation. If I frightened you. I received information that you might have—There was some confusion about some expense reports—"

Semele was studying Persephone. "You're the one who answered the phone," she said abruptly. "You made that crack about Artie."

"Yes."

"Is Zeus bothering you?"

"No!" Persephone said. "No, I'm just his moral support." She nodded at Hades.

Semele relaxed infinitesimally.

Hades, on the other hand, stiffened even further. "I apologize for the question," he said. "But perhaps we'd better get a few things stated clearly. Did you and Zeus have a sexual relationship while you worked at Olympus?"

"Yes," Semele said. "And yes, before you ask, he's Dio's father." She cracked a wintry smile. "Biologically, if in no other sense. That could easily be confirmed by a paternity test."

"Was it..." Hades cleared his throat, and gripped the armrest of his chair. "Was the relationship consensual?"

Semele sat very still. "Yes," she said, after a long moment. "I am not sure what would have happened if I'd said no. As it happened, I wanted to say yes. But—"

"But that doesn't make it any more right for Zeus," Persephone said, and Semele nodded at her.

"Yes. Precisely. I didn't really understand that at the time." She sighed. "I thought I did, of course. I'm a feminist. I'd had all the earnest discussions about workplace harassment and gender egalitarianism, written protest letters, gone on a campus march... but I couldn't make the link between that and my handsome boss kissing me in his office. It seemed like a different category altogether, like it occupied a different place in my head. There were the terrible things that had happened to other women, over there, and then me, right here, having an exciting affair with a powerful man."

Persephone thought about how easy it had been to recognize that what Hecate's mother had done to Hecate was terrible and wrong, and how difficult it had been to see the same thing when it came to herself and Demeter. "I think I understand," she said.

Semele looked at her hard, and nodded again. "Well, you can probably understand why I won't take this lying down."

Hades frowned. "Sorry? Won't take what?"

"I assume Zeus has sent you to tell me the payments will be stopping."

"Zeus doesn't know I'm here," Hades said, looking baffled.

Semele was looking equally confused. "Then why did you—" Her eyes widened. "Did *she* send you?"

"Who?"

"Hera!" Semele's hands clenched into fists. "If she comes near my son, I promise, I will drag Zeus through the courts *and* the media. I've got a dozen press releases ready to go."

"Okay, okay, whoa, no threats needed, no one sent us," Persephone said, flinging out her hands. "I think we might all be making some unhelpful assumptions. Hades, why don't you tell Semele why you're here?"

Hades blinked at her, but took the cue she was offering. "Zeus was using company funds to pay you," he said, ticking off on his fingers. "That's fraud, which I'm responsible for investigating as Olympus CFO. He had an affair with you, which is a betrayal of his wife, my sister-in-law and friend." He swallowed hard. "And I'm very relieved to hear you say it was a consensual affair, but you're right, it should never have happened. I came here to offer you my personal assurances that Dio and you will be financially supported as long as you need and want to be—and not by company funds or irregular under the table payments."

Persephone loved him so much. He'd put so much thought into this, thought so hard about what he could offer this self-contained young woman and her innocent son, who had both been neglected by his tool of a brother.

"*You're* going to pay?" Semele said, sounding less as if she didn't believe him, and more as if she couldn't.

"I'd be more than happy to. I can speak to my lawyer about setting up a trust fund on Monday."

"And you won't tell her about us?"

"Her? Hera?" Persephone asked.

Semele nodded tightly.

"I have to tell Hera," Hades said, back to confused. "Not about the trust fund, if you don't wish me to, but certainly about the affair."

"No."

"But he cheated on her," Hades said helplessly. He looked at Persephone and then at Semele. "What am I not understanding?"

Persephone had the terrible feeling she knew. "Semele," she said gently. "Why don't you want us to tell Hera?"

"She'll destroy us," Semele said. Her dark eyes seemed even larger in her pale face. "Zeus told me. She's crazy. Zeus told me what she's done to his other women, how she's harassed them and gotten them fired, how she's ruined their lives. He showed me some of the emails, when I wouldn't get an abortion. I told him I'd never sue him for paternity if he kept her away from us. You can't tell her. I need to find a job. And I don't want that bitch knowing about my son!"

Hades drew in a deep breath. "Hera would *never* do that," he said, and the force of it left them in no doubt of his belief. "Zeus was lying to you, Semele. He doesn't want Hera to know because she'll leave him."

"I saw the emails," Semele said stubbornly.

"*What* emails?"

"Hades?" Persephone said. "Can I have a word with you outside?"

263

It was the first Sunday of March, and the air was definitely warmer. The last icy slush of winter had grudgingly disappeared, and the spindly sidewalk trees, in their protective cages, were starting to put forward tight buds. There were kids everywhere. Small children, delirious with the prospect of being outside, were escorted by a parent or two. Pre-teens and younger teenagers dashed past in packs, laughing and arguing, and older teenagers sauntered by in twos or threes, intent on each other and oblivious to the world moving around them.

Persephone parked her butt on the concrete stoop. After a moment, Hades sat down beside her.

"Did you know your brother had had an affair with Aphrodite Urania?" she asked.

He went rigid. "No. When? Recently?"

Persephone grimaced. "When she was seventeen."

"Oh," he said quietly. "I really... every time that I think there can't be more, that this is as horrible as it can get, he's done something else." He blew air threw his teeth. "So, now there's this, and he's lied about Hera..."

"About that," Persephone said. Her stomach was tightening. "He might have lied about what Hera would do to Semele. Well, I'm sure he exaggerated, anyway. But Aphrodite did get some emails from Hera, threatening her and calling her some slurs."

The face he turned on her was absolutely blank. "Hera wouldn't do that."

"Aphrodite got the emails."

"She wouldn't."

"It was years ago," Persephone said hurriedly. "Probably things were really messy with Zeus; Hera would have been scared and angry. Probably she wouldn't do it now. But maybe it's not a good idea to tell Hera about Semele and Dio without thinking it through."

She couldn't really reconcile the vengeful monster that Semele had described with her own impression of Hera, reserved, cool, and emotionally contained. But she did have a temper. Persephone remembered the bite in Hera's voice when she'd told her about Zeus's stupid stunt on the way up the mountain. "

"She was angry with *Zeus*," Hades said. "She had every reason to be." His hands were clenched. He consciously relaxed them, flattening them on his knees. "Look, you didn't know Hera then, and you barely know her now. Trust me."

His flat refusal to listen was starting to get to her. "Trust *me*. Aphrodite's not lying."

He didn't say anything to that, and his silence felt like a wall. He was sitting right beside her, and yet she could feel him retreating, the warm, kind man she loved pulling back behind the stony mask.

Persephone took a deep breath. "We've both had a lot of emotional shocks lately," she said. "Your brother, my mom."

"Are you breaking up with me?" Hades asked. His voice was cool, and the gaze he turned on her seemed unconcerned with the answer.

Persephone flinched. "*No*. I'm saying, we might not be in the best place to make good judgments. I mean, I find it hard to believe that Hera could be like that too, but—"

"I find it impossible," Hades said.

He was so stern, so unyielding. Persephone felt tears prickle at her eyes. "There's a little kid involved," she said, her voice wobbling. "Hades, can't you wait until you can at least think about the possibility?"

"Get me the emails," he said abruptly.

Persephone flinched away from his tone.

Hades winced, the first sign of softening. "Sorry. That came out curt. I'd like—if Aphrodite is willing to forward the emails, I can have them forensically examined." He grimaced. "Persephone, no matter what's in them, I *have* to tell Hera about this soon. It's an even worse betrayal if I don't."

"But you'll wait? You'll think about how to do it?"

"I'll wait," he said. He grabbed the guard rail and pulled himself to his feet. "I'll tell Semele that now."

He went back inside without offering her a hand or waiting for her to go with him. From the intent look on his face, she didn't think he was trying to exclude her; he was focusing on the problem, and had no room for anything else.

No room for her.

The chilled concrete of the stoop was numbing her butt, the warming air a fragile illusion. Persephone hugged herself and tried not to think about a long winter blighting everything she'd worked for. Spring was coming. It had to.

When Hades reemerged, he looked surprised to see her still sitting there. His hand was warm when he extended it, and he tugged a little, so that she leaned into his embrace for a second, his chin tucked over her head. For a moment, as they went back to the car, Persephone thought it might be all right.

The moment didn't last. He parked outside her building, but didn't move to get out with her. "Do you mind I don't stay over tonight?" he asked.

"Of course not," Persephone said, ignoring the internal protest of her shaky heart.

"It's just that I've got to think about this." He looked at her. "I'm glad you're not breaking up with me."

"Why would I?" she asked, too confused to be less direct.

"This family," he said, and made a short, chopping motion with his left hand. "Zeus. Me."

"You are *nothing* like Zeus."

He gazed at her unhappily. "I'm fifteen years older than you, Persephone. You're beautiful, young, bright... It's impossible *not* to see the parallels."

"But I love you," Persephone said. The words didn't have the usual effect. Hades' eyes were still troubled, his beard-framed mouth turned down. "Look, it's been a bad afternoon. Call me later?"

He nodded, and she got out of the car, watching as he pulled away without looking back at her.

She tried very hard not to see it as a metaphor.

Aphrodite didn't do texting. Persephone dumped her coat on a chair and called her instead.

"Hey, girl!" Aphrodite's voice sang, vibrant and carefree, over the sound of artificial warfare. "We still on for that movie night at my place next week?"

"Yes, absolutely."

"Oh, good! Can't wait to meet your Hecate!" There was a whooshing and a mechanical cheer. "Get out of the— Okay, got it!"

"Should I call back?"

The sounds had ceased. "Nah, I've stopped. What's up?"

"I need to ask you a favor," Persephone began, and explained the situation. She carefully left out Semele's name, and Dio's existence, explaining

267

only that Zeus had had an affair, and the other party was worried Hera would be vindictive.

Aphrodite was quiet for a long moment after she finished. "You really think those emails could be fake?" she asked.

"I don't know," Persephone said. "Hades thinks so. I don't think he can bear to suspect Hera of that kind of viciousness, not when he's getting so much bad news about Zeus."

"I never thought it could be anyone but her," Aphrodite admitted. Her voice darkened. "Do you think that maybe Zeus—"

"Maybe. You've never said anything about the emails to Hera in person, right? Like, she's never confirmed or denied it?"

"Nah. I didn't see her much back then anyway, and I was definitely a junior model. Also, I mean, I *did* sleep with her husband, which wasn't great of me, and at the time I didn't realize just how gross a response those emails were. I sure wasn't going to bring it up. And since then, she's always been nice to my face, but I thought maybe she was just a two-faced bitch."

"Maybe," Persephone said, thinking of Hades's expression when Semele had blurted out her fears. If Hera *had* done this, it would hurt him so badly. "And maybe not."

"If she's the bad guy, is he going to take it out on you for telling him?"

"I don't think so," Persephone said. He'd looked so cold. It was hard, learning terrible things about the people you loved. But then... she hadn't hated Hecate. "No," she said, more firmly. "No, that's not his style. But... he brought up the age difference again."

Aphrodite snorted. "You don't care."

"No. Should I, though? Am I being stupid? I pretty much went straight from living with my mother to hooking up with this older man. Am I just trading one codependency for another?"

She heard Aphrodite's sigh. "Okay, well, for one thing, I don't know you *that* well, but—"

"Right, sorry," Persephone said, embarrassed. "I shouldn't have—"

"Bitch, shut up and let me finish my stupid sentence," Aphrodite said, yawning. "I said, *but* even not knowing you that well, I know that's not the chronology, okay? You met him, and *then* you left your mom and *then* you left him *because* you didn't want to be codependent. Then you picked up again with him, and a month later you were back to your mom, and now you've left your mom again. Right?"

"Right."

"Right. So he's steady. It's the mom yo-yo you've gotta watch out for. Besides, what do you mean, co-dependent? You live at your own place, right? You make your own money?"

"Barely," Persephone said, with feeling.

"Well, yeah, like, *exactly.* Babe, I know like eighty girls who would have already quit their jobs and tried to move in with a Kronion."

"They'd be wasting their time trying to move on this one," Persephone said, feeling a lot steadier. "He's mine."

Chapter Twelve

Hades paced. It was an annoying habit, one he thought he'd left behind, but he couldn't stop moving. He'd felt bereft the moment Persephone had stepped out of the car, wanting to follow her, to tell her he'd changed his mind and wanted to stay.

But he felt like a man made out of broken steel and ice. Touching him could only hurt her. He went down the stairs again, and only when he'd hit the bottom did he realize he hadn't looked at Persephone's mural on the way. For the first time he could recall since he'd first seen it, he hadn't even thought of it in passing.

It had to happen sometime, of course. The things in your home couldn't endlessly surprise you with their beauty and vitality. But missing it now felt like a terrible sign. He checked his phone, sighed, and wandered around the living room.

"What the hell is going on?" Don asked, appearing from nowhere.

"Holy *fuck*," Hades said, clutching his chest. He'd thought Don was out, with one of the many friends he'd made over the last months.

Don ignored the part where he'd nearly shocked his older brother into a heart attack and squinted at him suspiciously. "You've been weird all week, and now you're just running all over the house?"

"End of fiscal year," Hades said. "It's always stressful."

"It's *this* stressful?" Don demanded. "Every year?" He stepped closer. "Hades, you've *got* to work less."

"It's not this bad every year," Hades said. He was ashamed of the half-lie, but warmed by his brother's concern. If Don knew the real reason he was stressed... He would have to tell him, Hades knew, and after Hera that was his greatest worry. Proportionate response wasn't really Don's strong point.

"Did you and Persephone have a fight?"

"No," Hades said, then amended to: "Not exactly."

"Sit down, then."

"I can't," Hades said. Even standing in one place for the conversation was making him jittery. His fingers were twitching, and his eyes kept moving around the room.

Don eyed him. "Okay, then grab your coat. If you're going to walk, you may as well give your carpets a break."

It was good advice, Hades thought, though he was startled when Don followed him to the door. He hadn't realized that Don intended to walk *with* him.

Don didn't try to talk, but he set a blistering pace, his powerful legs easily carrying his big body down the pavement. Hades couldn't help comparing the neighborhood to the one he'd visited that day. Semele's street had cracked pavements and graffiti on the walls, but it was full of life and movement. Not like his own cul-de-sac, where everything was very tidy, expensive, and quiet.

Quiet had been the first thing on Hades' mind when he'd bought his house. He'd wanted an easy-to-maintain home with a good kitchen for the housekeeper, and a place where he didn't have to deal with the noise of large parties or the conversation of nosy neighbors. He'd opted for this street because it was mostly favored by professional couples and moneyed retired people. There were a few children around. He'd seen them visiting grandparents in the holidays, or getting into their parents' BMWs in the uniforms of various private schools. But the children in Semele's neighborhood had run and shouted, playing inexplicable games or gossiping loudly about their peers. Would Dio join those kids? The little boy in the playground pictures hadn't looked quiet.

Hades wasn't sure when it had happened, but *quiet* wasn't what he wanted any more. It might have even started before he'd met Persephone, when Mackie exploded into his best friends' lives, and thus into his, but Persephone had been a powerful catalyst. Whenever she was around, he wasn't afraid of change. Sometimes he even actively sought out excitement.

Hades stopped dead.

Don, evidently consumed with his own thoughts, took a minute to notice. Then he jogged back, the question clear on his face.

Hades didn't let him get it out. "Am I using her?" he asked desperately. "Am I an old predator?"

"No," Don said.

"I'm nearly 43. That's mid-life crisis time. I could be wasting her time, tying her to me just so I can relive some dream of youth, or depending on her to change me."

"You're not."

"You thought I might have been. How do you know you weren't right the first time?"

He was expecting a glib response, but Don took the question seriously. He started walking back home, setting a much slower pace. Hades walked beside him, waiting for judgement.

"I'm not sure I can *know*," Don said at last. "But I believe it. For one thing, man, you tied yourself in knots to make this aboveboard at work. And in your private lives, you don't try to take up all of her time. You don't patronize her, or treat her like anything less than an equal partner. You take her, and your relationship, seriously. Right?"

"Well, of course," Hades said.

Don shook his head. "No 'of course' about it, bro. That's not how mid-life crises work. Those guys don't want their girlfriends to be real people. They want women to be symbols of how they haven't lost it yet: sexy, exciting, young and gorgeous."

"Persephone's all of those things."

"Well, yeah. But to you, she's not *only* those things. And when she's not those things— when she's upset, or miserable, or fighting with her evil mom—you don't back off or lose interest. And in case you were wondering, she's not using you, either."

"I *wasn't* wondering," Hades said dryly.

"Well, don't start. That woman's eyes turn into hearts whenever she sees you." He grinned. "Honestly, it's embarrassing to be around you two. It's like the second-hand gooeyness is getting all over me."

"Thanks."

"No problem."

"She *is* changing me, though."

"Yes," Don said, obviously exasperated. "And you're changing her. That's how good relationships *work*. All good relationships, not just romantic ones." He punched Hades in the arm, possibly with a little more force than he intended. "You're changing me. And I'm changing your decor."

"You're changing more than that," Hades said gruffly. "I'm glad you're here."

"What did I tell you about saying emotionally healthy things?" Don said. "I feel like we have to go wrestle or something now. At least shoot some hoops."

"You can't give me excellent advice based on perceptive observation and then complain I'm being too open and honest with you."

"Sure, I can. I'm multi-faceted." Don picked up the pace again, forcing Hades into a half-jog to keep up.

Hades was fairly sure Don was joking, but he also didn't slow down, and by the time they got home, Hades was panting. Don, of course, was breathing as if he'd been out for a light stroll around the backyard.

"Feel better?' Don said.

"Only in spirit," Hades said, leaning over to catch his breath. "I might need to do more exercise. Come May, I'm going to have to walk up eight flights of stairs at least once a day."

"No elevator? Oh, wait, is this your heights thing?"

Hades looked at him sharply, but neither Don's voice or face were mocking. He was just asking a question, about a normal problem lots of people had.

"Yes," Hades said. "Heights and elevators." It felt like it should have been momentous, like Don should have started a slow clap or ushered in a trumpet player, but he just nodded and opened the front door for them.

"Hera thinks I should get therapy for it," Hades said, toeing off his shoes.

"Well, if Hera says it, she's probably right," Don said. "She's smarter than all of us, you know." His face had that half-fond, half-haunted look again, and Hades had to turn away.

***

The emails arrived early on Monday morning, dropping into Hades' personal email account with the unpleasant shock of a cold shower. He hadn't decided whether or not he would read them—it probably wasn't necessary—but the phrase "dumb bitch" caught his eye in the notification, and he was halfway through the first before he knew it.

There were only three, and they were short, but they were vile. The writer, whoever they were, had used every misogynistic slur with abandon, and "dumb bitch" was, in fact, the nicest thing they'd said. They'd compared Aphrodite's body parts to various animals, sneered at her intelligence and lack of education, graphically described what should happen to her in a just world, and made some serious threats about what *would* happen if she ever touched Zeus again or told anyone about the affair. The last email concluded, "And who do you think they're going to believe? Not you, because you're trash. People don't listen to trash. They just toss it in the garbage."

Hades put his phone down, and seriously considered whether he might throw up.

The nausea passed after a moment, but the shaky horror continued. Aphrodite Urania had been *seventeen* when this foulness had arrived in her inbox. The emails came from an address that had Hera's name in it;

275

the signature had an old photo of her and a link to a social media profile that had become defunct a couple of years ago.

But there was no part of him that believed she could have written them.

He picked up his phone, and walked past a yawning Don on his way into the kitchen, distantly grateful that Don was considerably less sharp in the early morning.

"Where are you going?" his brother mumbled, around an enormous yawn.

"Work," Hades said.

"At *this* hour? Hades, come on."

Hades looked at him, and reached a decision. "What were your plans today?"

"Didn't have any. Why?"

"Why don't you invite Hera over?" Hades said. He looked from his baffled brother to his sterile living room. "I've decided to give you carte blanche on renovation."

Don blinked. "What? Really?"

"Yes," Hades said, and discovered he didn't feel even a little regret at the sacrifice. "*If* Hera advises you. After all, she's smarter than both of us."

"That she is," Don said, still looking confused.

Hades got out before Don could go from confused to suspicious, feeling that at least he'd done one thing right today. Whatever happened, Hera would have someone with her; someone indisputably on her side.

***

Persephone hadn't gotten much sleep. For once, her alarm didn't need to drag her out of bed at 5 a.m.. She was awake when it went off, blearily pulling clothes out of her wardrobe and mentally swearing that tonight, she'd definitely remember to choose her outfit and lay it out in advance. The bus wasn't too bad, first thing in the morning—she was guaranteed a seat, and her fellow travelers were in similar early-rising fugs—but it was still mostly dark outside, the atmosphere lightening only to the dull grey of the pre-dawn.

It was just as quiet at Olympus, where Kitchens was the only department where early mornings were the norm. The yawning night security guard waved her in, and she went straight to the top floor, walking past Gary's empty reception desk, and into the huge, glassy room that held the outer office and Zeus's special sanctum.

She turned all the lights on as she went—the energy efficiency mandate hadn't made it to the top—but padded down the back corridor in the dark to her own tiny office, where she hung up her coat, did her makeup in a hand mirror, and put her handbag away in a desk drawer. All of that took a whole eight minutes, and now she was here for an hour, until Gary and the senior assistants came in. Polly typically used that time to triage Zeus's inbox, but he'd made it clear that definitely wasn't a task for an intern. Her job was to be here in case Zeus made one of his rare early morning appearances and needed someone to get him a coffee or grab the latest editions for his coffee table.

She wandered back out to the main office, sketchbook in hand.

Zeus was standing in front of his locked office door.

"Oh!" Persephone said, and hurried forward. "I'm sorry, Mr. Kronion, I hadn't got to unlocking that yet."

"No problem," he said. "I should really remember to bring my keys."

He wouldn't and they both knew it, but Persephone managed an accommodating smile and pulled the keys from Artie's immaculate desk. He could have got them himself instead of waiting for her, but that didn't seem to have occurred to him.

She unlocked the door for him and put the keys back.

"Persephone?" he called, from inside his office.

She walked in, sketchpad held in best note-taking position. It was a little large, but maybe if she pretended hard enough, it would look like she'd been prepared with a notebook, instead of planning to while away an hour of boredom. "Yes, Mr. Kronion."

Zeus shook his head, smiling. "Zeus," he said, his tone lightly chiding. "Call me Zeus. And close the door."

A chill stroked the back of her neck as she did it.

"Take a seat." Zeus was leaning against the front of his desk, his smile broad, his posture easy.

But his smile didn't reach his eyes. His eyes were cool, assessing her every action and expression. Persephone schooled her face as best she could.

It was difficult, when all she could think about was what a tool he was. What an entitled, selfish tool. He got to stand in his enormous office, watching the sunrise, while Semele cared for her little boy and tried to get a job with a salary that she could feed him on.

Hades would take of her–of them–but that shouldn't have been his job. It was this man, who cheated and lied, who should have done that.

She remembered what Hades had told her about their childhood. Zeus had once been a little boy without real parents, with a weak mother and a monstrous father, who'd been feted and praised, but deprived of true love and care. She could pity that child, but not this man he'd grown into. He was making his own choices, and they were cruel ones.

"So, how are you enjoying your time here?" he asked.

"Oh, it's a real privilege, Mr.— Zeus. Olympus was right at the top of my preferred programs."

"Hera liked what you did for the Winter Ball," he observed. His wife's name sat so easily in his mouth.

"I was happy to help."

"And are you learning much about the business up here?"

"It's much more complex than I thought," Persephone said, which was better than *no, your snotty assistants won't let me.* "I'm impressed that you manage so many details."

He took the praise as his due. "But it's the Art and Design department you want, right?"

"Yes."

"And you did that mural for Hades. I haven't seen it yet, but Hera raved about it." He chuckled genially. "Next thing you know, she'll want to hire you for our place." He steepled his fingers. "That would open some doors for you, I bet. My wife has a lot of influence."

Persephone nodded without speaking. It seemed safest.

"But she can be a bit capricious. If she's upset." He chuckled again. "No, you wouldn't want to upset her."

Shit, shit, shit. Persephone's skin prickled uncomfortably.

"I'd better—" she said, and edged forward on her seat.

"Artie told me you took a message from Semele," Zeus said casually.

"Who?" Persephone said. "Oh, yes, the one I forgot to write on the messages pad. I'm sorry about that." She wasn't a good liar, she knew, but hopefully she could act flustered enough to put him off the scent.

"Not a problem, not a problem," Zeus said. "Do you know what *is* a problem, Persephone? That you and Hades went to visit her yesterday. Why did you do that, hm?"

Persephone sat very still. "Okay," she said, after a moment. "You had someone watching."

"Well, yes. I heard you'd been sniffing around. I have a right to protect my investment." He gave her a calm, kind look, the kind that said he was an adult who knew how the world worked, and she was a little girl who needed his good advice. "Here's the deal, Persephone. You convince Hades to let this go and keep his mouth shut, and I get you whatever design position you want. Doesn't that sound fair?"

Persephone stood up. "I don't think I could do that."

Zeus pushed himself off his desk and strolled past her, placing himself between her and the door. "Sure, you could. I've never seen my big brother so smitten. You could get him to do anything you want, just by bending over in that top." He waved at her chest. "I mean, you're not really my type, but I can definitely appreciate the gifts your mama gave you."

Persephone stopped trying to be neutral, and hoped that her face looked as disgusted as she felt.

"And I'd be properly grateful. You get me?"

"Oh, I get you," Persephone said. "You're not subtle. But it's still no."

Zeus ignored her. "On the other hand, if you don't do me this little favor, you might find a lot of doors slammed in your face. After all, who are they going to believe? Some spoiled rich kid?"

Persephone was abruptly done with this conversation. She rolled her eyes. "You realize that could refer to both of us, right?"

"I love my wife," Zeus said, still smiling. "I don't need the dumb bitch my brother's fucking to screw up our marriage."

"Okay, yeah," Persephone said. "You're an asshole. I quit."

She tried to sweep past him, but Zeus stepped forward, looming over her. Persephone didn't often feel small, and she didn't like it.

"I'm going to go have a conversation with Semele about this little story she's telling," he said. "You can stay here and keep out of trouble while I do. Just remember, I tried to be reasonable."

"I said, I quit," Persephone told him, and darted forward.

He grabbed her wrist, just as she'd been dreading. Braced for it, she had enough momentum to drag him towards the door a few steps. "Hey!" she shouted. "Help me!" The outer office was totally empty. A movement caught her eye in the entrance of the dim corridor that led to the back room.

It was Gary, his beautiful eyes wide and terrified. Persephone lunged forward another step. "Help me!" she screamed, her eyes on his.

Gary shook his head, visibly shaking, and faded back into the darkness.

Zeus had a firm grip on both wrists by then. He shoved her towards his bookshelves, using the weight of his body as much as his hold on her.

Persephone fought. She got a few good kicks in, though he easily blocked the knee she aimed at his balls, shaking his head at her mockingly. When he let go of one wrist to push the button that opened the secret door, she punched him in the face.

It hurt like hell, but she had the satisfaction of seeing his head snap back and his smug expression replaced by a snarl. He hauled the door open and threw her into the secret hallway.

Persephone hit the floor hard, her breath knocked out by the impact. By the time she scrambled to her feet, the door had shut with a soft, definite thunk.

She tried the door at the other end, but the magnetic lock held fast, and she'd never been trusted with the keycard that would open it.

Her phone was in her handbag, on the desk in the back office.

Artie and Polly wouldn't be in for at least half an hour, and anyway, she couldn't count on them. Gary had seen her being actually assaulted, and been too much of a coward to do anything.

No allies, no way to call for help, no way to fight.

Persephone screamed, in rage and defiance, and hurled her body at the door.

***

"I'm not touching these until I get direct permission from the recipient," Heph Smith said, folding his bulky forearms. The IT security specialist had been contracted to come in that day, and Hades had hoped that he'd be willing to take on some extra work. He hadn't realized Heph would balk at privacy concerns, but he probably should have.

"I understand," Hades said. "But Aphrodite *has* given her permission, and this is rather urgent."

"No direct permission, no forensics," Heph said impassively.

"Okay, no problem," Hades said, and pulled his phone out. He should have asked Persephone for Aphrodite's phone number before, but he'd call Persephone now, and ask her to ask Aphrodite to call him... "Sorry, this will involve a bit of phone tag."

Heph shrugged. His massive shoulders made it a very definite gesture. "You're paying by the hour."

Persephone's phone kept ringing, and then went to voicemail. Hades frowned. Perhaps he should have texted first. Or perhaps... perhaps Persephone didn't want to talk to him right now. He'd been awkward on the phone last night, which wasn't unusual for him, but she'd sounded strange too. She was being careful around him, in a way she never had before, and he hated it.

"Hold on, let me see if I can get hold of Aphrodite directly..." The model appeared in dozens of spreads in various Olympus publications. Someone in the building had to have her contact details. Cherry could probably find them in eight seconds flat.

The problem was, Cherry wasn't here. No one was here. Even for him, this was an early start. Heph was here because he preferred getting in before navigating the crowded hallways made mobility more of a challenge.

Maybe someone in Kitchens could help? There'd been that Cooking with Aphrodite video segment last year...

His phone rang while he dithered, Persephone's name flashing up on the screen, and he hit the answer button. "Hi, sweetheart, just a quick questi—"

"I'm not Persephone," a whispering voice broke in.

Hades went rigid. "Why do you have her phone?" he snapped, in a voice that didn't sound like his own.

"She's on the top floor," the voice went on. The whisperer sounded terrified. "Zeus is mad. Really mad. He— I think he *hit* her." The whisperer's voice hitched. "You'd better come." The line went dead.

Hot metal flowed through Hades' veins. He dropped his phone and ran for the elevator, scarcely hearing Heph's alarmed questions behind him.

There was no time for stairs, and he hit the elevator call button with no hesitation. But even his rage at Zeus and fear for Persephone couldn't smother his phobia. It leapt to life as soon as the elevator jerked into motion, and he crammed himself into the back corner, clutching the handrail.

"Focus, focus," he muttered to himself, and concentrated on Persephone's face, her smile, the warmth in her voice, the joy of her presence...

And Zeus had hit her.

When the elevator doors opened, Hades was ready. He launched himself out with a single convulsive movement, using the momentum to hurtle through the empty reception space before he could freeze or retreat. He made it to the outer office without looking at the space outside, and nearly crashed into his brother in the doorway to his private domain.

"Hades? What are—"

The office didn't have anyone else in it. Hades grabbed Zeus by the front of his shirt and hustled him into the room. "Where is she?" he snarled.

There was a thump and a muffled shout, and Hades's eyes went directly to Zeus's stupid secret passage. He swung his brother aside and lunged for the button on the bookshelf.

Persephone tumbled out, and into his arms. She was breathless, sweaty, and red-faced, but his first frantic survey showed that she wasn't visibly injured.

"Are you all right?" he demanded.

"I'm okay," she said, and then her eyes widened in alarm.

Hades was already half-turning when Zeus tackled him.

He was expecting to hit the floor, but instead Zeus shoved him onwards, past his desk, until his back slammed into the windows.

Hades froze. Down there, way down there, was the ground, and the only thing saving him from the fall was this thin layer of glass.

Theoretically, he knew that the glass was not thin, that it was heat-strengthened and stress-tested, that very little could break through its double layers, and that even the combined weight of two men didn't have a chance of damaging it.

Practically, he was paralyzed with fear.

Zeus looked into his face and smiled. "Yeah, that's right," he said. "Look behind you."

"No," Hades got out. He meant it to be a shout of defiance, but it sounded like a groan.

Zeus braced him against the glass with his forearm and grabbed his jaw with the other hand, forcing his head around. The side of Hades' face ground against the glass. He screwed his eyes shut, chillingly aware of the void at his back.

Zeus laughed. "Look, you spineless shit. You dare to judge me? I saved this company. I saved our family. And you, who can't even look out the window, you and your fucking girlfriend think you can tell me what I can and can't do?" His grip, impossibly, tightened.

"Let him go!" Persephone shouted, and Zeus's hand left his jaw.

Hades heard the impact of the blow, and the stumbling footsteps. His eyes popped open instinctively. He saw Persephone falling heavily back against Zeus's desk and tried to move again, but he was still stiff with terror.

And Zeus had control now, and he never relinquished that easily. He used the momentum of Hades' movement to spin him, so that now he was facing out into the void and shoved him back against the glass.

Below, so far below, cars crawled down the streets, glittering like diamonds in the early morning light.

Hades could hear himself making a high, wild sound in his throat. He couldn't close his eyes now; the void would take him. He tried to fling himself backwards, but Zeus was behind him, the pressure remorseless.

"Look," Zeus was saying in his ear. "Look, look at this, Hades. This is mine, do you get it? Not yours. Mine. You're mine. You're going to back off, you and your nosy bitch, and I'm going to keep Hera. She's mine too."

"No," Persephone said, close by and oddly calm.

Zeus screamed. The pressure abruptly fell away and Hades scrambled backwards, crab-like, not caring how ridiculous it looked. He was only desperate to get away from the edge.

Zeus was leaning over his desk, clutching his upper arm. Blood was seeping between his fingers.

And Persephone... Persephone was standing in front of Hades, facing Zeus, his ridiculous lightning-bolt letter opener clutched in her hand.

There was blood smeared on its blade.

Without looking behind her, she reached her free hand down for Hades. He hoisted himself up, and caught the tremor in her hand.

"We're leaving," she told Zeus, and he glared hatred at her.

"What the fuck is going on in here?" a gruff voice demanded.

Heph was standing in the doorway, leaning on his forearm crutches, Hades' phone poking out of his shirt pocket. Behind him, Zeus's assistants were clustered, staring at their boss in astonishment.

"Nothing," Zeus growled. "Get out."

Hades tugged on Persephone's hand, and she moved backwards with him. Zeus looked as if he were done, but he had no desire to offer him their backs. The last thing he saw before Heph closed the door behind them was his brother turning around, ignoring them all to stare out his window at the rising sun.

***

Persephone had no idea who the broad man with the crutches was. He planted himself in front of the closed door and frowned at Hades.

"What happened?" he rumbled.

Hades closed his eyes. "It's a long story, and I can't tell you all of it yet," he said. "Can we go back to your office?"

"You stabbed Zeus," Artie said, staring at Persephone. "You *stabbed* him."

"I also called him an asshole and tried to knee him in the balls," Persephone said brightly. She put the bloody letter opener on Artie's desk. "By the way, Artie, you're a nasty bully and nobody likes you."

She ignored Polly and Artie's twin gasps, and looked at Gary, who was hovering behind them with her handbag. "Thank you," she said, meaning it for more than the bag. Only one person could have told Hades what was happening in time for him to get to her.

287

Gary gave her his small, rare smile. "You're welcome," he said, so quietly it was almost a whisper.

Persephone didn't like the grey tinge to Hades' skin, nor the way his hand was trembling in hers. "Let's go, love," she said, and was relieved when he opened his eyes to meet her gaze.

He kept his eyes on her face as they went back through the glass-walled reception space, and clutched her hand convulsively in the elevator, but let out a sigh of relief once they were on the eighth floor, where this Heph guy apparently had an office of his own despite not even being an official Olympus employee. She called Aphrodite and handed her phone to Heph while she looked Hades over—and checked herself while she was at it. Bruises and aches, she thought, but nothing serious.

She was sort of trying to forget that she'd stabbed a man. She hadn't thought the blade would go so deep. She hadn't thought much at all. She'd just seen Zeus tormenting Hades, grabbed the letter opener, and acted.

Her boss had assaulted her in his office. He'd *locked her up* and *hit* her.

For a brief moment, she wanted to go upstairs and stab him again.

Hades stroked her hair out of her face and smoothed his fingers down her cheek. It was more PDA than they'd ever done at work, but she had no desire to tell him to stop.

Besides, she'd already quit.

"Am I going to be in trouble?" she asked quietly. "For hurting Zeus, I mean?"

"No," Hades said, so firmly she believed him at once. "He hurt you, too. If he tries to get you in trouble, we'll also press charges, and Hecate will skin him alive." He leaned into her. "I'm so sorry. I shouldn't have tried to handle it alone, not up there. I should have realized I'd be easily

288

incacapitated. I just heard that he'd hurt you and—" He sighed. "I didn't think."

"Tell you what," Persephone said, in a voice that tried to be flippant. "The next time I'm locked up in a high-rise, you call for help *before* you come and rescue me."

"Deal," Hades said, and kissed the tip of her nose.

Heph had hung up and was typing on a noisy keyboard, fingers moving so fast they were nearly a blur. Strings of text and numbers scrolled across his screen in time with his clacking, then vanished.

"Okay," he said. "Got it."

Hades blinked. "That was fast."

"Amateur work," Heph said. "The ISP was spoofed, but those emails were sent from this building." He pointed to a cupboard that was humming in what Persephone considered an ominous fashion. "That server, in fact. And, while I can't say for sure, I'm pretty sure they were sent from the machine Zeus was using eight years ago. The sender tried to alter the metadata, but there's a hidden signature in the encryption engine." He shrugged at the confusion on their faces. "Never mind. Anyway, if you want a real forensic specialist, I know a guy, but someone sent these emails from Zeus's machine, in the middle of his work day, from his office. If there's still security cam footage from that far back, you could check to see who was in there." He left, carefully unsaid, that there couldn't have been too many candidates.

"We don't need to do that," Hades said, and then hesitated, looking at her. "Do we?"

Persephone hated the doubt in his eyes. "I never wanted to believe it was Hera's work," she said. "This is proof enough for me."

He sighed. "Then I suppose I have to do the hardest part now."

Persephone's heart broke for him, but he was right. "Let's go home," she said. "Hera needs to know."

Chapter Thirteen

T here was no way to make this easy, and Hera wouldn't appreciate the soft sell anyway. Hades asked Don and Hera to sit down on his couch, and began by telling Hera about Zeus's affair with Semele. She sat there, turning pale and still.

"How old is the child?" she asked when he was finished, her voice very controlled.

"Two and a half."

"So. The affair took place after we remarried." She looked at Don. "Aren't you going to say you told me so?"

Don's mouth was set in a grim line. "No."

"But you did tell me so. Everyone did." Her face was perfectly smooth. "And everyone was right. Marrying him again was very stupid. But he made so many promises. And I loved him." She stopped. "I still love him, even now. Isn't that foolish?"

Don turned away from her abruptly. Hades couldn't look at his face.

"Why didn't this girl sue him for paternity?" Hera said, pursuing the next step of the logic.

"I—," Hades said, and discovered he couldn't go further. It was such a fundamental betrayal, of her love, of her trust, of the marriage she'd fought so hard to restore.

"He threatened her with you, Hera," Persephone said. "He told Semele you were jealous and vindictive and that if she tried to pursued legal avenues you'd ruin her life. He said you'd done it before."

"I have never done anything to Zeus's mistresses," Hera said blankly. "It's... frankly, I don't care about *them*. I care—cared—about Zeus. I care that he *lied* to me." She looked at Persephone. "And now, apparently... about me."

Persephone nodded.

Something flickered across Hera's face. She looked at Hades. "There's more," she said. It wasn't a question. "It's bad."

"I—"

"Tell me, Hades. I want no more secrets or lies."

Hades handed her printouts of the emails. "We think he pretended to be you," he said, quietly. "I'm very sorry, Hera."

"Aphrodite Urania," she said, scanning the text. "I hadn't known that." She hesitated. "This date. She must have been young."

"Seventeen," Hades said, his throat tight.

Hera visibly steeled herself, and read the emails. "These are... This is horrible." Her voice was hoarse, and when she raised her face to meet Hades's eyes, she was crying. "Did he send these to his other women, do you think? Did he make them all believe I was like this?"

"Excuse me," Don said abruptly, and stood up.

"Where are you going?" Hera asked.

"Zeus and I have an appointment." His fists were clenched.

Hades saw his brother's face, and wondered if he was going to have to cover up fratricide.

Hera caught Don by the sleeve. "No."

"Hera, you can't defend—"

292

"I am not defending him," Hera said. "He deserves it. I very much want to hurt him myself. But you can't go to jail, Don. I need you." Tears gleamed wetly on her cheeks, but her gaze was steady. "Please."

Don's face was anguished. "Hera—"

"Besides, Persephone already stabbed him," Hades said.

"She what?"

"In the arm," Persephone said demurely. "With his letter opener. You can't fight him now, Don, he's injured. You'd never know that you'd beaten him for real."

Don stared at her for a moment, then wheeled on Hades. "Don't let this one go."

"I wasn't planning on it," Hades said fervently. Persephone slipped her hand into his.

Don sat down and crossed his ankles. The casual air wasn't fooling anyone—he was almost vibrating with murderous tension. But at least he wasn't roaming the city, bent on vengeance.

"Goodness," Hera said, blinking at Persephone. "What prompted that?"

"Oh, right," Persephone said. "We haven't told you about Zeus locking me in the secret passage. Or fighting Hades when he rescued me."

"There wasn't much fighting involved," Hades said, remembering again the terror that had frozen him in place. "Hera, I definitely need to see that phobias therapist you mentioned."

"I'll get you her number," Hera said. "Are you saying that Zeus *assaulted* you? Both of you?"

"In his office," Persephone said, and shuddered, the movement convulsive against his side. Hades tugged her into him.

"What the fuck happened?" Don asked, and when both Hades and Persephone started talking at once, he held up his hands. "All right. From the beginning."

Persephone looked up at him, and Hades felt everything around them dim into relative insignificance.

"I think the beginning was the soup," she said softly, shifting towards him.

"The beginning was your tattoos," Hades corrected, and touched the back of her neck. "I saw them, and came alive. I think I'd been dead for years."

Persephone's whole heart was in her eyes, glowing up at him.

"But the fight?" Don said.

Hera was watching Hades and Persephone, a peculiar expression on her face. "No, not now. We'll hear about the fight later. I'm going to go home, have the locks changed, and get very drunk. Don, you're with me."

Don jumped to his feet. "Yes, ma'am."

"We can—" Hades said, beginning to get to his feet, but Hera turned on him.

"Absolutely not," she said. "Today ought to end happily for *somebody*." She whirled on her spiky heel and strode from the house, Don in her wake.

"She's amazing," Persephone said, in the echo of the slammed door.

"Truly one of a kind," Hades agreed. He kissed her throat, and felt her shiver.

"Is Don in love with her?"

"I think so," Hades admitted. "I think he has been for a while." He pulled her legs over his, and ran his hand down the undersides of her calves.

"That's sad," Persephone said, and shivered again when he stroked the back of her knee. "Do you think—"

"Persephone," Hades said, "I will be delighted, or at least willing, to discuss my brother's fragile heart on another occasion, but we've both had a rough morning and it isn't even noon. It is my most fervent desire to take you to bed, get you naked, and keep you that way all day. What do you say?"

Persephone rolled off the couch and bounced to her feet. "I say, I'll race you there."

She won, both because she had a head start, and because he was enjoying the view of her spectacular hips working from side to side as she took the stairs. She jumped on to the bed and stayed standing, balancing against his headboard as she eyed him. "Come here."

"I hear and obey," Hades said, and sauntered forward, yanking his tie off and unbuttoning his shirt. Persephone's breath hissed as her eyes dropped to his chest, and when she looked at him again it was with naked lust.

Keeping eye contact, she grabbed the hem of her knit dress and pulled it up and over her head.

Hades' head spun. She was standing in black tights and a plain black bra on his white bed, all smooth skin and abundant flesh barely contained by the thin fabric. Color and life and joy and sex, for him. All for him.

He climbed onto the bed and knee-walked forward until his hands were at her hips and his face pressed between her soft thighs. He breathed, deliberately heavy and wet, and felt more than heard her sigh. With a sharp tug, he yanked down both tights and underwear, and set his mouth to her.

She was deliciously wet, sweet liquid sliding across his tongue as he delved inside her. He replaced his tongue with two fingers twisting inside her and licked greedily at her clit, feeling her moans reverberate through her pubic bone.

"More," she was saying, her fingers pressing into the base of his skull. "More, more, Hades, more, there, *there, don't stop*, yes, yes, *yes.*" She shuddered above him, then screamed, a long note of pure abandonment. He caught her when her knees gave way, and tumbled back, so that she landed with her knees either side of his waist, her hair falling around his face as she kissed him, the taste of her nectar still rich on his tongue.

Her heavy breasts pressed against his chest, impossible soft and smooth, and he rocked upwards, his cock sliding up her thigh. He dipped inside her, more or less accidentally, and when she moaned again, it took all his willpower to pull back.

Persephone reared back to kneel upright and twisted to rummage frantically through his nightstand drawer.

That was when he saw the bruises.

They were on the underside of her arm, a tight grouping of four little purplish points, where Zeus's fingers had dug in. Hades raised himself on his elbows, suddenly a little less mindlessly horny.

"You're hurt," he said, and touched the tender points, feather-light.

"So are you," Persephone said, and smoothed her finger over his cheekbone. He flinched as her gentle touch revealed a sore spot he hadn't noticed. He caught her hand before she could withdraw and kissed her fingertips, one at a time.

"Oh," Persephone said. He met her eyes, and hoped his own face was reflecting the joy he saw shining there.

"I love you," he said, just to make sure. "I love you, Persephone. I think this is it for me. I think you're it, forever."

"Oh," she said again. "Me too. You're my forever. Are we being stupid?"

"Sure. Let's be stupid together," he said, and sat up to catch her face in his hands, kissing her deeply.

She pulled back after a long, breathless moment, and handed him the condom. He reached between them and rolled it on, then helped her lift her hips and settle on him,

They both sighed when she sank down. Hades shifted, pulsing within her, and felt her clench around him. He was so deeply rooted he could barely move, and she rocked steadily against him. He cupped her breasts, glorying at the warm weight of them, and then teased her nipples, drawing them down.

"Yes, there," she said, her voice tight. "There, Hades, right there."

Hades licked at her throat, then scraped his teeth down the same route, and she came again, falling apart in his arms, this time with a bitten lip and eyes gone glassy with need.

And as she tightened around him, her muscles quivering, he was gone too, gone deep, body and heart. "Sweetheart," he said, barely conscious of the words as he let go with a pleasure so sharp it was nearly pain. "Sweetheart, my sweet Persephone."

She pressed him back onto the bed, moving her hips in lazy circles, a low purr rising from her throat. "You said all day, right?" she asked innocently. "Any chance we could make it a week?"

And he rolled her onto her back and kissed her laughing mouth, and knew, with a satisfaction more certain than he'd ever felt, that he was hers, and she was his.

***

Persephone sat up in bed and eyed her ringing phone balefully. It hadn't been a week. Barely 24 hours had passed before Olympus intruded upon them again.

She had a half-dozen texts from Terry that she really should respond to and a missed call from Aphrodite that had come while she and Hades were very much occupied with something that couldn't be interrupted, but she had no such excuse now. Hades was downstairs on a foraging mission, promising—with an endearing nervousness—to cook her something good for breakfast.

There wasn't much point in putting it off. "Hello," she said.

"Persephone, hello. It's Mark Hermes here." The resonant British voice was unusually hesitant. "I've heard some news. Is it true that you've resigned?"

"Oh, right," Persephone said. "I suppose I have some paperwork to sign. Do I need to do an exit interview?"

"Well, about that." She could hear him shuffling papers around. "Is there any way you could see yourself reconsidering? Perhaps if we gave you a week's vacation to decide?"

"I can't work under Zeus Kronion," Persephone said firmly, though the offer was reassuring. "Unless... has he quit?"

298

"I believe he's considering his options, but my best understanding is that he intends to stay as Olympus CEO."

Persephone sighed. It was probably too much to expect Zeus to do the right thing. In their lazy, sex-hazed talk last night, Hades had expressed hope, but no real belief, that he'd step down. "Well, then I'm afraid it's still no." She hadn't given any thought to what quitting meant, financially. She should probably start looking for something today. Come to think of it, there'd been a help wanted sign in that cafe she and Hades liked.

"Persephone, I've been given to understand that Zeus's intentions might not be unopposed," Mr. Hermes said. "What would you say to a deferment?"

"A what?"

"We put the internship on hold for a year. If, in twelve months, you don't want to return—for whatever reason—then that's fine, no problem. But if you feel you *can* come back, we'd be delighted to have you."

"This is a lot of work to keep one intern," she said suspiciously. There was the sound of conversation downstairs–Hades and a light, crisp voice she thought she recognized.

Mr. Hermes coughed. "Well, yes. But it's been put to me that perhaps I've been a little derelict in my duty of care to my interns."

"Does that mean you'll stop betting on us?" Persephone asked.

"Certainly not," he said, sounding genuinely shocked. "That's a hallowed tradition." He paused. "I might put a few more limits on it. But to return to the deferment. What do you think?"

***

Hades was trying to remember how long it took to scramble eggs when Hera walked into the kitchen and made him jump.

"Don gave me his key," she said with no preamble.

"Ah," Hades said. "How are you?"

"Hungover."

She didn't look it, dressed in an impeccable, dark pink suit with matching heels. Up close, her skin might be a little less radiant, her hair a little less glossy than normal, but her spine was straight and her shoulders square.

"Did you want breakfast?" he asked.

"No, thank you. We need to discuss a few matters."

He waved the spatula at her in a go-ahead gesture.

"So," she said, "I will be pursuing a fault divorce on the grounds of adultery. Unless Zeus contests the grounds, and I don't see how he can possibly manage that, the divorce should be relatively quick, and the settlement in line with what is laid out in our pre-nuptial agreement."

A no-fault divorce would certainly be less messy, but he could see why Hera wanted to go after Zeus through the courts. "I guess it will be faster," he said.

"I do not want the option of reconciliation," she added, her cheeks pinkening. "He's talked me around before. I don't want to be tempted."

"Well, you have my full support," Hades said reassuringly. "If you need me to make a statement or give testimony..." He faltered a little on the last, imagining being cross-examined in front of people, but no, he'd do it, to help Hera get away from Zeus. "Hera, I don't know if this needs saying, but I'm—I still think of you as my sister and my friend. I wouldn't blame you if you wanted to cut us all loose, but I don't want to lose you."

Hera stared at him as if he'd sprouted another couple of heads. "It didn't need saying," she said, after a pause, "but I am very grateful you said it. Now. Hades. What do you plan to do as regards Olympus?"

"I have to resign," he said, and shrugged uncomfortably. "I don't see how I can do anything else. I can't work for him anymore."

"Don't quit."

Hades blinked at her.

Hera was smiling, a wide smile with too many teeth in it. "You, Don, and Zeus own twenty percent each of the shares. Forty percent are owned by various other shareholders."

"Hera... if you think I can force Zeus out, you're wrong. Even if Don and I both vote to remove him as CEO, the other shareholders will support Zeus. Most of them won't care that he cheated on you or manhandled me or Persephone. Even the embezzlement... He's been good for the company; good for dividends. It'd be 60-40 in favor of him."

"Currently, that's probably true," Hera said. "But once the divorce goes through, I get half of everything Zeus owns. Including his shares."

Hades blinked hard as the implications hit.

"You and Don have forty. I will have ten. At that point it's us, versus Zeus and whatever support he can drum up from the shareholders. At worst, it's fifty-fifty." Hera smoothed her skirt over her hips. "I don't know about you, but I like those odds."

"I—"

Hera patted him on the shoulder. "Don't quit," she advised him. "Take leave–you must have months accumulated. Leave your competent second-in-command in charge. Redecorate your house. Explore some hobbies. Take your excellent girlfriend on a romantic vacation. And when you come back..." she shrugged. "Well. Things might be very different at Olympus."

He stared at her, and Persephone came into the kitchen, wearing her dress from yesterday, but padding barefoot over the tiles. "Hi, Hera," she said shyly.

"Hello, Persephone."

"I've deferred the rest of my internship for a year," Persephone said. Hades couldn't tell whether that was directed at him or Hera, but Hera looked satisfied. "I'll have to find some other work in the meantime. Love, you've ruined those eggs."

Hades sighed, and put his spatula down.

"Paint me a mural," Hera said. "I like lilies. Lilies and peacocks. Perhaps a formal garden view, rather than a forest?"

"Oooh," Persephone said, her eyes unfocusing slightly. "With, like, a slightly stylized Art Deco feel? Maybe some columns to indicate a peristyle?"

Hera shrugged. "Draw up some sketches, and we can discuss your ideas." She pulled a check from her handbag. "In the meantime, here's your deposit. That again on completion."

Persephone's eyes widened. "This is *way* too much," she stammered.

"I get the best; I pay for the best," Hera said, in the voice that didn't allow for compromises. Then she winced, and pressed her hand against her forehead. "If you'll excuse me, I think my painkillers are wearing off."

They saw her to the door, and watched her step into the backseat of her town car, perfectly composed.

"Is she—is everything really going to be okay?" Persephone asked as they hovered in the doorway, her voice small.

"I don't know," Hades said, and hugged her from behind. "But I hope so." Demeter probably wasn't done making trouble for them, and he thought Zeus might be poised to do a lot of damage on the way down, once he grasped that Hera was bent on toppling him from his throne. Hades was certain of Persephone, but of not much more.

Persephone leaned back against him, sighing happily at the touch, and he felt a warm glow that had nothing to do with the temperature.

"Look," Persephone said suddenly, pointing to one of the trees. A bird was hopping busily along a branch to a crook in the bough, small twigs sticking out of its beak. "He's building a nest." She turned in his arms and looped her hands behind his neck, smiling. "Isn't that great? It's finally spring."

Aphrodite Unbound

A snippet from *Aphrodite Unbound*, the next book in the Olympus Inc. series!

***

"I've been asked by my client to thank you for your assistance today," Ms. Eule said.

Heph nodded awkwardly. Minerva Eule was Hera Kronion's lawyer. She was brutally efficient, frighteningly intelligent, and about the same age as his moms, which didn't stop Heph from having a mild crush on her. He had a lot of respect for competence, which was what had got him to Eule and Spindle first thing in the morning.

Heph had some work to do at Olympus after this, and the delay meant he'd be arriving at the same time as everyone else, with all the added difficulty that meant for his mobility. But being able to impress—or at least not disappoint—Minerva Eule meant that it was worth the inconvenience.

"Let's begin by going over your actions of the morning in question. Hades Kronion requested your assistance in checking the provenance of some emails sent to Ms. Aphrodite Urania, is that correct?"

"Yes."

"And what happened after that?" Ms. Eule asked.

"I told him that I wouldn't do that until I could confirm the recipient had consented," Heph said.

"Very sensible," Ms. Eule said, and led Heph through a minutely detailed account of the rest of that bizarre morning that had led him to Zeus' office, and then back down to his own, safe den. And there, a bruised and shaken Hades and Persephone had learned the final truth about Zeus Kronion; that he'd impersonated his wife and threatened his ex-mistresses in her name. The emails were one of the ugliest things Heph had seen, and his career had led him to some fairly disgusting corners of the internet. It wasn't so much the content of the emails, although they were bad, but the absolute betrayal they signified.

"Can you confirm that Zeus Kronion wrote them?" Ms. Eule asked, and Heph grimaced.

"No," he said. "I can confirm that they were written in his office, from his network station. I can't guarantee that he was the one doing the typing."

"In your professional opinion, what is the likelihood of anyone else writing those emails?"

"It's not very likely at all," Heph said.

Ms. Eule made a note on the tablet she'd been taking notes on and clicked the recorder off. "Thank you for your time, Mr. Smith," she said, and got to her feet. "Would you be amenable to a further interview, if it should prove necessary?"

Heph felt as if a very busy raccoon had rummaged around in his brain, picking out the tidbits it wanted, and rearranging everything else. He couldn't think of what else she might need from him. "Sure," he said, and backed his chair away from the table. Ms. Eule opened the door for him and he wheeled into the small anteroom outside her office.

There were two women chatting out there; a small, pale woman in a black dress, and Aphrodite Urania. Heph didn't stop in his tracks, but only because the chair already had momentum. As it was, it took him a second to tighten his grip on the rims and control his motion.

"Ah, Hecate," Ms. Eule said to the woman in black. "Is that the report? Excellent. Would you mind waiting just a moment, Ms. Urania?"

"No worries," Aphrodite assured her, as the woman in black got up. "See you later, babe."

'Babe' was apparently the woman in black, who grinned at Aphrodite and then smoothed her face out to follow her boss into her office.

"Hey!" Aphrodite said, and smiled at Heph. "Nice to see you again, under different circumstances."

Heph's face must have done something, because she said, "We kind of met at the Olympus party in December. I had a fight with my ex and I didn't look where I was going, like a total dumbass, and I fell right into you. Remember?"

"Yes, I remember," Heph said.

He would never, ever be able to forget, and not just because the added weight had compromised the already faulty padding on his chair. His tailbone had momentarily hit the metal beneath, and the pain had been searingly bright, so sharp and intense that he hadn't even been able to scream.

And then he'd realized, as her weight shifted and the pain ebbed, that he was holding Aphrodite in his arms. Her long, red-gold hair had fallen around them, a shimmering curtain between them and the outside world. She'd looked right at him, her eyes startled and bright with tears, and he'd stared back, unable to speak or move.

And then she'd stammered an apology, lifted herself off him, and run.

He'd had to leave the party after that, firstly because he was in the kind of pain that needed strong opioids, and secondly because he wasn't quite sure what had happened. Logically, he knew that most men and a lot of women would have been just as stunned if Aphrodite Urania had literally fallen into their laps, but he couldn't shake the whisper at the back of his head that said it was more than just an accident.

"Did you get the fruit basket? I figured if you were on the guest list, the Events team would know where to find you."

"I did," Heph said, and because it seemed like something else was required, added, "Thank you." It came out surly, and he winced. He could never be charming, but at least he could be polite. The fruit basket had been lavish. He'd given most of it to the Olympus IT department, saying it was a gift, and letting them assume it was from a client.

He'd kept the card.

"So what are you doing here?" Aphrodite asked, and then her eyes tracked over his shoulder to Minerva's office. "Wait, are you here as part of the divorce stuff?"

"Um, yes," Heph said. "I, um, I forensically examined your emails."

"Oh, hey!" Aphrodite said. "You're the IT guy who needed to talk to me!"

"Yes," Heph said.

She beamed at him. "Thanks for checking with me that it was okay."

"Sure," Heph said. He wanted to say something cogent and impressive about privacy and how it was important and also how he thought she'd been brave to let a total stranger read those disgusting emails but before

307

he could think about any way to phrase it that also didn't make him sound like a condescending dick, Aphrodite's smile got even brighter, and he felt actually breathless.

"So now I owe you two favours!" she said. "One for crashing into you, and one for this."

The card had said "SORRY I OWE YOU ONE LUV APHRODITE." It had been written in marker, in wobbly capital letters with no punctuation. He would have thought it was the gift basket company, but when he'd handled it, he'd caught the scent of her perfume.

"You don't owe me anything for doing my job," he said brusquely, but an idea was percolating at the back of his head. "I think you know my sister. She used to be a model. Mellie Smith."

"Oh, Mellie! Yeah, I know Mellie!" She shook her head, her gold chandelier earrings tinkling slightly. "She helped me out on one of my first big jobs. She was super nice about it."

'Super nice' was not a phrase Heph would use to describe his sister, but Aphrodite seemed to mean it. "How's she doing?" she continued.

"She's great. Runs an events planning business now. Got married four years ago."

"You must be the genius little brother she bragged about. Didn't you graduate MIT at sixteen or something?"

"Eighteen," Heph corrected, momentarily touched that Mellie had bragged about him. The conversation had wandered away from where he wanted to point it, but Aphrodite unknowingly walked it back again.

"There's two other sisters, right?" she asked.

"Yes. Narnie is a researcher at a biological lab. Aoide is a singer."

Aphrodite blinked. "Aoide Waters? I love her stuff!"

Heph blinked too. He wouldn't have imagined Aphrodite Urania as someone into country-folk music. But he shouldn't stereotype; he wouldn't have thought her the kind of person to handwrite an apology note, either. "Yes. Well, she's getting married in four weeks."

Aphrodite's smile flickered for just a moment, then renewed. "That's awesome."

"Yes," Heph said, and nerved himself up. She had said she owed him a favour, and she did know Mellie. This wasn't creepy, just awkward. "She's very happy. I don't have a date for the wedding."

"She's happy you don't have a date for the wedding?" Aphrodite wondered, and then her glorious eyes widened. "Wait, are you asking me to go with you?"

"I—" Heph said, and then found that his courage could carry him that far and no further. "No. Sorry."

"Because normally I'd say yes, but, well, you saw the press conference."

Heph, still stumbling over 'normally I'd say yes', said "What press conference?"

Aphrodite laughed. He'd seen her laugh in a few social media videos that he might or might not have looked up in the week after the party, a shimmering, tinkling thing, like a wind chime in a gentle breeze. This wasn't that laugh. This was a delighted bark, abrupt and a little rough.

Heph stiffened, but she wasn't laughing at him.

"Duh, of course you have better things to do than watch entertainment news," she said, her eyes alight with amusement at her own misstep. "I did this press conference on Friday where I mentioned I was seeing someone new. Someone who was outside the industry, someone with a real job."

"Oh," Heph said, ruthlessly stifling a whisper of envy for the lucky person. "That's nice. Congratulations."

Aphrodite sat very still for a moment, and then leaned forward. The gold top she was wearing had a cowl neck, and it swung low. Heph kept his eyes on her face. "You work in IT," she said. "That's a real job."

"Yes," Heph said, and remembered that he actually did have a job, and should be heading to Olympus to do it.

"Would you say that you're trustworthy?" Aphrodite asked.

"I work in network security," Heph said. "I have to be."

"And you're Mellie's little brother," Aphrodite said, and lowered her voice even further. He had to lean over himself to hear her. "I made it up."

"What?"

"I made up the person I'm seeing. But now I need to see someone for real - well, no, I need to fake-date someone, but they have to be a real person, and they have to come to a movie premiere with me in three weeks. And you're a real person. And you need a date to Aoide's wedding."

"I don't understand what's happening," Heph said honestly.

Aphrodite grinned at him. "Would you like to go out with me? For four weeks? We'll go to my premiere and your sister's wedding, and then we'll break up."

For a moment, Heph considered it. If he showed up with a date, he'd be buying himself non-interference time until this time next year. But then there was the other part of the deal with his sisters, the part he actually needed to focus on...

"What were you thinking that would involve?" he asked.

"I hadn't thought about it," Aphrodite admitted. "Maybe... let's see, my schedule's pretty good at the moment, so maybe two dates a week where the paps can get their photos? Plus the premiere; that'd be a three-night trip to LA."

"I'm sorry," Heph said, with real regret. "My contract at Olympus is ending soon, and I need to hustle to find new clients. I can't spare that kind of time." The casual mention of the press didn't sound too good either, but he didn't want to say so to someone who spent so much time in the public eye. He was an ugly man who used mobility aids; he didn't want to know what the internet would say about him dating one of the most beautiful women in the world, even if it wasn't real. Especially if it wasn't real.

"Oh, okay," Aphrodite said, also looking regretful. Then her eyes lit up again. "Wait. What if I could *be* your new client?"

"What?"

"I'll pay you a hundred grand to go out with me for four weeks," Aphrodite told him. "What do you say?"

Find out what happens next in Aphrodite Unbound!

About the Author

Kate Healey lives in New Zealand and writes spicy contemporary rom-coms with a mythic twist. Karen Healey, who looks suspiciously similar, lives in New Zealand and writes fantasy romance, science fiction and young adult fiction. They both drink a lot of coffee.

Find more about Karen at http://karenhealey.com and sign up for her newsletter at http://thathealeygirl.com . You'll get the first news on new books, weird research rabbitholes, and occasional freebies!

Acknowledgments

I am grateful to a great many people who made writing *Persephone in Bloom* both possible and pleasant. I love Robyn Fleming for many reasons, and editing this book is probably the smallest of them. Alison Cooley created the gorgeous cover. Carla Lee, Marianne Kirby, Kristen Smirnov, Chloe Sutherland, and Rem Wigmore read it first and gave great feedback. Jessica Tai answered questions about art school, Jex Thomas answered questions about narcissism, and Abdul Aziz said "SICK!!" every time I told him my word count totals.

I could not have written this book without multiple supportive communities: the Best Ladies, the Ultimate Bitches, the Speculative Collective, the Healey family group chat, and the readers and subscribers of That Healey Girl. Thank you all.

Also by Kate Healey

Olympus Inc. Series:

Penelope Pops the Question (a newsletter freebie, available when you sign up at http://thathealeygirl.com!)

#1 *Persephone in Bloom*

#2 *Aphrodite Unbound*

#3 *Hera Takes Charge*

#4 *Ask Cassandra*

#5 *Love, Laodice*

As Karen Healey:

Movie Magic Series:

"Jingle Spells" (a newsletter freebie, available when you sign up at http://thathealeygirl.com)

Bespoke & Bespelled

Savory & Supernatural

The Hidden Histories Series (with Robyn Fleming):

The Empress of Timbra

The Spymaster's Apprentice

Young Adult:

Guardian of the Dead

The Shattering

When We Wake

While We Run

Made in the USA
Middletown, DE
11 October 2024